THE ANGEL IN THE STONE

R L MCKINNEY

SANDSTONEPRESS
HIGHLAND | SCOTLAND

First published in Great Britain by
Sandstone Press Ltd
Dochcarty Road
Dingwall
Ross-shire
IV15 9UG
Scotland

www.sandstonepress.com

The publisher acknowledges subsidy from
Creative Scotland towards publication of this volume.

ISBN: 978-1-910985-79-3
ISBNe: 978-1-910985-80-9

Cover design by Stuart Brill
Typeset by Iolaire Typography Ltd, Newtonmore
Printed and bound by Totem, Poland

For Craig, Jamie and Susanna

BLOCKAGE

'Someone's been coming into the flat.' Mary's voice was muffled. 'Things keep going missing.'

Calum Macdonald stopped working at the washer, slid out of the cabinet and looked up at his mother. She sat at the table, surrounded by the contents of the under-the-sink cupboard: old bottles of household cleaners, packets of sponges, mouldering dish brushes, rolls of bin liners, cracked Marigolds. Her fingers laced together, released and laced again.

'What things?'

'Documents. Money. Food.'

'Food?' It was impossible to hide his cynicism.

'Look at this.' She showed him the fruit bowl she kept in the middle of the table. It contained a single shrivelled clementine.

There was no evidence to support the break-in theory. He tried to reason with her again.

'Your windows are fine, your door is fine, nobody's broken in. Nobody's been in your flat.'

Her head moved from side to side. 'Maybe you're stealing from me, I don't know. You have keys, maybe you let yourself in when I'm out.'

'I'll hold my hand up and confess that I ate a banana when you weren't looking. We've been through this, Mum. I am not stealing from you. Where are you getting this idea?'

'I don't know, Calum.'

He wormed himself back into the unit again, eased the wrench onto the joint that connected the basin drainpipe with the main outlet pipe, exerting more pressure this time. It didn't want to give. He channelled anger into the wrench. Last week she believed he had stolen her chequebook. After a frenzied search, she found it in the freezer. Then she accused him of hiding it there.

Stealing had been Finn's game, not his.

He had to remind himself that she wasn't rational. Or maybe she was, but it was a rationale that came from a brain that was slowly consuming itself. He couldn't argue with her, even to defend himself. He never could, even before she got ill. Her moral high ground was so heavily fortified he never stood a chance.

Calum breathed in. A wet, smoky smell hung about the kitchen: last night's campfire on a rainy morning. 'Have you been burning something in here?'

Mary didn't answer. From his position, he could see her legs, sturdy trunks sheathed in brown polyester. She stood, shifted from one foot to the other, walked around the table, crinkled some newspaper and put it down again. Her anxiety was real enough, even if the cause of it wasn't.

'Mum?'

'Sorry, did you say something?'

'I can smell smoke. Have you been burning something?'

'Just some old papers.'

'Why?'

'I told you, someone's been in the flat. They could be stealing my bank details or anything. How do I know they're not taking everything I have?'

'We'll check your accounts, but I'm sure it's fine.'

'I've been burgled before, Calum, don't dismiss me like you always do.'

She had forgiven the so-called burglary all those years ago. She had swallowed the invasion and abuse it constituted, and he couldn't recall hearing her mention it since. She hadn't forgotten about it though. The fear was still there, even if the essential details were missing. What could you say about that?

Nothing. Say nothing. Let it go. Oblivion was the best place for some things. He clenched his teeth and gave a final heave on the wrench. The joint cracked and loosened, and a dribble of black sludge escaped. He pulled a basin over and worked it off completely. A mass of slimy, burnt paper and wet ash splatted into the basin.

He sat up. 'There's your blockage. Be thankful it was in the U-bend and not behind the wall.'

She bent forward and narrowed her eyes. 'What is that?'

'Burnt bank statements. How about we go buy you a shredder if you feel the need to destroy things?'

'Och, I don't see any need for more gadgets. A waste of money.'

Calum looked at her. A wee plump fairy godmother with a bun, specs on a chain and a whole pumpkin-load of bitterness. She had been old a long time, far longer than she deserved. Her losses kept her afloat, like strange life rings. Her God had picked her out for some special misery, there was no question about that. Still, she prayed. Believed He was Good. Came back to Him. Like a woman who sticks with a man who gives her a doing every Friday night.

'Okay, do me a favour and promise me you won't burn anything else in the sink. I'm not doing this again.'

'People have been in my flat. They're looking for evidence.' The hands were going again, making a dry snaky sound.

'Evidence of what?'

'My political affiliations. Your father's activities.'

'Oh for goodness sake, Mum, they're not.'

'I'm a woman on my own. I know you hate helping me.

3

You always have. You left me to deal with everything, both of them, on my own, while you were away. Doing whatever you were doing.'

'Your timeline's a wee bit off.'

Mary didn't acknowledge this.

Calum hid in the cupboard again and began reassembling the pipework. The plastic pipe cracked as he attempted to tighten it. 'Ah . . . ' He swallowed a curse, threw the pipe out of his way and sat up. 'That's buggered. I'll have to go see if I can get a new one.'

'I knew you'd break something. I knew I should have got a plumber.'

'Aye, that's right, you should have got a plumber. I had better things to do today.'

'You always do, Calum. You don't come for weeks at a time. You come when you have to, but you never want to.'

'I come to steal your bananas, remember?'

She only looked at him, her mouth working on unspoken words. He knew she would swallow her confusion because she was too embarrassed to admit to it. But here was the cruellest irony of all: the disease had made Mary even more Mary than ever. One day it would suck her empty, but right now it had inflated her with her own most dominant traits, so that she had become a great big festering balloon of herself. It might have been okay if it was as straightforward as losing her memory but right now she was remembering things that might be better forgotten. She had been angry since Dad died, and now she seemed angrier than ever. Maybe, Calum thought, they both were.

GLENDARACH, MAY 1986

They made their way through the oaks, Calum hanging back to walk with his dad and Finn running ahead, leapfrogging stones and swinging from branches like an adolescent Tarzan. Sometimes Finn doubled back, sat down and waited, legs jittering impatiently. Calum accompanied their dad slowly along the path as it rose and fell over the mossy steps and forest debris. They had walked these woods together hundreds of times but somehow even the place felt different now: more hazardous, more frightening. Jack stepped carefully, watching the uneven ground like a person twice his age, protesting as Calum reached for his arm.

'Leave me, I'm fine.'

'You look a lot better today, Dad,' Finn said, trotting back to them. He was on an upswing, when even the worst news in the world couldn't bring him down.

'I feel better.' Jack paused again. 'A wee bit of sun makes all the difference.'

It was the first properly warm day of the summer. They came down onto the sheltered beach below Uncle Iain's cottage and Jack stopped. He stood for a minute, breathing heavily, wiping sweat from his forehead. It had been nearly two years since he could work, and his body had softened with disuse. He stifled a wheezy cough, mouth closed, his chest heaving with spasms. This was new, and Calum and Finn looked at each other, marking another milestone in the cancer's progression. They had learned how to pull in their belts and live without his income. Soon they would have to learn how to live without him entirely. Nobody was saying it yet, as if talking about death would only speed its approach.

Jack turned his face into the sun and smiled as its heat fell across his cheeks. He knows too, Calum thought as he set the case containing Jack's pipes on a stone. He knows this will be his last summer.

'I'm going in,' Finn announced, pulling off his shoes and stuffing his socks into them. Peeling off his sweaty T-shirt, he revealed three parallel tracks of purple welts on his back.

'What happened there?' Calum asked.

'Just . . . football.'

'Were they using you for the ball, like?'

'Nah, it was a bad tackle or something. I don't remember.'

Jack turned to look. 'What is that, Finlay?'

'Just stud marks. It happens.'

'That looks intentional.'

'It wasn't, alright?'

Jack inspected the marks more closely: long, deep bruises edged by scabs. 'Can't you learn to stand up for yourself, lad?'

'I said it wasn't intentional, Dad.'

'Was it that wee ginger shitebag Thomson? Tell me and I'll sort him out for you.'

'Calum, just shut up, right?' Finn dropped his shorts and strode into the sea in his pants, dived in and came up with his dark hair sleek against his skull, lean and wiry as an otter.

'You go in with him, Son, I'll be fine here,' Jack said, testing the ground for stones with his feet before sitting on the soft sand.

Calum sat beside him. 'I'll give him a few minutes to stop being stroppy.'

'He's stroppy all the time now. Up and down like a damn yoyo.'

'He's thirteen.'

'You weren't like that.'

'Do you blame him?'

'I suppose not.' Jack coughed again, fist pressed against his lips.

'You all right?'

'Aye, aye. That sun feels braw, doesn't it? It's been a cold year. I never felt the cold when I was working, you know

6

that? That's the key to it. Whatever happens, you've got to keep yourself going. Promise me you will, right?'

'I will.'

They sat without speaking for a couple of minutes. Calum lay back and closed his eyes, listening for Finn's splashes, picking out the different bird songs, feeling the warm grains between his fingers and the sun burning his cheeks. Jack's breathing settled and he hummed a tune to himself like he always did. Calum felt sleep coming for him but he didn't want to give in to it. This day was too precious to sleep through any of it. He opened his eyes and pushed himself out of the sand. The sun glittered on the water.

'You coming for a swim Dad? I'll take you.'

Jack gave a soft laugh and thought about it for a moment. 'Nah. You go on.'

'Sure?'

'Aye.' He lay back on the sand and folded his arms behind his head. 'I'll just lie here and imagine I'm on the Med. I can see those lovely girls in their bikinis already. Tops off.'

'Dream on.'

'Aye, I will.'

Calum undressed and left his clothes beside Finn's. 'Right, then. See you in a bit.'

'Leave me the pipes, Son, I might have a wee blast.' Even now, Mary wouldn't let him play anywhere near the house.

Calum wondered if he would have the breath to play, but set the case on his T-shirt.

Jack patted the case. 'Aye, that's grand.'

We should give him a Viking funeral, Calum thought as he crossed the beach. No mouldy old priest humming and muttering a stream of lies to people who would believe anything. Dad would hate that. Pie in the sky, he'd say. He would laugh and make a flashing sign in the air with his hands. Christianity: Keeping Poor Folk In their Place for Two Thousand Years.

The sea hadn't warmed yet and it tightened like an iced metal vice around his shins. Calum paused, took a deep breath, then ran forward and dived in, swimming hard to catch up with Finn. They raced each other towards the tip of the headland, where the white sand fell away and the clear shallow water became huge and black. They stopped to catch their breath, treading water, rising and falling with the swell, and from the shore came the drone of the pipes warming up. They looked back at Jack. After a few skirly notes, he started into a *piobaireachd*: long mournful phrases, more chant than melody, a steady stream of sound like he was drawing breath from the earth itself.

'He's obsessed,' Calum said. 'Normal dads cook sausages and read the newspaper on the beach.' His voice broke.

'He's never been a normal dad,' Finn said without judgement or sadness, floating on his back with his ankles together and arms outstretched. Christ cast adrift.

'That explains you, then,' Calum said. He wanted to joke, or fight even, because Finn could never take a joke. But Finn just floated there, refusing to be drawn. Calum felt himself become heavy with the coming loss: a stone strapped to his back, ready to drown him. He let it pull him down, deep below the surface where the pipes were no longer audible, and tears leaked from his eyes, making tiny pockets of warm water in the cold sea.

PRETENDING
TO BE DEAD

Catriona Smith kicked her legs free of the cover, pushed the pillow onto the floor and lay flat on the bed, pretending it was a mortuary slab, pretending she was dead. Her fingers splayed against the sheet. After a couple of seconds they began to grip the fabric, so she turned her palms toward the ceiling. She tried to imagine her body withering and sinking down into the ground. The dead were empty. They felt nothing. They were safe. Death was the only place of safety in the world.

She could hear her mum clattering around downstairs, talking to the dogs, thumping across the kitchen floor in her work heels. Soon she would go out the door and even that small protection would be gone. Catriona thought she should get up, run downstairs before her mum left, tell her to stay, tell her everything, be the baby girl again, let herself be gathered in. But instead she lay on the bed and wanted to be dead. She imagined her body filling with cement and becoming impenetrable.

The heels were thudding up the stairs. Catriona hauled her cover back over herself and closed her eyes as her bedroom door creaked open.

'I'm off.'

Catriona pretended to sleep, but Jenny Smith had never been easily fooled. She sat down on the bed and stroked her daughter's hair.

'Cat, are you going to get up and do something today?'

Cat opened her eyes but didn't turn over. 'Is there something I'm meant to be doing?'

'You've done nothing but lie about the house since you got home. You don't look well.'

'I'm knackered, Mum.'

'You shouldn't be, unless you're ill.'

'I'm not ill.'

'Are you depressed?'

'No.'

'It runs in families.'

'That's another thing you can blame my dad for, then.'

'Cat . . . '

'It has nothing to do with him, and I'm not depressed.'

Jenny gave a huffy breath. 'Well in that case, you might consider getting off your backside. It wouldn't be the worst idea in the world to find a job for the summer.'

'Where?'

'Anywhere. A shop, or a café. Ask some of the guesthouses if they need a maid.'

'I'm not changing other people's dirty sheets.'

'Don't ever think you're above it, young lady.'

She groaned. 'God, Mum.'

'I could ask in the office if they could take you on part-time in reception for a few weeks. It'd be good experience for you, and I'm sure we'd both appreciate some extra income.' She paused and waited for Cat to respond. 'Cat . . . '

'Do we have to do this again? I just want to relax for a few days.'

'Yesterday you watched television, all day as far as I could tell. It's no wonder you've put on weight.'

Jenny was always on about her weight. The little sniping remarks, never calling her fat outright but suggesting it. You've got that from him too, she would say: another hotspot of regret and resentment. Catriona thought about letting the weight pile on. She thought about forcing her body to ooze and swell until she became repulsive in the eyes of men. Until she was too big to fit through the door, until she was so massive her legs couldn't hold her up and her neck subsided into her chest. Then she could slip down into the great soft fortress of her own flesh and hide inside forever. Her parents could rage and blame, Kyle could try to carry her away, her friends could pester her to come out, her lecturers could prattle on about ideas of no consequence, and none of them could touch her. She could never be moved by another human hand.

She sat up and stared past her mother toward the wall that she had painted powder-pink when they moved into this house. She was thirteen then, girly, aspiring to prettiness.

'I think I'll decorate my room.'

'Get a job and pay for it yourself.'

'It's only a bit of paint, Mum.'

Jenny rubbed the lines on her forehead, as if to remind Catriona that they were her fault. Another thing on a long list. 'Catriona ... I have supported you on my own your whole life. Maybe you could think about helping me for once.'

'Dad helps.'

'Your father is as helpful as a chocolate fireguard.'

'He gave us money. He still does.'

Jenny's voice climbed. 'If you think raising a child is all about money, you've got a hell of a lot of growing up still to do.'

'You could have let him come back when he wanted to.'

'And so could you, but we didn't, and that's that.' Jenny

sighed. 'Will you at least make an effort? Pop down to town and ask in a few shops.'

Catriona lay down again. 'I feel a bit sick.'

'You're not pregnant, are you?'

'No! I'm not bloody pregnant.' But her stomach turned over. She easily might have been.

'Well in that case, whatever you're feeling sorry for yourself about won't be helped by lying in bed for days. Get up.'

Catriona turned over, curled her back toward Jenny. 'Whatever. See you later, Mum.'

Jenny said nothing else, and Catriona lay still until she heard her leave the house. Then she went to the bathroom, knelt in front of the toilet, waited for the sickness to consolidate and rise into her throat. When it didn't come on its own, she put her middle finger down the back of her tongue and made herself gag. Clutching the rim, she heaved brownish liquid into the bowl. There was nothing inside her, nothing to bring up, nothing to flush out, but still she felt like someone had sprayed her with raw sewage. Her skin was saturated with it. When she got undressed she could smell something rotten, like a dead animal on the beach.

She showered, lathered and scrubbed herself until she was red and irritated, then dressed and went downstairs, made tea and sat at the table. The morning sun coming through the kitchen window warmed her face. It was tempting to sit out in the garden, but the fence wasn't high enough. People passing on the back street could see her. Kyle could see her. She'd never given him her address in Aberdeen but he was clever enough to sniff her out. He hadn't phoned for a couple of days. That should have brought some kind of relief, but it didn't. When he left three or four voicemails a day, at least she could keep tabs on him. Silence was worse. He could be watching her right now. Her stomach contracted again and she pulled down the blind.

12

Her mum would go mad if she stayed indoors another day. Then there would be a performance, with tears and guilt and the same old single mother script, and Cat would finally have to tell her what had happened at that big house in the woods, and she couldn't bear to think about that.

Maybe she could go away for the summer, find a job in a hotel somewhere quiet and clean, where they would give her a room and meals and pay her minimum wage. There were worse jobs than changing other people's sheets. She thought about her dad, whom she hadn't seen since that Christmas five years ago when she'd said so many awful things. She could go stay with him, away out on the west coast, miles from anywhere. He might be so grateful to see her that he'd let her stay with him and not harass her to get a job. Either that, or he'd tell her to get lost and slam the door in her face.

INSIDE THE WALLS

The calls came every day near teatime: several seconds of silence and then a voice. Not quite a human voice, maybe some kind of robot or computer. *You have been identified through a government database,* it said. And then something about her boiler and her walls. Mary didn't understand. They wanted to get inside her walls.

'Hello,' she said, but the machine was unresponsive. 'Hello? Can anyone hear me?' She pressed buttons but the machine spoke over her.

She hung up. They would call back the next day, and the next.

Maybe they were watching her. They were trying to get in, trying to get inside her walls. They'd install tiny cameras. She imagined an enormous room filled with thousands of screens. She'd never read *Nineteen Eighty-Four* until Finn became obsessed with it, and when she did it unsettled her terribly and gave her nightmares. The vision was so bleak it could never be possible, but now it was starting to seem probable. Orwell had been right all along, just ten years too early with his predictions.

Ten? It was more than that. Why had she thought ten? It must be fifteen now, or more. What year was it? The millennium had passed some time ago. Of course it had; there had been a ceilidh, and then those lads had nearly started a riot with their fireworks. Feral thugs. Most boys were brutes now: uncontrolled, selfish, vicious creatures. They ran in packs like dogs, they didn't work, they knew nothing about work, they knew nothing about the land. Their hands were soft. They took drugs. They had nearly killed her Finlay with their drugs.

When she turned on the television, the news talked about Scotland more than it normally did. There were people on the streets of Glasgow and Edinburgh, and people with banners and people arguing. These same feral boys and girls, waving flags and shouting and talking about independence for Scotland. It had to be some kind of trouble. These kinds of things could lead to a war.

She and Jack had marched for peace. They had marched for solidarity, not division. He wouldn't have liked this business. These young people didn't know what they were asking for.

They didn't know they were being watched. Those calls, those voices on the telephone, they were all part of it. Computers trying to get inside the walls.

She left the flat and walked down to the precinct. It was full of old people pulling their messages behind them in tartan trolleys, peering in the windows of vacant shops. They didn't know. Nobody told them anything because they were old. They'd be the first to starve when the young people went away to fight.

There was Jean Crawford going into Boots. Beside the door there was a man with a blue badge that said Yes on it. He was handing out leaflets. He was trying to speak to Jean.

'Don't speak to him, Jean,' she puffed, out of breath from hurrying to reach them. 'He's one of them.' She said it in Gaelic so the man couldn't understand. 'Don't tell them where you live or write anything on that paper. Don't give them any information.'

Jean and the man looked at her with matching blank expressions. They looked like they'd taken some drug.

'Mary, dear.' Jean placed her hand on Mary's arm. 'I'm afraid I don't understand Gaelic. And neither does this young gentleman.'

The young man with the leaflets laughed. 'More's the pity. It'll be different when we become independent. We won't have to be ashamed of it anymore.'

Mary switched back to English. 'Jean, these people are troublemakers.'

'I seem to recall a time when you were a bit of a trouble-maker yourself, Mary. You and that man of yours, God rest his soul. He'd have appreciated this campaign.'

'I know what my Jack would have thought,' Mary said. What did Jean know about her Jack? What had she told this man? She turned on him. 'I know what you're trying to do. You won't get into my house. I won't have you spying on me.'

He opened his mouth but she turned away sharply to cut him off and hurried in the other direction. She had wanted to go into Boots but couldn't remember what she needed. It would come back to her once that dreadful man had gone.

'Oh, poor Mary,' she heard Jean say to him. 'Such a shame to see them go that way.'

Poor Mary indeed, she thought. There's nothing poor about me. I still have ears. I hear you. I know what's going on.

PUSSY CAT

Catriona woke in the wee hours. She lay under the duvet with her phone and surveyed Kyle's activities on Facebook. He had been to Croatia with his parents: pictures of a yellow villa, turquoise water, brown skin. Bare-chested selfies beside a skinny bitch in a bikini. Perfect white teeth. Rich people could buy perfection. Something alien surged through her, as if someone had injected her with poison. The phone pinged in her hand and a message popped up: *I know you're logged on, Sneaky Cat. Come on, enough of the silent treatment. Go and answer your phone, eh?*

'Fucking bastard,' she said aloud. Then she switched off the phone, pried off the back and pulled out the SIM. She chucked the phone onto the pile of clothes on the floor on the other side of the room and lay back, breathing hard. Blood thrummed so loud in her head it was all she could hear.

In the space of two months, Kyle had taken over every aspect of her life. He lived with such urgency, consuming everything around him with a voracious appetite – books, politics, coffee, women, alcohol – that you'd think he was trying to squeeze a lifetime into a few weeks. The referendum debate fuelled him with the kind of enthusiasm that you couldn't argue with, even if you wanted to. Even his smell was intoxicating. Catriona thought back to the night they met, in that club down the Cowgate. She should have known

17

then that he was too good to be true. She *had* known, but she'd let herself be sucked in anyway.

EDINBURGH, APRIL 2014

'You look far too interesting for a place like this.'

Catriona took a sip of beer and looked up at the boy. He was tall, lithe, admirably cheekboned. The inflections in his voice suggested he'd grown up surrounded by money and confidence, but it could be put on. Pretty much everyone at Edinburgh University was putting on some kind of act. It was hard to imagine that he'd be interested in her for any other reason than the fact that she was easy prey, sitting on her own. Still, a little blue badge on the breast of his black shirt said Yes, and a quick glance at his feet revealed a pair of Dr Martens Chelsea boots. In politics and footwear, at least, they had something in common. He might merit speaking to.

'I can't be bothered with it,' she said. 'My pal dragged me here and now she's bagged off with some guy.' The club was thronging with girls in negligible dresses and monumental heels. Chart anthems thudded out of the speakers. It was Avicii at the moment: 'Hey Brother'. A decent song the first two hundred times you heard it. Emily and Todd were practically giving each other hand jobs on the dance floor. 'I'm about to ditch them.'

'If I buy you a drink will you stay?'

'Maybe.' She held up her bottle. 'Same again, if you're offering.'

'I'm offering.' He held out his hand. 'I'm Kyle.'

'Cat.'

'As in Stray Cat or Wild Cat? Or ... Pussy Cat?'

She laughed. 'I don't know you well enough to tell you that.'

18

His lip curled into a smile and his eyes narrowed. 'I'll be right back.'

She watched him go to the bar. Jostling bodies parted to let him through and he got served almost immediately: a trick she still hadn't mastered. Being over six feet tall and male would help. Cat sometimes had to resort to hanging her tits over the bar to get served, but she wasn't tall enough to do it comfortably and so she felt like a wee girl playing at being an adult. She didn't understand the attraction of clubs like this, where sex and violence were so close to the surface you could practically taste their associated bodily fluids. Last weekend she had punched a guy who had groped her arse and Emily told her off for it. Emily said she should have been flattered. Flattered. Honestly?

Take off your combat boots for once, Cat. Just be a girl for Christ's sake.

Kyle drifted back over with two bottles of lager and slid into the booth beside her. 'That was cheeky of me, wasn't it? Pussy Cat? If someone hit me up with a line like that, I'd think he was a dick. I bet you've heard them all before, anyway.'

'Once or twice, but I'll forgive you.' She accepted a bottle and clinked it against his. 'Thank you.'

'No, thank *you* for giving me hope that tonight might be salvageable. The people in this place are so unbelievably dull. And listen . . . listen to that . . . they're playing One Direction. It doesn't get any worse. Manufactured English pop for babies. It's not music, it's capitalist neuro-programming, designed to brainwash any individuality right out of you. It's like saying, "I have no identity. I am incapable of having a single thought of my own. I am a drone." Please tell me you don't like this, Cat.' He grabbed her hand and his eyes pleaded with her, pupils huge in the dim light. 'Please give me hope for our generation.'

'Oh my God, for once somebody here has said something

19

sensible!' He was still holding onto her hand, squeezing it hard like he was afraid of letting go. 'The bar just down from our flat has an open mic on a Friday night. They get some great songwriters in there, performance poets, people doing things that are original and political. I wanted to go there, but apparently I'm like . . . a freak or something.'

'I'd go,' he said. 'I'd go there any night of the week. When we get independence, the first thing I hope we do is ban the BBC. It's just a mouthpiece for the Tories and the Royal Family. Have you ever noticed how they force feed us this disgusting, fawning idea of Britishness and we're all supposed to be so cosy and unified, watching *Strictly Come Dancing* and *Comic Relief* and the *Last Night of the Proms* . . . and we're all meant to say aw, look at us, all happy together on our wee island? One big happy family. It makes me want to puke.'

Cat's head moved up and down emphatically. Even drunk, he managed to articulate the things she could never quite string together coherently. She felt she could devour his words.

'My dad, right? My dad's a musician. He's like . . . the best musician you've ever heard, he can play any instrument with strings on it, I'm not kidding. He comes from the west coast, and he's like . . . he should be famous. But he's not, because he plays Scottish music and the music industry isn't interested. It doesn't value anything that comes from Scotland. He could never even make a living from it. He had to go and work on the rigs, and in America and stuff, so I hardly even got to see him when I was growing up.'

She didn't know why she was telling Kyle about her dad, why she was almost bragging about her dad as if he was someone to be proud of. He wasn't. He had never been the slightest bit interested in her. He never bothered hanging around more than a few days at a time. It was five years

20

now since she'd seen him. More than five years. She'd been fourteen the last time, and it had been an almighty disaster. Sometimes she wished she could forget about it and pretend he didn't exist at all.

But Kyle said, 'I like him already.' Then he leaned toward her and suddenly they were kissing. Her back was pressed into the corner of the booth and Kyle had his hands on either side of her, his tongue slipping between her teeth, his body radiant and damp. He smelled of beer and sweaty maleness, and he looked so good in his jeans and tight black shirt with the sleeves rolled up muscular arms. He pressed himself hard up against her, as close as he could get with clothes on, and slipped his hand under her dress.

She manoeuvred herself away from him, dizzy, waving her hand in front of her face, laughing. 'Okay ... that was unexpected.'

'Damn, girlfriend,' he groaned. Pupils huge in the dim light. 'I almost forgot we were in public.'

He was back in Edinburgh now, campaigning for independence. If she was a braver person, she would go down and see him. They might talk about what happened, because maybe it hadn't really happened how she remembered it. If they talked about it, maybe they could piece the night back together in a different way. He could convince her that it had been a misunderstanding. He could convince her of just about anything.

She lay there listing her failings: afraid, gullible, naïve, desperate, careless, stupid. Maybe if she kept the list going long enough, she'd eventually get to sleep. Twenty minutes passed, then another twenty. Fed up, she snuck down to the kitchen, ate a packet of crisps and spooned Nutella straight from the jar. The house felt hostile, more like a prison than a sanctuary. She opened the back door and faced the early dawn sky: a wash of indigo and gold. Dew beaded on the lawn and roses. She sat on the chilled concrete step and huddled into herself, body jittering with sugar and anxiety. She felt swollen and tight, like a boil in need of bursting.

After a few minutes she went back inside, took out a bottle of vodka and mixed at least a double measure with Diet Coke. It burned all the way to her stomach but she forced it down. She needed it to unlock the confusion that tightened around her like the coils of a python.

Or Kyle's arms. They'd been snakelike around her that night in the shower, gripping her hard enough to bruise. She closed her eyes and tried to trace each detail of what had happened at that party. She remembered a dining room as big as her mum's whole downstairs, and a seething crowd of posh, loud people. She remembered repeatedly filling her glass with whatever came to hand. At some point, somebody brought out a bag of hash. The details after that point became hazy. She had wriggled a bit when he lifted her off the couch, but she had also laughed at him. He laughed too, she remembered that. She had turned her face into his chest and let him carry her. And she remembered thinking, he's mine. She remembered hoping the girls he'd been messing about with earlier were watching.

She emptied the glass and stood up. The floor rushed up to meet her, like when you jump in an ascending lift. Her knees buckled and she sat down hard. Too much vodka too fast, too late at night. It was more than a double. Maybe a treble. Or a quadruple. Did they even measure it like that? She leaned her back against the cupboard door.

'Oh for the love of God, Cat.'

Catriona opened her eyes. Still on the kitchen floor, she pushed herself upright. Blood pulsed around in her head.

Jenny squatted beside her, her face frozen, suspended between sympathy and rage. She was capable of either but less capable of controlling which came out first. Catriona's eyes found the vodka bottle, still standing where she'd left it.

'I'm sorry, Mum.' Tears were very close to overflowing and she let them.

Jenny's rigid shoulders fell a little. She put her hand on Cat's cheek. 'Fit ye daein, quine?' Jenny's Doric was purposefully reassuring. She never spoke like that except in those rare moments when she wanted to make herself softer and more maternal than she was by nature.

'I don't know.' Catriona gathered her knees in and wrapped her arms around them. 'I couldn't sleep. I thought it would just help me get back to sleep. I'm sorry.'

Jenny grasped her hands and pulled her to her feet. 'Come on, up you get. Can you manage tea?'

Catriona settled herself at the kitchen table and nodded, then turned her eyes into her hands to block out the bright morning light. 'I'm sorry, all right? It won't happen again.'

Jenny switched on the kettle and dropped three tea bags into the pot. 'It's all right, Catriona, stop apologising.'

'I thought you'd be raging. You get so angry all the time.'

Jenny looked out the window for a moment. Sun fell on the creases at the corners of her eyes and she sighed deeply. 'I'm trying not to. All right? Please just ... tell me what's going on. I'm worried about you. '

'I know. I'm fine, Mum. I will be fine, I'm just ... getting over someone.'

Jenny took this in. 'A boy?'

'Aye, a boy. Do you really think I'm into girls, Mum?'

'Sometimes I don't know, Cat. You never seem that bothered about anyone, to be honest.'

'Well I was bothered about him.'

23

'I'm sorry, love.' Jenny made the tea and brought out mugs and milk. 'What happened?'

'I don't know ... the usual story. I met this guy and it was like ... intense for a few weeks, and then we went to this party and he messed around with these other girls. And then he ...' Her voice trailed into silence and she reached for her mug.

'And then he what?'

'Well he just ... screwed me over. That's all. I need to get over it. I'm being an idiot. I thought he was somebody special and he turned out to be a bastard, like they always do.'

'Not all men are bastards. You'll find a good one someday.'

'If you honestly believe that, how come you never did?'

Jenny lifted her mug to her lips, sipped and swallowed. 'I thought I had.'

'My dad? Jesus, Mum, get over him already.'

'Well, after him it felt like more trouble than it was worth. Listen to me, love. Don't waste another minute of your life on this guy, okay? If he's stupid enough to drop you for someone at a party, he doesn't deserve you. Don't ruin your summer over him.'

Catriona stared at her hands. She could feel Kyle's fingers around her wrists. 'Mum ...'

'What?'

'Nothing.' She snatched her mug and tea sloshed onto her fingers. 'Never mind. You're right.'

'Get yourself out today. Kate and Eilidh will be desperate to see you. I'll give you a little money. Go buy yourself some new clothes and cheer yourself up.'

'I guess. I need a new SIM for my phone.'

'Why?'

'I want to change my number so he can't call me.'

'He's not stalking you, is he?'

'No! Well ... no, he's not, but ...'

'But what? Is that why you're afraid to leave the house?'

Catriona closed her eyes and tried to compose herself. 'No. I just don't want to have to talk to him, all right? Don't get your knickers in a twist.'

'Fine.' Jenny shrugged and shook her head. 'If you say so. Listen, I have leave booked for the end of the month. Why don't we go away somewhere? We could get a late deal, something cheap and cheerful in the sun.'

'Maybe,' Cat said, even though baring herself on the beach was the last thing in the world she wanted to do. 'I was thinking about going to see Dad.'

'Oh aye.' Jenny took a couple of seconds to realise she wasn't joking. 'Honestly?'

'Maybe.'

'Okay ... that's a new one. Have you spoken to him recently?'

'No.'

'Mmm,' Jenny murmured again, and the beginning of a huff was audible. 'Well. It's up to you.' She turned away and dumped the remainder of her tea in the sink. 'I have to get ready. Go out and do something today, Catriona. I'm fed up seeing you lying about.'

'Do you really give a shit?'

Jenny paused on her way out of the kitchen. 'If I say I do, you won't believe me. So think what you like, all right?'

POSITION STATEMENTS

Julie rolled away from him, got out of bed and stood naked by the window. Calum turned onto his side and watched the late evening sun cast a soft copper glow through the hairs on her forearms. She clasped her fingers behind her neck and stretched her hands over her head, her little breasts stretched almost flat across her chest.

He lay down again and extended his legs beneath the quilt. 'I thought we weren't going to do this anymore.'

She raised an eyebrow. 'You weren't complaining five minutes ago.'

'I'm not complaining now, I'm just reminding you what we said last time.'

'Remind me why.' She lifted her jumper from the heap of clothes on the floor and pulled it over her head.

'I can't remember.'

The phone rang. Calum saw his mother's number flash onto the screen and groaned, 'Oh God.'

'Aren't you going to answer that?'

'It's ten o'clock at night.' The phone rang seven times and stopped.

'She could be ill. She could have fallen.'

'She has an emergency alarm button. If it's a genuine problem, she can use that and they'll call me.'

'Calum . . .'

'Julie, you have no idea what this is like.'

The phone rang again. Julie sighed, picked it up and handed it to him.

'Thanks,' he muttered. 'Hi Mum, are you all right?'

'Where were you?' Mary demanded. 'Why didn't you answer?'

'I'm in my bed. You know what time it is?'

'You never go to bed at this hour. It's still light.'

'It's midsummer. I've been working all day, I'm tired. What's up?'

'I think someone's been into the flat again.'

He draped his forearm across his eyes. 'Have you heard someone?'

'No, of course not. They come when I'm out. Jack's pipes are missing, and a box of photographs I had.'

'Dad's pipes? I haven't seen them for years. They must be somewhere.'

'I'm telling you, they're not here. I've looked everywhere.'

'Mum, has your door been forced?'

'No. I don't think so.'

'And you haven't left a window open?'

'You know I never do.'

'We'll have a look, all right? You'll have put them away and forgotten. When was the last time you had a look in your loft?'

'I can't even get up that ladder anymore. I won't have put them up there.'

'You sure you haven't done something daft like give them to a charity shop in one of your cleaning frenzies?'

'Calum, they were your grandfather's during the war and they're precious. I'm telling you, someone's been in here. I get a bit frightened. Will you come round?'

'Mum . . . I'm sorry, I can't. It's too late. Honestly, I'm shattered. Please just . . . lock the door and go to bed. You remember your alarm, right? You know how to use it.'

'I won't be able to sleep.'

'Look—' he broke off, sat up, ran his fingers through his hair. Julie had gone into the bathroom and he could hear water pattering in the shower. 'If you're feeling that worried about being on your own there, maybe we should talk about finding you somewhere else to stay.'

'You mean a nursing home? You want to put me in a nursing home?'

'No, I don't.'

'That would make your life easier. I know I'm a burden.'

He could feel his pulse at his temples. 'It's not about me. I want you to feel safe.'

'I suppose you'll do what you have to, Calum. If you think that's for the best, I'll just have to . . . '

'Mum, I'm not going to make you do anything against your will. I'll come see you in the morning. We can talk then, all right?'

'What time are you coming?'

'Let's say eleven. Why don't you write yourself a wee note so you remember?'

'Of course I'll remember.'

He took a deep breath. As often as not, she was out when he arrived, dotting around Fort William picking up bits of shopping or having a cup of tea. She was still agile enough, and determined to maintain her independence. She didn't like him waiting in the flat on his own and would accuse him of snooping, or worse. Alzheimer's twisted her lack of trust in all the wrong directions. Now it was only his word against hers. 'Right, I'll call you before I leave here and let you know I'm on my way.'

He lay for a minute longer after hanging up, wishing Julie hadn't conveniently removed herself from the room. It was a deliberate removal; she didn't want to know the gory details

28

of Mary's decline or its implications for him. He and Julie were birds of a feather: solitary creatures who came together for one purpose only. They had agreed that they were not partners, only grown-up friends. In bed, it worked. Out of bed, it was either not enough or too much, depending on his mood or hers.

He pulled on a pair of shorts and a T-shirt, went downstairs and poured two glasses of cabernet. While he was waiting for Julie, he sat with the laptop and checked e-mails. There were four gig invitations: a ceilidh, a wedding and two Yes campaign events. There were also e-mails about a kitchen installation, a loft conversion and a rant in Gaelic from the mother of one of his fiddle students. He put on his reading glasses and tried to fathom it. He could still understand Gaelic well enough when he heard it, but reading it gave him a headache. Vaguely, he gathered that Morag had to be nagged to practise even ten minutes a day and spent all her time in her room listening to pop music. Poor kid, he thought. At the age of twelve, finally rebelling against the most overbearing parents Calum had ever met: pop-up Highlanders, who had moved their sustainable architecture business from Edinburgh, learned Gaelic and home-schooled their children.

He thought momentarily of Finn standing out on the headland playing 'Another Brick in the Wall' on the Highland pipes and Mary listening from the front door, arms crossed over her chest, asking, 'Pink Who?'

He wrote back in English, 'Why don't we try guitar lessons?'

Then he flicked onto Facebook and brought up Catriona's profile. It was a painful, necessary daily exercise, one which sometimes choked him with all the words that went unspoken. This voyeuristic little portal was the only contact they had with each other. He didn't know if she looked at his profile. If she did, she would see photographs of otters and eagles, his kayak grounded on various beaches, occasional links to articles from the *Guardian* and even more occasional photographs of himself at a gig somewhere. It was his life and it wasn't. It was a surface-skim, a position statement that represented where he wanted to be more than where he was.

From her own profile, he knew that she'd spent her first year in Edinburgh drinking, clubbing, partying, maybe occasionally studying. There was chat about boys and bands, all reassuringly predictable teenage stuff. Selfies with pouty faces, dim light, backdrops of dance floors and laughing students. Sometimes he clicked 'like' just to let her know he was paying attention. He never commented and she never acknowledged his presence. Her silent message was clear enough: a Facebook friendship was all he deserved. It was better than nothing.

But it was gone now. Most of it, anyway. At first he thought there was some fault with Facebook, but as he clicked through her profile he realised that she'd taken down as many of the pictures as she could and removed all of the personal information about herself: school, university, home town, relationships. Her most recent post, from several days ago, said, *Cat is Gone. Fuck Edinburgh, Fuck Uni, Fuck You.*

Julie came into the kitchen and picked up the glass of wine he'd left at the end of the table. 'I'm down to Glasgow first thing tomorrow.'

'So just have the one.'

'I'm not staying over.'

'It's up to you, as always.'

'What do you mean by that? Are you saying none of this is your choice?'

He took off his glasses and looked up at her, determined

30

that her hackles were still up and that retreat was his only option. 'No, it's fine Julie. Forget I said that. Here, have a look at this.' He showed her Cat's profile. 'What do you think this means?'

Her face became pointy and keen. 'She's fallen out with someone and she's gone home. It's the end of term, right? Maybe she's finally realised that Edinburgh is full of pretentious tossers.'

'Come on.'

'Honestly. What are you looking at her profile for anyway?'

'She's my daughter.'

'It's creepy.'

'It's not. If you put stuff on here, you have to expect folk to look at it. I just wonder why she's changed her tone so abruptly. Something's happened. I hope she's all right, that's all.'

'Phone her if you're so worried.'

'She won't speak to me.'

'What is it about women that makes you so passive aggressive?'

'I beg your pardon?'

She laughed as she brought her glass to her lips. 'If you're concerned about her, phone her. Go see her. Make a move, Calum, don't just spy on her from your safe little hidey-hole and pretend you give two shites about her.' The Glasgow in her took over when she gave advice. There was no diplomatic dance around the issue, only heartfelt opinion delivered like a knuckle to the nose.

She took another sip of wine and put the glass down, then gathered her bag and her keys. 'I'll see you in a couple of weeks. Keep an eye on the house for me.'

'Okay.'

She kissed his cheek and lingered for a couple of seconds, waiting for something else. A hug, a word, an indication that he was capable of feeling anything other than this leaden ambivalence. Sometimes he wasn't. It wasn't about her. At least he was honest about that.

He touched her arm. 'See you, then.'

'Aye. See you.'

When she was gone, he sat with his guitar and let disconnected riffs and segments tumble out. When he felt in danger of drifting too far, music brought him back. It was one thing he knew he could rely on and he was grateful for it. The guitar's shape against his belly was a comfort and the faint smells of beer and smoke emanating from the wood helped him recall times of genuine happiness. They were precious as gems, stitched into a cloth that seemed otherwise chaotically woven and easily torn. His clearest memories were supported by music: lyrics and melodies you could hang moments on to keep until you needed them again. A single verse could bring back the best times of his life, and some of the worst.

GLENDARACH, 1986

Mary sang 'An Eala Ban', the White Swan, and her face was the colour of porridge. She didn't cry. Calum had heard her weeping alone in her bedroom every night since his dad died, but she refused to let anyone see her grief. Caring for Jack had taken its toll; it was visible in the shadows around her eyes and the hollows of her cheeks. Still, she was determined to be seen to be unbroken. She was stoic and gracious in the church today, and now, with the house full of relatives, neighbours and friends. As she sang, the people in the room were still, frozen in time. Her voice was high and thin and pure, and nobody made a sound to dilute it. Auntie Helen, his dad's sister up from Glasgow, had tears streaming from her eyes. They created sludgy mascara tracks but she didn't wipe them away. She just sat there looking like a demented clown, with her voluminous ginger perm and streaky cheeks.

It all felt like a play. A big show, a fiction, a joke even. Like Dad would spring through the front door in the middle of his own wake and shout, 'Surprise!' It would be the kind of thing he'd do, the ultimate practical joke, trying to catch them all out. He'd have something to say about all of this, for sure. The funeral mass, the churchyard burial, the mourners in black. It wasn't Red Jack's style. The priest promising life everlasting. Steaming pile of superstitious shite, he would say. Another myth cooked up to keep us in our place.

When he stopped trying to convert Mum to atheism, they knew he was really dying. Let her have her way about the funeral, he'd finally told Calum. It'll make her feel better, and I won't know the difference anyway.

Calum looked for Finn, scanning as far to each side as he could without distracting everyone from Mary's song. He'd caught Finn slugging whisky straight from a bottle just after they came back from church and given him a half-hearted reprimand.

'Don't embarrass Mum,' he whispered, grappling the bottle away from his brother. Finn replied with that smirking laugh, a suggestion that he knew something nobody else did, and drifted out of the room. Calum hadn't seen him since.

There were two or three seconds of absolute silence when Mary finished her song, broken by Auntie Helen wailing, 'Oh my brother, my big brother,' and others moving to comfort her. This too was for show. She didn't have to be so melodramatic, just like Mum didn't have to be so stony. Most of all, he would miss Dad's realness. Dad never lost his ability to be exactly who he was in any situation, knowable and solid, even as his cancer became terminal. If he was here now, he'd cough up a sarcastic remark, put his boots on and find something useful to do. He'd chop some wood or paint the shed, and leave the mourning to the rest of them.

Two more weeks, Calum thought. Two more weeks and he'd be away from here, maybe forever. He wished he could pack up right now and sneak away while everyone was distracted. He had offered to postpone university for a year so that Mum and Finn wouldn't be left alone so abruptly.

'Your dad would have wanted you to go,' Mum had said, with barely a suggestion of martyrdom in her voice. So he was going, and glad. He was claustrophobic here, fettered by the judgements of people who had watched him grow up and thought they knew him. You were a fish in a net here. If you stayed, you would be ensnared forever by your family's name, the reputations of your parents and your aunties and uncles and cousins, the whispered memories – or made-up stories posing as memories – of the people whose genes you carried.

He opened a bottle of lager, lit a cigarette and stepped out the back door. It was a beautiful September day, the sun filtering lazily through a thin gauze of cloud. Not that summers were ever aggressive here. The heat was always fragile, blown away on the slightest whim of the Atlantic. Days like this were easy, gentle and kind.

He was expecting it to be cold in Aberdeen when he arrived. Everyone said east coast cold was something different. They said it was a meaner thing altogether and that the North Sea wind cut you like a blade no matter how many layers you wore. Calum sucked on the cigarette and blew away a shiver of anxiety. He refused to be scared about going away, even though it felt like everyone wanted him to be.

They warned him about the weather, they warned him about men with knives, they warned him about girls who might try to trap him, they warned him about venereal diseases, they warned him about city traffic and burglars and foreigners who came off the ships and unscrupulous landlords and Americans. Dad had warned him not to be seduced by the capitalist oil barons and their promises of fat paycheques. Mum had warned him not to be seduced by cultists and evangelicals who preyed on young students. They warned him not to drink too much, they warned him not to study too much and forget to have fun. Finn warned him not to turn into a wanker.

'Have you seen your brother?'

He turned around. Mary stepped out beside him, a mug of tea between both hands. 'Nuh.'

'Mmm.' She looked across the garden toward the woods. 'Your father's just died of cancer and you're standing in my kitchen smoking.'

'Sorry.' He dropped the butt into the dregs of his beer.

'Promise me you won't smoke when you go to university, Calum. Just stop it now while you can.'

'I will.' He wondered how old he'd have to be before she stopped issuing directions and assuming she knew best. He wondered when they'd be able to have a conversation that meant anything.

'Calum . . .'

'What, Mum?'

She stared at him, mouth half open. 'Nothing. Never mind. Would you go see if you can find Finlay? I'm worried about him.'

'He's fine. You know he doesn't like crowds.'

'Just go and find him.'

'Aye, okay.' He touched her arm. 'Are you all right?'

'Of course I'm all right,' she snapped.

35

Ask me, he thought. Ask me and pretend you really care about the answer. Just for once, pretend you worry about me the way you do about Finn.

She didn't. She wouldn't. Calum sighed. 'I'll go look for him.'

He found Finn where he expected to find him, on the beach below Iain's house. Only three months ago, Jack had been standing right here with his pipes under his arm. It was the last time he ever played them. From his lungs, the cancer invaded his bones. The pain was excruciating in his last few weeks. He drifted in and out of morphine dreams until Mary finally cut him loose with a gentle shove: Let go, my love. It's all right to let go now.

Finn was sitting on the sand, smoking a joint. Calum sat beside him and for a few minutes they ignored each other. From here you looked straight out towards Skye's toothy profile. From this distance, the Cuillins looked small enough: piranha teeth rising out of the sea. Calum had walked the ridge for the first time only about a month ago, balanced on a blade of stone, quietly terrified as the wind buffeted his shoulders and tried to shove him over the edge. At one stage, he'd found himself unable to step forward or back, so weak with panic that all he could do was sit down and renew contact with something solid. His friend Gary ripped the piss out of him badly, but Gary's dad sat beside him, poured him some tea from a flask and told him never to be ashamed of a healthy fear of heights. He'd never been so genuinely afraid of dying, but then he'd never had to watch someone he loved dying before either.

He watched his brother suck on the joint and wondered what he was supposed to do about it. 'If you share that, I won't tell Mum you've got it.'

Finn handed it over, got up and strolled to the tide line,

gathered a handful of flat pebbles. Then, without bothering to roll up his trousers, he waded into the water up to his knees and began skimming stones over the gentle waves. He threw stone after stone, and as the hash took hold, Calum saw him throwing away tiny pieces of himself, one after the other.

UNFINISHED BUSINESS

Catriona filled the bath until water dripped into the overflow, slid down until her chin was submerged and closed her eyes. Heat surrounded her and the steam was so thick that it stole oxygen from the air. With the light off and the blind drawn, the bathroom was pitch dark, and the darkness was protective, like a womb. She tilted her head back so that her ears were underwater and all she could hear was water sloshing against the sides of the bath and her own breath inside her head. If she wanted to, she could let herself sink. She forced herself down so that the water covered her nose and mouth, and stayed down as long as she could. After less than a minute she pushed her feet against the end of the tub and sat up. It wasn't as easy as it ought to have been. Sometimes such bleakness came over her that she couldn't imagine living another day. But then she thought about all the unfinished business there was. If she topped herself now, she wouldn't wake up to an independent Scotland on the 19th of September. She would never get Kyle back for what he did. She squeezed water out of her eyes and pulled the plug.

It was after ten already, but she dressed again in a pair of black jeans and a hoodie, stumped downstairs and poked her head into the living room. 'I'm going to meet Robbie.'

Jenny drew her eyes away from the television. 'Robbie? What's he doing now?'

'Working.'

'Uh huh.' Jenny waited for more. 'Doing what?'

'Just . . . in a bar.' Catriona hoped Jenny wouldn't ask for details. She'd given her virginity to sweet Robbie Brown in fifth year, mostly because they were both seventeen and felt like they were missing out on something everyone else had been doing since third year. He had embarrassed himself trying to put the condom on, and the deed itself was tentative: it didn't hurt but Cat had gone home wondering what the fuss was all about.

'We're just going to have a drink and maybe go for a coffee when he gets off.'

'Oh . . . well . . .' Jenny glanced at the clock. 'Be safe, then.'

'Yeah.' She ducked out of the room and left, striding as forcefully as she could. The sun was a pinkish glow behind heavy mist but she was grateful for the light it provided; it was a half-hour walk into town and the streets were quiet. Her senses were on high alert, catching shadows and footsteps, snippets of conversation, the passing whiff of a stranger's perfume, and as she told her legs to move forward, some deeper force made them want to skip sideways into a doorway or break into a run. She was in the grip of something that wasn't normal or rational; she'd never been anxious like this in her life. She'd walked this road hundreds of times, even late at night, and she'd never been scared before. Maybe she'd just been too stupid to know that she should have been.

The streets were busier as she neared the city centre: buses and taxis hissing over damp tarmac, groups spilling out of pubs, Wednesday night revellers. Waiting to cross Union Street, she thought she heard a man's voice calling her name. A flood of adrenaline drove her from the corner and she darted between stationary traffic. On the other side, she paused, searched and listened. A drunk man was calling to his mate, shouting something that sounded like *Cat*, but he was older and fat and it clearly wasn't meant for her. He wasn't Kyle.

She wondered why she'd thought it was Kyle. Then she wondered why that should frighten her so much. Kyle was in Edinburgh. He was no threat to her. Surely he wouldn't . . .

He wouldn't what?

She remembered him carrying her in arms like pythons. She couldn't have broken away from him even if she'd tried.

She swiped her fingers under her eyes and hurried the rest of the way to Robbie's bar. It was a small place tucked away down a side street: a shabby chic combination of rickety wooden tables, metal chairs and velvet sofas. The clientele and staff were obviously gay, confirming what she'd always secretly known about Robbie. She saw him behind the bar in his tight black T-shirt and jeans, hair in a perfectly sculpted quiff. It was a relief as the door shut out the street behind her. At least the men in here wouldn't grab her bum or slaver in her face.

Robbie came around the end of the bar and hugged her. 'Here's my girl.'

'Hey Rob. You look amazing.'

'You like?'

'The women of Scotland are in mourning.'

He grinned. 'Sorry.'

'I'm happy for you. I knew anyway.'

He rubbed her arms and inspected her. 'You look rough, by the way.'

'I know that too.'

Robbie patted a bar stool. 'Sit. Drink. Tell. What you having?'

'Make me something sweet.'

Robbie mixed up a concoction involving gin and frozen raspberries, and topped it with fresh mint leaves. It tasted dangerously non-alcoholic. He left her to serve other customers and by the time he came back it was nearly gone.

'What's up with you, then?'

'I fell in love with the wrong person and he hurt me.'

'I hate him. What did he do?'

'It doesn't matter. I just need to forget about him, but for some reason it's like...he's following me around. In my head.'

'So you need to tell him to get to fuck. For real. Phone him and tell him you're never going to think about him again. Make the break on your terms.'

'I wish I could.' She closed her eyes and imagined facing up to Kyle. She'd bugger it up, like she always did. She'd open her mouth and no sound would come out, and he'd laugh at her. That's what would happen. Kyle would laugh at her and she would hear him laughing at her forever.

'I wish I could be someone else, Robbie.'

'Who do you want to be?'

'Someone who takes no shit.'

He laughed. 'I have an idea. Wait till I get off.'

It was light again by the time she finally took the towel off her head and stepped in front of the mirror. Robbie stood behind her, echoing her expression. Shock, excitement and horror jolted her in equal measures. They'd bought supplies at an all-night supermarket on the way back to his parents' house: gin, bleach and dye. She drank while he massaged her head, fingertips hot and strong beneath her hair.

'Do you trust me?' he asked.

She said, 'Yes.' So she sat there and allowed him to snip her hair short, imagining each cut lock releasing an evil spirit from her brain. Then she bent over the bath while he bleached out her own mousy colour and replaced it with an electric cherry red.

'Oh my God,' they said in tandem. Her fingers went to her forehead and lifted a lock. 'Oh my God!'

Robbie slid his fingers into her hair and pulled it out into spikes. 'It's fucking amazing.'

'My mother is going to go off her nut.'

He pressed his cheek against hers. 'And?'

'And I don't give a shit.'

'Correct.' He giggled. 'Repeat after me, Catriona. I take no shit.'

'I take no shit.'

'I take no shit from anyone.'

'I take no shit from anyone,' she echoed, but her voice was meek and thin.

'You have to mean it.'

'I do.'

Robbie looked at her and she knew he didn't believe her. The air felt too thin to power her vocal chords. Her lungs dragged in meagre sustenance and her body wilted. She leaned into his chest. 'I promise you, I mean it.'

MATCH

Mary knew anything could incriminate her. Those years she'd spent going around the folk clubs, singing the songs her mother and aunties had taught her, sharing tables with poets and communists. The teaching. There were books she'd taught, books they wouldn't like her to have taught, words they wouldn't have wanted her to keep alive. Jack's trade union associations. Those campaigns he'd involved himself in, the strikes, the rallies, the marches, the times he'd got himself arrested. There were letters, old posters, photographs, ticket stubs, programmes. She had been too sentimental about it all, and it would be her downfall. They were trying to get inside her walls.

She carried four shoeboxes into the kitchen, opened the first and lifted out a photo of herself on a stage, singing. Her eyes closed, her hands open, palms up. Hair like the fine waving tail of a bay horse, parted in the middle. She remembered the time she'd been called the Highland Joan Baez by an Edinburgh promoter, and Jack had shouted out from the front table that Joan Baez was the American Mary Macdonald. A fond ripple of laughter went around the room like an embrace, a rise of song, a purpose shared. Back then, starting a revolution felt innocent and hopeful.

Those days had occupied her mind lately, memories coming to the surface like messages in one of those Magic

8 balls the boys used to have. Some days, the past was more vivid than the present. Some days she felt wrapped in cotton wool, fuzzy in her mind, like you always felt on New Year's morning. She went into rooms and forgot why. She went for shopping and came back with an empty trolley. It would be those tablets they made her swallow from the wee plastic boxes, three for every day of the week, all different colours. They were all in on it, maybe even Calum. Maybe he was letting them in. They were trying to get inside the walls. They were watching everything she did.

What had she been thinking, keeping hold of all this evidence?

Mary struck a match and held it to the bottom corner of the photograph.

THE ANGEL

Against his better judgement, Calum finished off the bottle of wine he'd opened for Julie and chased it with a couple of whiskies. In the morning, things were blurry, clouded by fumes, partially rubbed out. A squally little front had blown over during the night, hammering at the windows, manufacturing noisy dreams before waking him with the early dawn. But it had gone on to the east now, leaving mist hanging low over glassy, silicon water. He dragged the kayak over the beach and pushed it into the water, climbed in and paddled out into the bay, watching the ripples roll out across the surface. He dipped his fingers into the water and splashed his face, closing his eyes as the cold droplets ran down his neck and into the collar of his cagoule.

Maybe all memory is fabrication, he thought as he tried to paddle back to sobriety. Maybe we go through our lives forgetting the most significant details, and imagination steps in to fill the gaps. Maybe the events in our lives never really happened the way we remember them months and years later. He'd read somewhere that human senses only perceived the world partially and that the brain made assumptions about the rest, and he wondered if maybe nothing really happened the way you thought it did. If that was the case, you could make up any old story and it would be as true as anything else.

Maybe Finn's madness wasn't really madness, delusion wasn't really delusion and an angel did come for him after all.

GLENCOE, 1991

'She climbs with me,' Finn said. They were in the Clachaig Inn and more than a bit drunk after a day on the Buachaille Etive Mòr. The noise around them had risen on a tide of beer and whisky: the singer was belting out Corries songs, people were laughing and shouting at each other to be heard over him, and the heat was like an enormous, muffling duvet around them.

Calum hadn't really been sure he'd heard Finn right. An angel made of stone. He had to be taking the piss. Finn was at the peak of one of his up phases, buzzing with manic energy and speaking in a single unpunctuated stream that shifted subject without reason or warning. His *craic* was magnanimous and people who didn't know where it came from were drawn to him like midges to an over-bright lamp. Calum's university mate Andy was sitting on Finn's other side, and other climbers and mountaineers had gravitated around their table as the night progressed. His reputation was already preceding him.

Finn was nineteen and had been climbing for just over a year. Calum had suggested it, as a way of levering him out of the house during one of his depressions. To say he took to it naturally was something of an understatement; he moved up the rock like Spiderman. He was a perfect climber: long and lean, with oversized hands and a pathological lack of fear.

Looking back now, it was easy enough to see it for what it was, but back then it was thrilling and more than a little contagious. Finn made them all better climbers, pushed them up harder routes, challenged them to stretch beyond what they thought themselves capable of. And when he climbed, all you could really do was tilt your head back and watch. Almost immediately after taking up climbing, Finn emerged from the blackness of his depression and into a jubilant, if surreal, celebration of life.

Late into a wild night in the Clachaig, long after last orders had been called, he told them about his guardian angel. 'She's in the stone,' he said. 'Actually in it. She moves through the stone beside me.'

'What, like a ghost or something?' Andy asked. His voice was like tyres on gravel. He'd smoked a joint earlier and was prone to any kind of freaky rock jock bullshit.

'Nah.' Finn closed his eyes and leaned his head back on the bench, and his hands rose into the air in front of him, fingers illustrating the way they gripped the tiniest of holds. 'I mean ... the rock is alive, my friend. She is the rock ... they're one and the same. That's how I know I'm safe. I won't die.' He laughed. 'Not climbing.'

'Dude, that's *holy*,' said another nameless guy with Jesus hair and a goatee, and the noises around the table indicated appreciation and belief.

'You don't half spew some rubbish, Finn,' Calum said for the benefit of the others, annoyed that strangers took Finn's weirdness for spirituality. 'You're safe because I'm belaying you. If you fall, I'm the only guardian angel you've got.'

'No offence, brother, but you're irrelevant. I don't need you, I don't need gear. I'm *protected*. Know what I mean?'

'Mate, he *is*,' said Andy. 'How else do you explain it? He shouldn't be able to pull off the moves he does. It's like he stretches ... like elastic. He can hold on to bloody *nothing*. Thin air. He could free climb a glass skyscraper.'

'Don't give him ideas.'

'You're just jealous, dude. You could climb your whole

47

life and never be able to do what he's learned in a year.'

'Andy, you don't know anything about it, all right? I mean it, don't encourage him.'

'Aye, don't encourage me, Andy,' Finn chipped in, grinning. 'I'm no right in the heid. I'm mad, so I am. Loopy. Ha haha.' His laugh was forced at first, then became real. A silent rib-splitter that drew tears from his eyes. 'Calum can't see them. He can't see what's all around us, man.'

'See what?'

'The angels.'

'Finn . . . ' Calum cleared his throat. It was getting embarrassing now. 'You're fleein'. Let's go crash, eh?'

'Open your mind, bro, it's a beautiful thing.'

Andy guffawed and slapped Calum on the back. 'He's an engineer, Finn; if he can't put it into a formula, it doesn't exist.'

Calum drained his pint and stood up. 'So are you, and you should know better. Come on, Saint Columba, let's get some kip.'

Calum lay beside Finn in their tiny two-man tent, watching his brother sleep. It was a relief when he finally slept; for a few hours, at least, he was quiet and in a safe place. Sleep evaded him most of the night as he thought about the unexpected switchbacks on his brother's road and wondered where the next one would take him. Possibilities materialised like yellow eyes glowing in the darkness, each more frightening than the last. He dozed and dreamed of Finn peeling off a slick rock face and falling backwards in slow motion, arms outstretched, waiting for the angel to extend her hand.

The mist gathered in the tops of the trees and magnified the sounds of early morning on the bay: oystercatchers, water sloshing against the boats, Hugh MacNeill coughing like a bull seal as he rowed out to his lobster boat. Calum paddled gently for a few minutes, gliding through the translucent water, eyes scanning for life beneath him. Sometimes on these placid mornings a seal or an otter would come to investigate him, bobbing up alongside him with no suggestion of fear. Last week he'd crossed paths with a basking shark: a prehistoric phantom slithering through the water, the size of a bus, passing so close to his kayak he could have reached out and stroked its speckled back. These meetings with wildness touched the same thing in him that climbing had when he was younger and braver. Like a drug, they lifted him and steeled him against his more pessimistic days.

He left the mouth of the bay and pushed out into open water, pulling harder now. The wind drew tears from his eyes and he paddled until his shoulders ached and his lungs felt ready to burst. He kept going against the current as long and fast as he could, then stopped and slouched forward, chest heaving and sweat trickling down his back. He drifted for a minute until he heard a distinctive peep above him and looked up. A massive shape rose from a rocky outcrop on the headland to his left, drifted like an immense shadow down towards the water no more than twenty metres from him, then rose again and circled above him. The eagle's pale tail flashed like a salute as it extended its fingered wings into a span more than half the length of his boat. There was a pair nesting in a tree just over the headland, and by the size, he guessed this to be the female. Calum held the boat as still as he could and watched her, and she appeared to be drifting for the pure joy of looking down at a flightless human. She surveyed him from her lofty position. She surely knew him by now and understood his habits as well as he understood her own. He watched her sail away to the north and disappear into the mist, then he dipped his paddle into the water, turned and skimmed with the current back towards the beach.

He grounded the kayak and extricated himself, pulled the boat back over the sand, hoisted it onto its trailer and wheeled it over the road. Leaving the kayak upside down at the side of the house, he went inside, peeled off his damp clothes and left them on the tiled lobby floor, then went for a shower.

Dried and dressed, he made coffee and sat with it at the kitchen table, sipping slowly. He picked up a pencil and drew a sketchy eagle on the back of a torn envelope, a few lines to indicate the water and the island. He liked his drawing and smiled at it. The telephone rang and his smile soured.

He answered it and a woman with a Glasgow accent asked for Mister Finlay Macdonald.

'Pardon? Did you say Finlay?'

'Yes, Finlay Macdonald. Are you Mr Macdonald? The son of Mrs Mary Macdonald?'

'Eh ... no, I'm Calum, Finlay's brother. He's ... not around. Who is this?'

'Mr Macdonald, my name is Angela Moore and I'm phoning from Belford Hospital. I'm afraid your mum's had a bit of an accident early this morning and has been brought in to us.'

Calum's first response was to silently curse the addled old bitch, but he was immediately ashamed by the callousness of his instincts. He closed his eyes and took a deep breath. 'Is she all right? What happened?'

'She appears to have started a fire in her kitchen. She's not injured, but she's confused and a bit shocked. She doesn't seem to know why she's here.'

'That would be because she has Alzheimer's,' Calum muttered, pressing his fingertips into his eyes. 'You don't have any record of that?'

'I see. Given the hour, we haven't accessed her medical records yet.'

'Right. Was anyone else hurt?'

'The whole block had to be evacuated, but thankfully there were no other casualties. I don't know what damage there was to the flat itself.'

'Okay ... ehm ... ' He struggled to think clearly. 'Tell her I'll be there as soon as I can. I'm about an hour away.'

'I'm sorry, but she has asked for your brother. Will you let him know, or can you tell us how to reach him?'

'No, I'm afraid I can't,' he snapped. There was no point being angry at Angela Moore, whoever she was, but he needed someone to be angry at. 'He's beyond reach.'

'Oh ... I am sorry, I didn't ... '

'No, you didn't. Just tell my mother I'm on my way.'

A FACE IN THE
CROWD

Eilidh and Kate had been working all year and had money to blow. Catriona trailed around the Union Square shops after them, sweaty and flushed in the changing rooms as they tried on tops and jeans from the full price racks. They traded gossip about friends from their high school class, tallying the successes and failures of their first proper adult year: Amy Gillis and Daniel Begg had got engaged, Charlotte Jacobs had written off the Golf her parents had bought her for her eighteenth, Ryan Gilchrest was working offshore and getting drunk, Leah Malley was pregnant.

Catriona let the information wash past her, indifferent, feeling detached as a soul shaken loose from its body by some brutal force. She liked the look of her red hair in the mirror, but it hadn't made her feel any more substantial. Now, on top of everything else, she felt guilty about breaking her promise to Robbie. She hadn't been back to see him and didn't want to become the depressive friend who wept into her glass at the end of the bar. She tried on a single T-shirt from a sale rack. The twelve was too tight across her chest and she was embarrassed to pick up the fourteen.

'Don't like it,' she told the girls, leaving it on the hook in the changing room, pulling her hoodie back over her head. It was an oversized boy's one from a charity shop, which was as far as her student loan and her small allowance would stretch. 'I'm skint anyway.'

A year ago her life had felt like a flower unfolding. She could remember what the happiness felt like but couldn't imagine ever feeling it again. Everything was heavy now, even the stale air of the shopping mall as it dragged against her limbs. A flutter of nausea hung around the top of her stomach, sometimes moving up towards her throat. They sat in a coffee shop and she nibbled a bit of cake as her eyes drifted over the faces of the passing people. They were strange and familiar at the same time, like she'd forgotten how to distinguish features.

Then she froze. Kyle had materialised from between the ranks of shoppers, drifting casually towards her with his usual languid gait. He was alone and walking towards her. Catriona wanted to bolt away but she couldn't move. Her legs were disconnected from her brain. Blood thundered between her ears and her vision curved in at the edges, threatening to black out completely. Kate and Eilidh continued to chat, oblivious. He was ten feet away now, staring right at her, smiling. There was nothing she could do now except tell Kate and Eilidh. If he spoke to them, they'd never believe her. His chat was sleek and quick as mercury, his face so perfect that they'd fall at his feet. Any girl would.

She opened her mouth but no sound came out. Bile spilled onto her tongue.

Kyle walked straight past without even pausing. She was wet with sweat and her whole body felt limp.

It couldn't have been him.

What if it was?

If he was following her, he surely wouldn't have let her see him. Unless he was trying to scare her.

Kyle wouldn't do that. Most likely he'd forgotten her

already. She was seeing things. It was a panic hallucination. 'Can we go?' she blurted.

Eilidh tipped her cup back, shook the last of the foam into her mouth. 'You've gone all peely-wally.'

'I don't feel very well.'

'You fancy this film, then?'

'What film? Sorry, I wasn't listening.'

Kate laughed. 'Oh my God, Catriona, you've missed the whole conversation.'

'I'm not up for the cinema. I think I'll head home.' She retrieved her bag from the floor under her chair, slipped her phone and keys into the front pocket of her hoodie, wanting to move in the opposite direction from the Kyle lookalike.

Eilidh stood up. 'Are you all right? You want us to chum you home?'

'No ... no, I'm fine, I just feel a bit sick. You can stay.'

'I feel bad.'

'Don't. I'll text you later.' She turned her back on the girls and hurried away. They would speculate behind her back but all she cared about was getting as far away from here as possible. She found the quickest route out of the shopping centre, paused at the door and glanced behind her. Strangers moved past, laden with shopping bags. Opposing campaigners stood on either side of the door, one saying Yes and the other saying No Thanks. There was no sign of Kyle so she pulled up her hood and ran for the bus.

At home she bolted the door and drew the blinds. She sat down in the living room but was afraid to take her shoes off. The dogs wriggled around her calves, bumping against her and whining for attention. They needed a walk but she couldn't do it. She couldn't open the door or be seen in the street. The silence of the house pressed down on her. To dispel it, she put on *The Hunger Games* DVD and tried to imagine herself being as hard and brave and resourceful as

Katniss Everdeen. Katniss wouldn't curl up and spend the rest of her life on the sofa.

Katniss would kill the bastard.

Catriona lay on the sofa and imagined dropping a nest of wasps on Kyle while he slept.

MARY MACDONALD'S FAREWELL

As Calum drove, his mind was a confusion of memories and emotions, all punctuated by the same sense of falling through open space that came to him in dreams. Sometimes when he took a corner too fast, he felt the wheels lift off the road and the vehicle turn in slow motion onto its side, roll and sail out into nothingness. The loss of control frightened him, forced him to lift his foot from the accelerator and wipe his sweaty palms on his jeans.

He found his mother on a bed in A&E, turning the pages of a gossip magazine. She was dressed in a hospital gown and sitting on top of the sheet, knotted white legs sticking out in front of her. Her toenails were long and neglected and he wondered for the first time whether she was even managing the basics of personal hygiene. The acrid stench of burnt plastic radiated from her hair.

'Hi Mum.'

She looked up at him and seemed surprised. 'I wasn't expecting you. How did you get here so quickly?'

'I drove.'

'From America?'

He sighed. 'From Glendarach. What did you do?'

Her eyebrows drew together. 'What do you mean?'

He pulled up a chair beside her bed and sat down. 'You started a fire. Jesus ... I *knew* this would happen. You promised me you wouldn't.'

'Ocht, don't be daft. I've done no such thing. I'm here for tests.'

'Tests ...'

'Yes, tests.'

'Right.' Calum sighed and glanced around for a nurse.

'Well if you visited more, you'd know.'

He looked at her again. 'I saw you last Sunday. I spent most of the day with my head under your sink.'

'Well I don't remember. I must have blocked it out because you were unpleasant, as usual.'

'Aye, no bloody wonder.'

'Language!' she said in an exaggerated stage whisper. Nothing wrong with her hearing, anyway.

'What's happening then? Are they keeping you in?'

She made an exasperated sound. 'They don't tell you anything in these places. I expect they're waiting for Finn to arrive to take me home.'

Calum rose from his seat. 'Jesus Christ, what's the matter with you?'

People in surrounding beds stared. Calum drew the curtain beside his mother, sat down again and took a deep breath. 'Finn's gone,' he said, very softly. 'Don't you remember?'

'What do you mean he's gone?'

'Mum ... he's dead. You know that.' It was not news he'd expected to have to deliver a second time.

Mary's hands shook as she fingered the sheet. 'He's ... no ... that's not right, Calum. Why would you say that?' Her voice crumbled and she moved her head back and forth. 'Why would you do that to me?'

He lifted his hand and held it above hers, afraid to touch her. 'It's been twenty-one years.'

She continued to shake her head, but her eyes had filled with tears and her lips trembled. 'I ... of course ... I *do* remember now. I don't know what I was ... oh dear ... I don't know what came over me. I think I must have dreamed about him last night.'

Calum allowed his fingers to settle over hers, tried to expel his temper with a long, slow breath. 'It's all right.'

Her eyes narrowed as the recollection seemed to solidify in her mind, and he turned away from her so he didn't have to see the accusation that would inevitably accompany it. Perhaps this creeping amnesia would cure her of the need to blame him for something that had never been his fault, but right now he could feel her gathering her energy for an attack.

The arrival of a young doctor diverted her attention. By the state of his stubble and crushed shirt, he looked to be nearing the end of a very long shift.

'Now then, Mrs Macdonald, I see your son has arrived. I'm Dr Robertson. You must be Finlay.'

'No, I'm Calum,' he replied tartly. He wanted to walk away and leave Mary to the mercies of the NHS and Highland Council's Social Work Department. He wanted to claim no further knowledge of his mother or the dilemma she now posed for ever-dwindling public budgets. He gripped the sides of his chair and held himself down. 'My brother Finlay passed away in 1993.'

'Oh ... ah ... ' the doctor glanced down at his clipboard and quickly composed himself. 'I'm sorry, she ... asked for him.'

'Mrs Macdonald is having some problems with her memory,' Calum said, and glared at his mother.

He arrived home after nine, poured himself a large whisky and subsided onto the sofa. One massive clusterfuck of a day;

58

there was no other way to describe it. His utility room was now filled with bags of clothing, towels, blankets and linens, a fraction of what would have to be washed, everything infused with charred plastic and electrical fumes. Dad's pipes were still missing, too. He was sure they were still in the flat somewhere, but even after several searches of the loft, they hadn't turned up. He swallowed his whisky in two gulps, leaned his head back, closed his eyes and thought about the latest succession of disasters.

Mum's flat. Thank goodness it was only Mum's flat and not the whole building. It wasn't a total write-off but it wouldn't be habitable for a while. The worst of the damage was confined to the kitchen but the rest was damp and smoke-cured, and he suspected the wiring was buggered throughout. Expensive insurance job, *if* any sensible insurance company would agree to cover the fire-raising tendencies of a demented old woman. It seemed a pretty big if in his book. Mary would have to be found somewhere else to live for a while, or possibly permanently. The question of whether she could ever live on her own again hung like a sledgehammer over his head.

Disaster number two: the insurance. Mary couldn't remember who provided her buildings and contents insurance or where she might have stashed the documents. Calum wasn't surprised: that would have been altogether too easy. She had been adamant that all of her files were in good order in Granny Ina's roll top desk in the spare room, but he had opened the desk to find a heap of paper, which slid out onto the floor when he began to shuffle through it. There were pension documents, official-looking envelopes, which had never been opened, guarantee certificates for kitchen appliances she no longer owned, but nothing resembling an insurance policy. He had no idea what you were meant to do in this scenario. Was there a number you could ring, or some other way to track down your policy? A quick Google search brought up a dozen ads for insurance companies, but nothing of use. He would end up making the repairs himself at this rate.

Defeated, he had allowed himself to be distracted from his search by a single box of photographs which, thankfully, she hadn't yet got round to torching. In their childhood years, Mary had kept beautiful albums. She had kept one of herself and Dad, one for Calum and one for Finn, and had rigorously archived the evidence of their lives: pictures, school certificates for music or maths or sport, little boys' drawings and home-made Christmas cards. She had stopped updating these after Dad died, and in fact he realised now that she must have stopped taking pictures altogether. Calum's album stopped when he was eighteen: leaving school with a shocking eighties mullet and a rebellious scowl. Finn's stopped in his fourteenth year. It didn't even see him past his adolescent spots.

The only photos from after that time were ones he had given her copies of, and these she had stored unceremoniously in a shoebox at the back of the hall cupboard. He had lingered over one in particular: himself and Finn climbing on Skye. It had been one of those translucent midsummer evenings, maybe nine o'clock at night with the sun still high above the north-western horizon, casting rose dust across the mountains and turning the sea to molten gold. Andy had taken the picture of Calum belaying and Finn climbing: all long fingers and balance, gripping the rock with his toes and left hand as his right hand stretched upward for the next hold. He climbed like a gymnast with barely a care for the gear, so quick you could hardly belay him fast enough. Calum may have talked his brother into taking up climbing, but Finn had elevated it to something beyond sport.

Calum had slipped the photo into his jacket pocket and

taken it home. Now he stared at it, remembering that long, cloudless day on the Cuillin. It was what ... twenty-two or twenty-three years ago, but its details were still sharp. You got maybe one day like that in a thousand, and when they came you had to suck them dry and hold their nourishment right down deep inside you to keep you going through the dark months. They'd made their camp high up the ridge that night, sustained by laughter, songs and Andy's hip flask, and in the morning had looked down on a layer of sea mist like a wool blanket covering the world below them.

Mum had a thing she used to say, perhaps to keep herself going through the heavy times: *Mol an latha math mu oidhche.* Praise the good day at the close of it. That had been a day for praising, and yet he hadn't thought about it for a very long time.

He'd lost touch with Andy after Finn died. Now he wondered where he was, whether he was still climbing, what kind of a hand life had dealt him. Andy was a structural engineer and had been fostering an ambition to emigrate to New Zealand, where fault lines and wobbly earth meant plenty of work and plenty of mountains. Calum often thought about Dougie and Alison too. They'd been good friends, but lost touch when he moved to America. He'd always meant to get in touch again, but life got in the way. He'd made excuses. You put your life into the hands of others so easily in the mountains, but back on flat ground you let them go again. Was that normal, he wondered, or was it just him?

He put the photo and the empty whisky glass onto the coffee table and stood up, wandered into the kitchen and stared into a mostly empty fridge. He'd eaten only a soggy, packaged sandwich in the hospital canteen in the middle of the afternoon.

Crisis of the Day, number three: Mum had been admitted for further evaluation and moved to a ward, but was now refusing to eat or to speak English. He had been intercepted at the door by a perplexed nurse, who knitted her eyebrows and suggested Mary may require to be sedated and fed by IV if it continued.

She had become a delinquent child overnight. In stunned silence, he'd turned his shoulder on the nurse and found his mother sitting on the chair beside her bed. She was watching *Cash in the Attic* with her arms crossed over her chest and her lips pressed together like a bairn presented with a plate of spinach. He shut the curtain, sucked in his breath and willed himself to be calm.

'What's the story, Mum?'

She studied him, and for a freakish moment seemed not to recognise him. Then she smiled and shrugged, and answered in Gaelic, 'These people are holding me against my will.'

He was aware of the nurse hovering outside the curtain and dropped his voice, although he was fairly certain she couldn't understand. 'Why will you not eat?'

'You don't know what they might be putting in my food.'

Fair enough. He'd had enough hospital food himself to be suspicious of it. 'You'll make yourself ill.'

'You can bring food in for me. I'll make do with bought sandwiches if that's all you can manage.'

'I'll do my best, but the rest of the time you'll have to eat what they give you.' At least she seemed to have got over the idea of Finn coming back from the dead. 'I can't come every mealtime. I don't know how long you're going to be here and I've got to work.'

She sighed, shrugged again. 'It'll suit you that I'm here, being kept quiet. I'll just have to do my best to survive, won't I?'

He pressed his fist over his lips and sat on the edge of the bed, struggling to dredge up the right words. His mastery of Gaelic had never extended to this kind of situation. In fact, even his English was faltering. 'They only want to help you,' he blurted after a mute minute. In English, loudly enough for any eavesdropping nurse to hear. 'You'll have to speak to them.'

'Why don't they speak to me in my language, then?'

He almost laughed. Mary Macdonald, latter day Highland rebel. 'Because unfortunately they are not among the chosen few who can speak God's own tongue. You'll just have to condescend to speak English.'

'I don't have to tell them anything.'

'They'll sedate you with drugs if they think you'll cause damage to yourself, or anyone else while you're at it.'

'They can do what they will.'

Calum didn't know how to respond to that, and decided this wasn't the right time to press her about the insurance. It would only confirm her suspicions. 'I'll be back in a minute.' He opened the curtain and walked up the ward, between rows of beds containing shrivelled, sickly figures. The charge nurse was at her station, writing notes on a chart. She looked up at him with raised eyebrows.

'How did she seem to you?'

'Completely fine, apart from the crazy paranoia. She seems to think she's being held prisoner.'

'Mmm.' The nurse nodded. 'Does she understand what's happening to her? With the Alzheimer's?'

'She refuses to believe it.' His eyes were still stinging after a morning in the smoky flat, and he rubbed them. Guilt nibbled at his conscience; Mary had been showing signs for a couple of years before the diagnosis but he'd avoided talking about it or bringing it to her attention. To be fair, until recently it hadn't really progressed beyond a sort of irksome forgetfulness. Total denial had worked well enough for both of them until now.

A sudden tide washed over him, turning his legs to jelly.

There was a hard orange plastic chair beside the nurse's station and he sat on it, dropped his face into his hands. 'I'm not ready for this.'

The nurse nodded, and placed one broad, plain hand on his shoulder. 'Nobody is, hon.'

He wondered, not for the first time, whether learning to call everyone *honey* or *love* or *my darling* was an official part of the nursing curriculum.

'We'll be doing some assessments over the next few days. We'll sit down with you to discuss options for when she leaves hospital. It would help if she was willing to talk to us.'

Calum looked up at her and wanted to tell her he couldn't do this. 'Is there anyone on staff here who speaks Gaelic?' he asked instead. 'They might get more out of her.'

The nurse raised an eyebrow. 'I didn't think there was anyone left who couldn't speak English.'

'She speaks English more perfectly than anyone I know, she just doesn't want to.'

'It may change by tomorrow. They take notions ... they pass.'

'Aye.' He laughed bitterly. 'Apparently.'

He abandoned his search for anything palatable in the fridge and made a bowl of porridge instead, sprinkled it with brown sugar and tucked into the sweet beige mush. He would wake hungry in the night, but at least it warmed his belly and put a temporary hold on the nagging anxiety in his gut. After he had eaten, he opened his fiddle case and sat with the instrument on his lap for a little while, fingering the strings. He let his fingers explore a new pattern of notes, and he hummed along until this random sequence began to coalesce into a tune. It was a slow, tripping march in 6/8 time, with some curiously blue accidentals thrown in. He played it around a few times until it resolved itself, and then recorded it so that it wouldn't disappear overnight.

He listened to the recording and concluded that the tune was decent. In fact, it was better than anything he'd written for a while. At least one good thing had come out of the day.

He smiled and decided he would call it *Mary Macdonald's Farewell to Her Marbles*.

I NEVER ASKED FOR THIS

'Mum, can I come in with you?'

Jenny stirred, a shadowy figure in the bed faintly illuminated by the blue dawn seeping through the blinds. She dragged the heels of her hands across her eyes and glanced at the clock.

'Cat?'

Catriona slipped into bed beside her. 'I can't sleep.'

'No wonder. You sleep all day.' Jenny sat up and looked at her. Catriona closed her eyes to shield against potential anger, but Jenny's fingers gently touched her forehead and moved across it. Hot tears squeezed between Catriona's lashes. There was a dark place in front of her, a place where the world and time collapsed into a sinkhole. She had to turn back from it but she didn't know how. She needed someone to pull her back but that would involve saying things she didn't know how to say.

Jenny said, 'My wee baby. I wish you'd tell me what's wrong.'

Other girls could tell their mothers anything, but it wasn't like that with Jenny. She wasn't soft and accepting. It was like she had spent nineteen years rejecting the label of Mum. I never asked to be a single parent, she said so many times,

66

regret bending the ends of her words so it came out something like a slide guitar riff. You could read into that whatever you wanted, but you could never fully trust her. At any time she might turn around and say *I didn't want you anyway*.

'I've decided to go and visit Dad.'

Jenny sat very still and her breath shook. Then she got up and went to the window, tilted the blinds and looked out at the street. The early morning light was dull blue-grey. Jenny's fingers tightened around the windowsill.

'I think it's bad idea,' she said.

'Why?'

'You know what he's like.'

'He's better.'

'I doubt it.'

'I've seen him on Facebook.'

'You can't tell by that. Catriona, right now you're so depressed I'm worried about leaving you alone in the house.'

'Well I won't be alone, I'll be with him.'

Jenny sniffed, her shoulders tensing and lifting toward her ears. 'You remember last time he was here? You were so upset you couldn't stand to have him in the house. You were disgusted by him and you told him so. What makes you think he'd want to open his door to you now? Why should he?'

'He's my dad.'

'Aye, if you say so. He's never put himself out of his way to be a parent to you, Catriona; he's only ever been concerned with suiting himself. He should have stayed in Aberdeen, not taken himself away out to the middle of nowhere.'

'Mum, sometimes I think you're just horrible about him for the sake of it.'

'I'm not being horrible. He's not able to cope with other people. That's just how he is. I should have realised that before I allowed myself to fall pregnant, but I was too young. I was naive and he took advantage of me.'

Catriona's eyes drilled into her mother's back. 'So he forced you to have sex with him?'

Jenny turned toward her. 'No. No, of course not. That's not what I meant.'

'Then shut up! Don't you dare accuse him of that!' She launched herself off the bed and threw her body towards the door, wanting to clatter against it and feel the reverberations of the wood in her bones. Her fingers gripped the door frame, nails digging into the paint. 'You always come out with this shit, and you never stop and think how it makes me feel. Like you only had me so you could have someone to blame for everything bad that's ever happened to you. You want to know why I'm depressed? Think about yourself.'

Jenny sagged. Her backside rested against the window-sill and her shoulders slumped forward under an invisible weight.

Catriona waited in the doorway, quivering, waiting for some kind of response but knowing it could never satisfy her. Before Jenny could speak again, she said, 'I'm going back to bed.'

'Cat...'

'Forget it, Mum. Sorry I woke you up.' In bed, she drew the quilt over her head and turned her face to the wall, blocking out sound and light, subsiding into the close, drowning heat. Only deep in the cocoon of her bed could she allow herself to remember the last time she saw her dad.

ABERDEEN, 2009

'How long have you been back?' Jenny asked.

'A few days. A week, I don't know.' Calum sat at their table, his hands wrapped round a mug of tea. He looked bloated and unfit, with yellowish shadows under his eyes

68

and too much greying stubble. Like a man who had just risen from his sickbed or walked out of prison, with a whiff of alcohol hanging around him. His shoulders were hunched and he didn't meet their eyes.

'A *week*. And you haven't wanted to come see your daughter before now?'

'I've been dealing with some stuff.'

At the other end of the room, Catriona slid down the settee and turned the TV up. Her dad hadn't been home in close to two years, and this fusty old man with a flat Americanised accent was almost unrecognisable. Their phone conversations had been short over the last few months, his voice strange and weak like he couldn't catch his breath. She'd assumed he'd been in too much of a hurry to speak to her.

And now this. She and her mum had only moved into the house in the summer, and finally they lived in a neighbourhood where there were girls worth being friends with. Kate and Eilidh often came round for her in the evenings, and they would go to the park or just sit on her bed and talk. For the first time in her life she felt like she fitted in somewhere. It would be a disaster if they came to the door right now. Having to introduce him would be the worst kind of mortifying.

'You've been on a bender,' Jenny said. Her voice was still low but Cat could hear her starting to simmer. She was liable to go off like a whistling kettle at any moment. 'You still do that? Two weeks on, one week drunk, one week off?'

'I don't, Jen, honestly.'

'Well.' She sat back with her arms crossed over her chest. 'Let's hear your explanation, then.'

'For what?'

'For what?' Jenny gave a whoop of laughter.

Catriona spoke to him for the first time, raising her voice

over the television. 'Have you looked in a mirror lately?'

His eyelids were heavy and his shoulders moved back and forth with each breath. 'I haven't been so well. I've been off my work for a while.'

'How long?' Jenny demanded.

'A few months.'

'What's wrong with you?'

He glanced at Catriona, then shrugged. 'It's ... a bit complicated.'

'Are you dying?' Catriona asked, raising her voice across the room. She wanted him to be so ill that his life replayed itself in front of his eyes and he could see the details of every single day that he had missed with her. 'You look like you are. You look like you have cancer or something. Is that why you came to see us? I hope you're only here to say cheerio.'

'Cat,' Jenny said. A half-hearted warning, at best.

She flicked her eyes at her mother, then turned on him again. 'I hope you've left me something in your will, or does that American Barbie-bitch get it all?'

His body swayed like a branch disturbed by a gust, but otherwise her words appeared to make no impact on him. 'I'm not dying. It's not that kind of illness. Sorry to disappoint you.'

'You mean to say your fancy private shrinks in California can't cure you?' Jenny shook her head slowly, the queen of the post-punk sneer. 'What do you want, Calum?'

He looked out the window, like he wished he could fly through it. 'It's probably a lot to ask, but I was kind of hoping you'd let me stay for a wee while. Michelle and I broke up, and I've decided to come back to Scotland. It would just be ... you know ... until I get somewhere else.'

Jenny softened. Her shoulders lowered and her arms dropped from her chest. She might have given a different answer if she'd been allowed to have her way.

70

'You can't stay here.' Catriona flounced off the settee. 'We only have two bedrooms. Mum, tell him. What about Alec? He wouldn't like it.'

'Who's Alec?' Calum asked.

'Mum's *boyfriend*,' Catriona took delight in the word. 'Anyway, we're going away soon. He's taking us to Cyprus for the New Year.'

'Jesus, Cat, you haven't half lived up to your name.' Calum's laugh was painful. It was the first time he'd registered any emotion since he'd come through the door.

Jenny exhaled. 'If you're really stuck, you can have my bed for a couple of nights. Catriona and I can share.'

'No we can't! Oh my God, Mum!'

'Just for a few days, sweetie. Your dad knows that's all it's going to be.'

'Oh no way. That's so unfair.' She felt herself withering with humiliation and injustice. The unfair thing was him showing up like this, all fat and slow and ill in some way he hadn't fully explained but which Jenny seemed to understand. The broken promises were unfair. He was always going to fly her out and take her on a road trip up the California coast. He promised that every year and every year there was some reason why it didn't happen. And it was unfair how he'd proved Jenny right in everything she'd said about him. He'd promised Disneyland and surfing and San Francisco and sea otters and redwood forests, but he only ever sent pictures of himself seeing those things with his wife. The wife with the plastic tits and fake white teeth.

She wanted to slap him and pull that horrible greasy grey hair out of his face. 'Mum doesn't want you, here, okay? She just feels sorry for you, that's all.'

'Oh come on, Cat, give us a break, eh?'

'Why don't you give my nose a break. You're stinking. No wonder Michelle dumped you.'

71

He clapped his hands slowly, five or six times. The pocket of air between his palms made a deep, percussive pop. 'Nice kid you've raised there, Jen. Good job.'

Jenny stood up and lifted the mug from between his hands. 'I think you'd better go.'

'Jenny . . .'

'No, she's right, I don't want you here. I'm sorry for whatever you're going through, Calum, but I can't help you.'

He didn't move from the chair. Jenny carried the cups into the kitchen and Calum sat there, breathing heavily, staring at the table top. Catriona was afraid to look at him. She stood against the wall and chewed her lip.

When Jenny returned, she was carrying his coat. 'Here.'

Calum stood up and took it, lifted his eyes momentarily and offered Catriona a shaky, apologetic smile. 'I'll call you when I've got somewhere, and you can come stay anytime you want.'

'Aye, that'll be right. Don't bother.'

'I'm sorry,' Jenny said. She touched his shoulder, but he brushed past her and let himself out. When the door shut, she turned on her daughter and said, 'You stupid little brat.'

Lately Catriona wondered if she'd thrown her lot in with the wrong parent. Most of the time they'd got on well, the two of them together in their closed little unit. Jenny was younger than most of her friends' mums, sometimes more like an older sister or a youthful aunt. She was lively and fashionable enough to impress Catriona's friends. She *was* a friend, sometimes her best friend. But other times she got so angry that she became a snake who shot venom from her mouth. She could knock you down with a word. She could make you so tiny you might disappear through the cracks between the floorboards. She could make you believe that everything wrong with her life was your fault.

Calum had never done that. With the exception of that day, his words to her had only ever been kind. No wonder he never wanted to see her again after that day. Jenny had done her job well; with her judgements, pronouncements about his character, labels she recycled over and over until they stuck, she had turned Catriona hard and fast against him. He hadn't even been there to defend himself.

He wasn't there because he chose America. He chose a big money job and a big money wife. He made those choices, as Jenny was so fond of reminding her.

Neither of her parents had ever given her a satisfactory explanation for their breakup, or for their failure to get married in the first place. It wouldn't have worked was as much as they would ever say. Or simply: because we didn't. Non-reasons. Typical parental responses. They thought children didn't need the truth.

The truth was that her mum got pregnant by accident and they never would have been together otherwise.

Not my accident though, Catriona thought.

She and Kyle might have had their own wee accident to deal with. The thought made her feel nauseous. Jesus freaking Christ, what if that had happened? She would have nipped it in the bud early, before anyone had to know, and there would be nothing to have to explain to anyone. It would be a non-person. A non-event. Kyle was a non-event.

She hid in her room until Jenny went to work, drifting between thought and dreaming so that they became indistinguishable from each other. Later in the morning, she got up and wandered from room to room, listening to empty sounds – the whir of the refrigerator, the tick of the wall clock – and imagining that these might be the sounds of the rest of her life. Something had to give. She went upstairs and took her big rucksack down from the loft.

73

VERTIGO

'What will you do?'

'No idea,' Calum muttered around the nail he was holding between his teeth. He'd been telling Johnny the sorry tale of Mary and her flat to keep his mind off his present location, fifteen feet from the ground. A gust of wind pushed at him.

A distant echo of his own voice came down some kind of wormhole and battered him around the ear. Damn you Finn, would you slow down! Chill the fuck out! If you fall from there, you're toast!

If you fall!

If you fall . . .

He focused his attention on his hands and knees, his points of contact with the sloping byre roof. Stay here, he repeated silently. The only way to get through these moments was to stay in the present. Mindfulness was the word he'd learned. Mind where you are, not where you've been.

On the roof. He was on the roof. The old slates were coming loose and many of them were cracked. The whole bloody thing would need replacing.

He could get someone to do it.

That would be a waste of money. He should be able to do it himself. Dad would have laughed to see him sweating up here. He'd have said, 'Stop pissing yourself and get on with it, Son.'

He banged in a new fixing and secured another slate, then manoeuvred himself gingerly up towards the peak where Johnny sat straddled, apparently completely at ease on his perch. Behind him, the oaks bent in the breeze and the rising tide burbled into channels of sand. Calum kept his sights firmly affixed to the roof and the placing of his knees and hands.

'Nursing home?'

'What?'

'Would you put her in a nursing home?'

'It seems too soon, but . . . I don't know what choice there is. She needs somebody with her every day.'

'She could come and stay with you.'

Calum allowed himself to look up for a moment. 'You're having a laugh, right?'

'It's an option. You've got plenty of room.' Johnny sounded uncharacteristically serious. He was only thirty-one and his life was still balanced in favour of shiny youth. Old age, with its odours of stale soup and piss, was something that you read about in the newspaper.

'Not happening. No way.'

'Okay,' Johnny replied slowly. He was silent for a moment, watching as Calum shifted his position and paused to wipe sweat from his forehead. 'You're white as a sheet. You really don't like being up here, do you?'

'No, I really bloody don't.'

'Get yourself down, then. I'll finish this. You've broken the back of it.'

Calum thought he should protest, but didn't bother. He took a deep breath and unbuckled his tool belt, handing it up to Johnny. Vertigo had claimed another victory and he knew when he was beaten. He uttered a breathless word of gratitude and crawled back down to the ladder, placed one foot squarely on each rung, then the other, and climbed down feeling like an old man. The afterburn of fear made him shake and he leaned against the wall for a moment, closed his eyes and waited for his legs to decide to support him again. Then, because watching Johnny crawl about on the roof was nearly as bad as being up there himself, he went inside the byre – which he now used as a shed for tools and wood – and began splitting logs. The hammering continued above him, moving from place to place as Johnny checked and secured the slates torn loose during a turbulent winter.

It was getting worse, the vertigo. It was like you could feel the thing happening: the loss of contact, the flight, the fall. It was a flashback into a distorted memory. It seemed crazy so long after the fact, but that's exactly what it was. Crazy. A part of him was crazy. Michelle had pestered him for years to see someone. There was no shame in it, she said. Until he lost the plot completely and there was no choice but to see someone. She was ashamed then.

It might have all panned out differently if he'd taken her advice sooner, but it was what it was now. Most likely they would have ended up apart anyway, and he was always going to be a little bit crazy.

Mum was crazy too, that much was apparent, a kind of crazy that wasn't going to get better with any amount of counselling. The connections in her brain were slowly disintegrating, taking with them memory, reasoning, songs, stories, humour, love, all of the things that defined who she had once been. And it was all connected, her craziness, his, Finn's. This was the thing to really send you spinning: not down but out and away into space. The vertigo got worse when he thought of Finn, and he was thinking of Finn far more than usual lately. If Finn hadn't

76

fallen, he wouldn't now be facing their mother's illness alone. Damn that boy, he thought. Damn his childish, beautiful mad soul.

Coire an t-Sneachda (The Corrie of the Snow), July 1993

Finn stepped over a large stone and took no notice of the mountain hare that darted out from behind it. He was oblivious to everything except his destination. The shoulder of the corrie rose steeply and became littered with scree, but his strides quickened. Even burdened by the weight of his climbing gear, he almost ran up the hill. Calum kept a steady pace behind him, refusing to be rushed. He watched the hare scamper towards the brow of the corrie and disappear into the heather. Then he let his eyes move up the slope of Cairn Gorm far to the left, following the line of the chairlift. In summer, the lift looked derelict and the mountainside disfigured by human pursuits.

We shouldn't be here, Calum thought. He looked back to Finn. He watched Finn's head twitch from one side to the other, a jerky tic that started when he was agitated. Periodically Finn's voice punched out a single detached word in response to a conversation he was having with someone in his head. Agitated was an understatement. Today he was crazy, bordering on unhinged. You weren't supposed to say that, especially about your own brother, but that's what he was.

We really shouldn't be here, he thought. Not today. Maybe not at all.

'Finn!' he called.

Finn didn't reply. He probably hadn't even heard. This trip had been a mistake from the start. It had been Finn's idea, his way of trying to make amends for the guitar. Calum wished he hadn't allowed himself to be talked into this, but Finn was so cut up about the guitar he said he couldn't live with himself until they made up.

It was only a guitar. Calum had been trying to remind himself for weeks. A wooden box and six strings, not worth disowning your unhinged brother for.

But it was a Martin. A Martin D-28, the guitar he'd wanted since he'd first learned to play, and its loss still caused a pain akin to grief. His birthday present to himself in March, it had been his for such a short time. It had cost him close to a month's pay, but he had money to burn and it sang like a honey-throated woman in his arms. Five weeks ago he had returned from a stint offshore to his flat reeking of smoke and unwashed bodies, and an empty corner in the living room where the guitar should have been.

Finn didn't even try to deny responsibility. His illness made him chronically untruthful but also incapable of telling a convincing lie. He betrayed himself like a guilty dog. Some mates came round with a few cans and a few pills; it got loud and he went for a lie down in the bedroom. He didn't mean to sleep all night but he crashed out hard and when he got up in the morning everyone was gone. It was Cookie who took the guitar; Cookie had debts he couldn't pay.

'You tell me where I can find this Cookie,' Calum had barked. Words erupting from him like vomit. Finn could only shake his head; he had no idea where Cookie stayed. He didn't even know Cookie's proper name.

'He's your dealer. You gave it to him.' Calum wanted to break his brother's nose. 'You gave it to him, didn't you, Finn? Didn't you?'

Finn wept. He melted into a gelatinous heap on the sofa, covered his face with his hands and wept, incomprehensible words spewing from his mouth. Calum raged, a pot burning empty over too hot a flame.

'They're not your mates! You don't have any mates, Finn. I'm not your mate. Not anymore.'

'You're my brother, Calum.' A stalactite of mucus extended from his lower lip.

'Unfortunately so, but it doesn't make us friends.'

He'd driven Finn from Aberdeen back to Fort William, re-installed him in their mother's flat and told her that he needed a break. He didn't tell her about the guitar and he doubted that Finn would. The last month had been one of solitude and only the faintest murmur of guilt. When Finn finally phoned two nights ago and said he wanted to go climbing, Calum nearly hung up.

Now he wished he had. They'd bickered all the way up the road this morning, Calum strafing Finn with accusations and advice, Finn responding with semi-rational promises. He'd been reading Orwell, which couldn't be a good thing. He was paranoid and jittery, his heavy black eyebrows twitching, his fingers flexing, grabbing his trousers or rubbing his face. Anxiety danced in Calum's stomach.

Finn reached the base of the climb, let his pack thump down onto the scree and stared up, fingers raised towards the grey rock chimneys, feeling the route. He was conversing with someone, probably the infamous guardian angel. Calum pretended not to notice. He stepped up beside Finn cautiously, afraid of spooking him, eased off his own pack, took out his water bottle and sipped while he waited for his breath to settle.

'I could solo that,' Finn said.

Calum studied him. 'Not on my watch.'

'God, you're so boring.'

'Find someone else to climb with, then.' He found a flat-tish boulder and sat down, dug out a bar of chocolate and nibbled on it.

Finn swapped his walking boots for his climbing shoes and

scrambled around on the lower rocks, muttering, giggling and showing off. He climbed up seven or eight feet, shouting 'Big Brother! Oi, Bro! Calum! Caaaallluuummm ... '

Calum had learned from experience that attention only fuelled the mania, so he ignored Finn as well as he could and watched the sunlight glinting on the surface of the lochan. The air was unusually still for the Cairngorms, the sun soft on his bare arms. He filled his lungs and tried to exhale the sense of foreboding. Far below, a fleet of little sailboats bobbed lazily around Loch Morlich. Aviemore had been thronging with people, but up here they were alone.

Finn jumped off and strapped himself into his harness. 'Oh for the love of God, would you get off your arse!'

Calum crumpled his chocolate wrapper and shoved it into the pack, put on his own climbing shoes and began the process of roping up. He checked Finn's harness and knots like a drill sergeant inspecting a recruit's uniform.

'You want to lead for a change?' Finn asked. It was a rare offer.

'No, I want you where I can keep an eye on you.'

'You know you don't have to, right?'

'You know she's in your head, right? This angel of yours?' He tapped the side of his brother's skull. 'She's only real in there, poor creature.'

'You are mistaken, Big Brother. You are sadly and pathetically mistaken.' Finn gave him a saintly smile and turned to face the rock.

'Take it easy Finn,' Calum said. 'Just ... please, go easy.'

'As you wish, Big Brother,' Finn said, and then he took off, straight up. He moved like a cat: graceful, nimble and so fast his fingers and toes barely touched the rock. Within a few seconds, he was fifteen feet up.

Calum cursed. 'Damn you Finn, would you slow down

and get some protection in! Chill the fuck out! If you fall from there, you're toast!'

Finn ignored him.

'Finn, get some protection in!'

Finn barely slowed. He inserted a cam into a crack, clipped on and shot up again. Calum took a single breath. The sun made his eyes water and he glanced away momentarily, squeezed them shut, then looked up again. Finn made a wild move, launching himself upwards at full stretch for a hold far above his head. His feet lost contact. His right hand grasped at slick stone and failed to gain purchase. He peeled off and fell backwards.

'Oi, Macdonald.'

Calum lowered his axe and straightened up. Johnny's wife Abby leaned in the doorway, her sleeves rolled above her elbows, her arms crossed over her chest. 'I've hung out that last load of sheets, but I can still smell the smoke. It's foul, it's like burnt chemicals. They might all need another wash.'

'They might be better off in the bin. Thanks though.'

'That's what we're here for. However ... ' She pointed upwards. 'Tell me why my husband is up there while you're safely in here playing lumberjack.' She reinforced her Essex drawl when she wanted to project a kind of jocular assertiveness. It seemed incongruous for a woman wearing jeans under a patchwork dress. Abby and Johnny had moved up from London to build a house around the same time Calum had come back from America, and her transition from urbane graphic designer to new age crofter was nearly complete. Children would come soon, and Calum figured they would be allowed to develop dreadlocks and run around in pyjamas and batman capes until they were twelve.

'I had a wee panic to myself and he made me get down.'

'It's not very high.'

'It's high enough.'

'Poor love. Take your mind off it. How are you and Julie?'

'You know how we are, Abby.'

'No I don't.'

He glanced towards Julie's empty cottage on the other side of the gravel drive they shared. 'She's away more than she's here and that's how she wants it.'

'Are you sure?'

'Aye.' He hoped a monosyllabic response would head off one of Abby's deep, painful conversations. In her quest for a more meaningful existence, she gave herself permission to peer into your no-go areas. She was young enough to believe you could talk yourself into happy endings.

'What about you? How do you want it?'

'Part-time does me fine.' He positioned a fat log on the block and took a swing.

'Maybe all you have to do is ask for more.'

'Would you give it a rest?'

Shock crossed her face so he straightened up again, sighed, swung the axe deep into the log and left it quivering. 'Sorry. We're not cosy domestic material. Neither of us. I've been there, I'm not going there again. Please just . . . stop trying to matchmake.'

Abby took his hand and squeezed it. 'You try so hard to be a curmudgeon, and you fail miserably.'

'No I don't. I happen to think I'm quite good at it.'

She shook her head and led him by the hand out into the yellowy light. They stood back to watch Johnny descending the ladder.

He handed Calum the tools. 'Done. She's pretty sound.'

'That's another favour I owe you.'

'I'm keeping a list.' Johnny dusted cobwebs from his

82

knees, wiped his hands on the belly of his shirt and glanced towards the house. 'What's for eating?'

Abby dusted his back. 'Carrot and cardamom scones, just made.'

'What's the matter with plain old cheese?' Johnny muttered.

'No plain old anything for you, my love,' she said, and kissed him on the lips. 'Let's go put the kettle on. So, Cal ... when's Mary coming to stay? She is, isn't she? Obviously she won't be able to go home for a while. If she needs help, you know, please ask us, right? We're here for you.'

He snapped. 'Don't call me Cal.'

'Ooh, I've hit a sore one.'

'My wife called me Cal because she thought Calum sounded too foreign, and my mother is not moving in with me.'

'She's your *mum*, where else would she go?'

He let his hands fall helplessly to his sides and walked towards the house.

REMINISCENCE

From Jack's spells in hospital, Mary remembered needles and beeping machines, tubes attached to pouches of fluid, a succession of nurses and doctors delivering bad news with brusque cheer. She remembered messages of hope: there was always another treatment, another medicine, another possibility. Chemo knocked the cancer into remission three times. Hope finally died when the coughing started and the shadows appeared in his chest. Then ifs became whens and years became months.

It was different for her. She felt no pain and the air came into her chest cleanly. And yet they treated her as if her tenure in the world was drawing to its end. They didn't come with medications, they only came with questions. Questions about the past, about her family, about Jack and the boys, her home, her songs, her life on Skye and then in Glendarach. She might have been an old book they'd unearthed at the back of a library. As if her knowledge was of greater value than her body.

A woman called Fiona came and spoke in Gaelic with her. She wasn't a nurse exactly, she had some title that meant nothing to Mary, but she was kind and conversation was easier without the hard edges of English. She knew some of the old hymns and they sang together and looked at the photographs that Calum had recovered from the flat. They lingered over one of Finn playing the pipes, kilted, perhaps thirteen years old.

'He'd have made a fine piper,' Mary said, and her finger trembled as she touched his cheek. 'He gave up, not long after this.' Her lip began to quiver and Finn's face blurred. When she closed her eyes, she could only see his face as it was later, thin and shadowed, crossed by lines like tiny knife cuts.

Fiona handed her a tissue. 'Would you tell me about him?'

'Finn was sensitive,' Mary said. 'You know what I mean by that?'

'Yes.'

'Even as a tiny boy, he sensed things. He had a way of knowing things. Of feeling things. He saw angels. He . . .' she paused, closed her eyes, reached for solid memory. It eluded her, left her grasping echoes. 'He suffered badly after Jack died. Sometimes he was . . . wild, and sometimes so sad he could barely get himself out of his bed. They said it was a disease. Manic depression?'

'Bipolar disorder,' Fiona corrected.

Mary shook her head, didn't understand the need for such technical names. 'He just . . . understood more than most people. I believe the Lord spoke to him, that's all. He was picked for a reason.' She smiled, moved her finger over Finn's hair and tried to remember the feel of it under her skin. She tried to remember the tone of his voice, but all she could hear was Calum's. Louder, stronger, always more dominant.

'He was only twenty-one when he died.'

Fiona nodded, placed her hand over Mary's. 'I'm so sorry.'

'Calum should never have taken him climbing.'

'Calum told me he was a wonderful climber.'

A sudden anger filled Mary's throat. Who was this woman and why was Calum telling her about the family? 'Why have you been speaking to Calum? He has no business speaking to strangers about Finn.'

85

'He and I had a conversation this morning, Mary. He told me that you've been having some problems with your memory. We need to know a little bit more, so we can work out how best to help you when you come out of hospital.'

'It's nothing to do with you, or Calum. He has no interest in helping me.'

'He's been here every day, Mary. He's a good son. I wish my own son was as attentive to me.'

'I told Calum not to take Finn climbing. He didn't listen to me. He's disregarded everything I've ever said to him. I knew what would happen. I *knew*.'

'You can't blame him, surely.'

'If I was a better Christian, I would forgive him.'

The woman called Fiona, whoever she was, looked at her strangely and muttered some irrelevant response. Mary's attention drifted to the sun coming through the window, the glimmer of light on the bonnets of the wet cars outside and the faint rainbow hovering over the town. The summer days were so precious and she was stuck in here. She couldn't understand why they were keeping her here when there was nothing wrong with her.

'I'm hungry,' she said sharply. 'It's past two and they haven't brought my dinner.'

'They told me you'd had lunch already.'

'Well I haven't.'

'I'll see if I can get someone to bring you a cup of tea and some toast.' Fiona stood, patted her shoulder. Mary flinched away from her. People were always touching you in here, poking and prodding, violating your privacy.

When Fiona had gone, she got out of bed, pulled back the curtain and walked up the ward. Heads bobbled on feeble necks, cloudy eyes watched her walk to the window. She opened the latch and pushed the pane outward, drew in a deep breath of sweet, moist air. If she had her shoes, she could just climb out and go home. Her flat was only a few minutes' walk away; she could practically see it from here.

Then suddenly a nurse was at her back, grasping her by the shoulders, saying, 'Come on then, Mary dear, let's get back to bed.'

'Stop touching me!' Mary wrenched herself free. 'I'm only taking some air. Goodness knows what germs are circulating around in this horrid room. It isn't cleaned properly. You people should be ashamed of yourselves.'

The nurse was smiling, nodding at her. 'It's all right, love. It's all right. Come back to bed and have a little rest.'

'Did you hear a word I just said? I don't need a rest. I'm tired of resting. I should be going home, there's nothing wrong with me.'

'Mary, there was a fire in your house. Do you remember the fire? You'll not be able to go home for a wee while. We won't keep you here long, we'll find somewhere nicer for you.'

Another nurse came, a big woman with masculine hands. She gripped Mary's arms and steered her away from the window. 'Come on then, my love. Don't upset yourself. Here we are.' Mary found herself pushed firmly back onto the bed. 'Let's put the telly on for you.'

'I don't want to watch the telly,' Mary said.

The second nurse nodded. 'Oh here, it's *Cash in the Attic*. You like this, don't you? I'll leave this on for you.'

'I hate that programme, and you incompetents haven't brought my dinner.'

'You had your dinner, Mary. You had a lovely plate of mince, don't you remember?' She lifted Mary's legs onto the bed and straightened the pillow. 'And ice cream. I can tell you've been a feisty lady in your day, haven't you, my love? A wee handful. I'll be keeping an eye on you from now on.'

WRITTEN IN STONE

Calum arrived home from Fort William with another load of Mary's smoke-cured possessions and foreboding like a lead weight in his gut. She would be discharged tomorrow and for lack of a better option, she would come home with him until her flat was habitable or another arrangement was made. He poured himself a whisky, opened the back door and looked over his patch of moss, rocky heather and wood. It looked wilder now, happier, finally recovering after generations of sheep that ate the vegetation down to the roots, caused erosion and prevented any possibility of regeneration. The grass had been short then, tidy, almost like a lawn. Mary had created a rock garden and planted bulbs and bedding flowers, an oasis of apparent cultivation in an incorrigible land.

Now you could just see the raised area of the rock garden beneath swelling vegetation. Mary would criticise his neglect. She would walk the perimeter of land, hemmed in by the memory of the barbed wire fence that Calum had taken down, her forehead creased by scowl lines, and she would make a list of everything he had failed to do. His failure to maintain the croft to her standards would come to symbolise all of his other failures, and his own failures mirrored the failures of his generation: selfishness, individualism, promiscuity, Godlessness. Everyone could see it, she would say.

Aye, he thought. One day archaeologists would come and they'd cut away at the peat and moss, survey the stones and determine that an atheist slob lived here in the age of David Cameron, and that he displeased his mother greatly. Might as well write it all out for them and bury the note in a glass jar to save the guesswork.

He wanted a cigarette. Michelle had convinced him to quit smoking, a condition for agreeing to move in with him. Even years later, moments of anxiety still brought on a craving more intense than the need for sex.

To distract himself, he wandered into Julie's garden and surveyed the house, checked the doors and windows, then pushed open the door of her workshop and stepped inside the cold, dark building. The light flickered on and he paused in the threshold, breathing in the thick, moist smell of stone. There were chunks of raw granite and sandstone on the floor and workbench, and finished or partially finished sculptures standing around at the far end of the table or on the floor. This was an intrusion. Julie was very private about work in progress, even with her friends. He'd never been past the studio door before.

He walked around the sculptures without touching, unable to decide whether he liked the raw, angular figures, often only half emergent from their blocks. They were women, mostly, skinny with oversized hands and wide, tormented eyes: prostitutes, grieving mothers, anorexics, survivors of the myriad horrors that befell women. They were a commentary, effective if not particularly subtle, made for confrontation with people who were comfortable, fat and unhappy for reasons that were less than tangible. You have no idea, said these poor, demented souls. You have no clue, you bourgeois bastard, you don't know you're born.

Julie's current commission was a greater than life-sized representation of James Young Simpson, the pioneer of anaesthesia, a man credited with transforming the experience of childbirth for successive generations of women. How would Julie, who had experienced the pain of childbirth but none of the joy of motherhood, portray him? Would he be the saviour who offered respite or just a dealer of fancy tricks and dodgy medicine? It was her biggest project yet, a bit of a breakthrough as she'd described it, though not without its irony. It was too big for her wee studio here; she had to work on it in Glasgow.

He moved to the far end of the studio, where a number of smaller sculptures sat huddled on a dusty shelf. One towards the back caught his attention because its style was markedly different from the rest. It was smooth, polished, with fluid lines and soft curves. He pushed a couple of others out of the way and pulled it to the front of the shelf. Not quite two feet high, carved in sparkling grey granite, an angel leaned out of a rock face, extending her hand down toward a climber, a young man, reaching upward. Their fingertips, intricately rendered, just touched.

He wrapped his arms around the sculpture and carried it to the workbench to see it in better light. A strange flutter started in his stomach and moved to the tops of his legs. The story he had told Julie only once, an explanation of the dreams that still ripped his nights open, was written there in stone in minute detail. Finn's eyes were enormous with fear, or possibly wonder. His left hand gripped the rock but his feet dangled: if the angel failed to lock onto his hand, he would fall.

Calum had replayed the scenario a million times but this was the first time he'd seen the angel's face. She was dispassionate, almost bored. Maybe she had become complacent too: Finn *never* fell.

He expelled the breath he had been holding, left the sculpture on the workbench and pulled the studio door closed behind him. Brimming with anger, he went home and phoned Julie.

'I was in your studio just now,' he said when she answered, dispensing with the usual niceties. 'Were you going to tell me about the sculpture of my brother before or after you put it on public display somewhere.'

There was a pause. He could hear her suck in a breath. She didn't know what to say. Good, he thought.

'I wasn't going to display it anywhere.'

'Why did you make it then?'

'Because it's a beautiful story.'

Artists were parasites. They grew fat on other people's traumas. He should have known that.

'No it isn't, Julie. Finn *died*. I watched him die and it wasn't fucking beautiful.'

'Calum, I was going to give it to you.'

'What do you want me to do with it, put it on the mantelpiece?' She should have asked. She should have bloody asked.

'Well that's up to you.' She sounded wholly unapologetic. 'How are you, anyway? How's your mum?'

He paused, not quite ready to give up on the argument. But it was pointless. The sculpture couldn't be unmade.

'Mum is coming to stay tomorrow, until we can figure out something else. She keeps forgetting about the fire and can't understand why she can't go home. Nobody thinks it's a good idea for her to live on her own again, but that leaves us with a problem. I'm just ... trying to hold it together, if you want to know the truth.' He wasn't sure she did.

'You will. You'll be fine.'

'If you say so. How's Mr Simpson coming on?'

'Rough, huge and intransigent. Right now I hate him.'

'He's paying your rent.'

She laughed. 'It violates a lifelong principle of mine to be dependent on a man for money. So tell me what you thought of The Angel, anyway? I was practising a more realist style.'

His brother's death reduced to a practice piece, and she wanted his opinion on its technical merits? He floundered. 'I . . . liked the hands.'

'The hands?'

'Aye. Finn had good hands. They were the only reliable part of him.' He closed his eyes, pinched the bridge of his nose, thought of the stack of bills and invoices he'd neglected since his mother's fire. 'I've got a bunch of work to do, so I'm gonna go.'

'Right, well . . . good luck tomorrow.'

'Aye.' He was aware that his voice had become clipped and abrupt. 'Have a good night.'

'Bye then,' she said, and terminated the call as tactlessly as he'd started it.

The laws of magnetism held as true for relationships as they did for everything else; as hard as Abby or anyone else might try to bring them together, he and Julie would always bounce off each other. Julie had her reasons for being the way she was, just as he did. Good reasons. On his better days he understood her, even loved her for her hardwired resilience but right now he just wanted somebody soft and accommodating. Julie's response to this came through the inert telephone: If you want a woman without a backbone, Calum, buy a bloody Inflate-a-mate.

KITCHEN SESSIONS

Mary stood in the kitchen, facing a glass wall where the mahogany dresser used to be. It was like someone had flayed the stone skin off the cottage and left it open to bleed. The woods seemed to have moved closer too, scavengers closing in. They could almost reach in with their branches and grab her. The woods had frightened her as a child, when they'd first moved from Skye. The trees were like old hags, oaks and birches that had been stunted and misshapen by the sea winds, coloured by lichens and fungi. Deep in the woods there were ruined crofts, steps obscured by moss, an old cemetery where the graves had been almost consumed by vegetation. At night animals prowled and called: owls, pine martens, foxes, wild cats that looked like they should curl up at your fire but would take your finger off if you cornered them. Her mother called these the witchy woods and said the Wee Folk would take her if she went into them at night.

She went into the woods alone at night for the first time when she was fifteen, to meet Jack. She remembered how she felt, hot inside like there were coals glowing in her belly, and light as a balloon as she ran along the path to the agreed meeting place. Remembering brought back a little of that heat. Just enough to remind her that it had actually happened.

She turned away from the window and it was gone. There was only Calum, sitting at the table, fingers tapping on his thin little computer. 'What have you done with the blue teapot?'

'It was in your kitchen. I'm afraid it had to go in the bin.'

'That was my mother's.'

'I know.'

It was an ordinary thing, not fancy, cobalt blue, a stained and robust servant. Its loss pained her. Tea was important, objects from the family were important. A teapot held stories and stories were important.

'All this glass will make the house cold.'

'It brings the sun in. It's a lot warmer now.'

'Anyone can look in. You should at least put up blinds.'

'There's nobody here to look in. Julie's away most of the time.'

'Who's Julie?'

'The woman who lives in Donald's house.'

'Where's Donald gone?'

'He died years ago, Mum.'

'Nobody told me,' she snapped, but even as she said it something materialised like a figure from the fog. She *had* known. Of course she had, she'd been at his funeral. Where did these reactions come from? Sometimes it felt like someone else was speaking through her mouth, like there was another person inside her head, telling her lies, obscuring the facts of her life.

She turned away from the window and closed her fingers around the edge of the worktop, anchoring herself to something solid. 'Ocht, what am I like? I'm a daft old woman.'

'You're not daft, Mum. You've had a trauma.'

'Aye, I suppose I have. I don't know how I managed to get out.' She could still smell the smoke in her nose. 'I'll have to make you a mug of tea since you've thrown out my pot.'

He rose. 'I'll make it.'

'I'm capable, Calum!' She filled the kettle and switched it on. 'Did they work out how the fire started?'

He looked at her strangely, mouth half open like he wanted to say something. Then he shook his head.

She could always tell when he was lying. 'I'm sure it's something to do with the phone calls and all this business on the telly.'

'What business on the telly?'

'This carry-on with the signs and the ... people waving banners ...' She faltered. The words darted away from her.

'The referendum?'

'Aye, that's it.'

'Jesus. It's nothing to do with the referendum, I promise.' He chuckled but stopped himself quickly.

Why would he laugh? 'Calum, it's not funny. Why can't you ever take me seriously?'

'Oh, I do,' he replied, and closed his eyes. 'There's a meeting in the hall on Thursday about the referendum. A debate. There will be people from both sides, and everyone from the village will be there. Why don't you come? You'll see there's nothing to be afraid of, and you'll catch up with a few folk and get a wee cup of tea after. All right? That'll be nice, won't it?'

'Angus MacBride will be there, I'd imagine.'

'Oh, you bet he'll be there. He's a councillor now, did you know that? He'll be at the top table. No doubt holding forth on the virtues of this great union of ours.'

Mary wasn't sure which union Calum was referring to, so she refocused her attention on the tea. The blue teapot that usually sat beside the stove was nowhere to be seen, so she plopped the teabags straight into mugs and pried open a small biscuit tin. The pungent smell of coffee escaped, along with a handful of hard black beans. She didn't know anyone else who ground their own beans. It was another one of Calum's American affectations. She sighed and scooped them back into the tin. 'Where are the biscuits?'

He came over and took a packet of digestives out of a cupboard. 'He had his eye on you, didn't he, Mum?'

'Who?'

'Angus MacBride.'

'Angus?' she laughed. 'He fancied me something rotten. I never cared for him, I have to say. He was . . . puffy and soft. Like unbaked bread.'

'He's even puffier now.'

'He was never very bright. My mother preferred him to Jack, of course.'

'How's that?'

'Well, the MacBrides had money. And they had the Gaelic. She thought I should aspire to a man who wore a suit and tie. An apprentice electrician was common as muck.'

'Granny was a snob.'

'It wasn't snobbery,' she said sharply. Calum took so much for granted. 'You've never known hunger.' She studied her son and saw Jack's wide cheekbones and coarse shoulders, her mother's deep set blue eyes, something in the turn of his mouth that she had seen in the old faded photographs of her grandfather: familiar features that hung like ornaments over workings she didn't understand. He had never been open to her like Finn. For all his troubles, Finn had been accessible in a way Calum never was.

Finn might come into the church someday.

No. She was forgetting again. Twenty years, more than twenty years, were folding in on themselves. Maybe she was trying to fold them out of existence like the way you used to fold a strip of paper into ever tinier squares until you couldn't fold any more.

She looked into her tea, saw her own face and reminded

herself, Finn is with God. His bones lie in the churchyard in Arisaig beside his father's.

Two sons went up that mountain, one came down.

One came down. One. Why only Calum? What turn of events had led to that conclusion?

She stared at him. He saw what happened that day. He knew the truth.

He *knew*.

'Calum ... ' she said, and stopped. There was a jangle in the lobby. The same doorbell her father had put in, attached to a pull cord. Mary's heart skittered. 'Goodness me. Who's calling at this hour?'

Calum went away to answer it and there were voices in the lobby, male and female, the clatter of claws on the floorboards. Calum came back into the kitchen followed by a younger man, ginger and bearded, a girl with yellow plaits and a wiry brown terrier.

'Hello lovely lady!' the girl exclaimed, delivering a cake to the table and a kiss to Mary's cheek. *English*. 'I'm so glad you're here safe and sound. How awful about your flat!'

'They still don't know what caused it,' Mary said.

'Oh ... don't they?' The woman glanced at Calum.

'They're working on it,' Calum muttered, then smiled brightly. 'Mum, you remember my friends Johnny and Abby? We play in the band together. And this wee man is Oscar.' He clapped the dog's flank.

'Of course she remembers us,' Abby said, reaching for Mary's hand and squeezing it. Mary resisted the urge to withdraw it rudely. Why would she remember these people? These incomers were always so forward.

Johnny held up a guitar case. 'We've come to coax a song out of you, Mary. It's not often we get to sing with a legend.'

'Och.' Mary waved away the praise. Her cheeks grew a little hot. 'I can't remember any of the songs I used to sing.'

'I don't believe that for a minute,' Abby said. 'I bet when you open your mouth, they'll all come pouring out.' She flipped the catches on a rectangular case and lifted out a small button box accordion. Johnny took out his guitar without even waiting for tea and cake to be served, and they began tuning up. Fragments of melody fluttered out like songbirds from a cage, patterns of notes ascending and descending, rolls like dancing feet.

Mary sat and listened. There had always been instruments in the house, long sessions in front of the stove to pass the winter nights, songs passed from her grandmother to her mother to her. She'd fallen in love with Jack for his piping as much as anything else. The Highland pipes were fine, best outside at a distance, but when he first brought out his small pipes and played a set of reels, he transformed in front of her. A modest working man grew larger and more beautiful like a tree unfolding its leaves. It was a marvel the way his broad fingers flickered so swiftly over the holes.

Calum brought a bottle of whisky and a jug of water. He poured a single finger-width and handed her the tumbler.

'Mum?'

'Put some water in it for me, love,' she said. 'Right up to the top.'

She watched him pour the water. She had been meaning to ask him something, but it was gone now. It nagged slightly, this lost question. How could something feel so urgent one minute and be forgotten the next? It would be the tablets that were making her so forgetful. The doctor had prescribed her so many tablets, she couldn't remember what they were all for: acid reflux, thyroid, God only knew what else. So many chemicals going into her blood. They could be doing anything to her. They could be experimenting on her for all she knew.

But the whisky tasted good and she remembered the way its heat spread down through her arms and legs. It had been years since she'd drunk whisky, maybe even since before Jack died.

'Come on Mary,' Abby urged, 'Give us a wee song.'

'All right then. You may know this one.' She began to sing 'Fear a Bhata', which she thought might be the only Gaelic song these people had heard before. Johnny quickly found the key and played along, a sparse and gentle accompaniment that responded to the boundaries of her voice without restraining them. Then Abby joined in. Mary closed her eyes and continued singing, waiting for Calum's fiddle. At the end of the song, she opened her eyes again and looked for Calum. He had disappeared from the room.

Abby beamed. 'That was beautiful. You still have the voice of an angel.'

'I won the Mod when I was young,' Mary said. 'I could have been a professional singer.'

'You *were* a professional singer, Mary.'

'I mean, full time. I could have toured the world, if he hadn't come along.'

'Calum, you mean?'

'Aye. Where's he gone?'

'Out,' Johnny said, sipping whisky.

Mary's stomach contracted. 'Out where? He didn't tell me he was going out.'

'Only for a little walk.'

'He's always going off somewhere. He never tells me anything.'

'He won't be long.' Abby patted her leg.

'Stop touching me.' Mary jerked away. She was tired of strangers touching her. They were never finished manhandling her in hospital.

'I'm sorry.'

Mary stood and pulled the hem of her cardigan down more firmly over her waistband. 'Och, I'll make a cup of tea. Would you like tea? I'm sorry, I've forgotten your names. Calum will be back shortly, I expect. I can't think where he's gone. You're welcome to wait.'

MEETING

'We're isolated enough as it is,' big Angus MacBride was saying, his voice slurred with what might have been drink or might have been the hangover of the stroke he'd recently suffered. 'Our young people still move away to find work; we have no opportunities to offer them. How will independence change that, except to make it worse? You think London will still take them when we're a foreign country? They'll end up like refugees, in one of those detention centres.'

The village hall was crowded, overheated with bodies and arguments, some sensible and some less so. Calum shifted uncomfortably on the metal folding chair. His knee complained about the cramped position, his belly complained about the lack of food and the debate, now well into its second hour, showed no signs of concluding. He'd never known such contention in the village, or heard such political passion from people who generally kept the contents of their minds safely veiled. Mary sat beside him, hands folded in her lap, turning her head right and left like a spectator at a tennis match. Her eyes were very bright, but it was difficult to know how much of this she was taking in. She nudged Calum's arm.

'Is that Angus MacBride?'

'Aye.'

'I didn't recognise him. Look how fat he's got.'

'Mum . . .'

'Why is he at the top table? What makes him an authority?'

'He's a councillor. They're all councillors.'

She replied with a surprised, 'Hmm,' and fell silent, fidgeting a little.

'They already are foreigners in London, Angus,' Johnny was saying, 'And enough of them are sleeping under bridges. I know that too well because I was one of them. If we were independent, we could build our economy properly so they wouldn't have to leave. Westminster will never invest in the Highlands. They'll never fund roads and railway extensions up here, they don't even bother to get us proper broadband. It's in their interest to keep us remote, so the rich buggers can have their pretty playgrounds. Folk down south used to tell me they'd like Scotland if it weren't for all the Sweaty Socks. That's what we're up against.'

'Ocht, Johnny, there's plenty Scots hate the English as well,' Davina Nicholson replied. She had the tone of a grandmother already. She had been in Finn's year at school and was as prim and dull now as she had been then. 'What makes anyone here think Edinburgh will invest in the Highlands? Holyrood has no more interest in us up here than London does, and they'll have an awful lot less money at their disposal.'

Mary nudged Calum again. 'How much longer will this go on? I need the toilet.'

'Just go, Mum.'

'I don't want to be rude.'

'It isn't about having more or less money, it's about what we choose to do with it,' Georgie Richardson shouted, half rising from her seat. 'We need a government that listens to our priorities. Like when we tell them where they can stuff their bleeding weapons of mass destruction.' This evoked appreciative whoops and applause.

102

'You'd leave us as an isolated backwater with no military deterrent,' Angus said.

Georgie's voice crackled with emotion. 'Is the capacity to launch a retaliatory strike after our whole country has been annihilated really a deterrent? You're talking about mutually assured destruction. Surely the best deterrent is to be a small, peaceful nation which has moved on from its colonial past.'

'An independent Scotland would need its own defences, nuclear or not. Where would the money come from?'

'There'd be plenty of money if we kept the oil,' said someone else, a young man Calum didn't recognise. 'It's our oil, isn't it? It comes out of our sea.'

'Anyone who banks on the oil is a fool,' Calum said.

The room turned to look at him and the young guy looked disgruntled. 'What do you mean, pal?'

Calum crossed his arms over his chest. 'Oil is the past. You all know that, even if a lot of you don't want to admit it.'

'I thought you were a Yes man, Calum,' said Angus, 'or are you coming to your senses at last?'

'I support independence, but certainly not because I think we're going to get rich on oil. We have an opportunity to create an economy based on fairness and equality and sustainability. We have a chance to say to the world that we respect ourselves and each other, and that we value people who are vulnerable just as much as the people who do well for themselves. It's not about money, it's about the kind of nation we want to be. It seems to me we'll never get this chance again in our lifetimes.'

Angus MacBride pursed his lips. 'Don't pretend you didn't go away as well, to make your money from the oil.'

'Aye, I did, Angus, that's no secret. And I've seen how it works with my own eyes. The big money goes into the pockets of a very few rich men, who are getting richer by the

103

day while the rest of us scrape by. The industry is merciless and I guarantee you, the bottom line is all that matters. The people whose lives are destroyed by the spills, the accidents, not to mention climate change . . . you think they'll ever see a benefit? We're not Norway; we haven't been intelligent with our oil profits.'

'So what are you saying?'

'I'm saying the sooner we move away from dependence on fossil fuels, the better. We'll have wind and wave power forever in Scotland. Energy generation should be for the common good, not for corporate profit. I'll vote yes even if I think we might be poorer for a while, because we may well be.'

Angus's wattles vibrated. 'I see you've come into Red Jack's idealism late in life, Calum Macdonald, but we've got to eat.'

At this point, Mary sat up and said in clear, haughty Gaelic, 'You eat very well these days, by the look of you, Angus.'

Angus huffed and shook his head, cheeks wobbling, while the four or five other people in the room who understood tried to stifle their laughter. Whispered translations made their way around the room. Calum covered his eyes with his fingers and laughed until tears ran down his cheeks.

When the debate was drawn to a non-consensual stopping point, people congregated around plates of shortbread and tea and coffee in paper cups. Many of the younger ones were eager to continue the discussion, while others seemed grateful to return to village gossip and more mundane concerns. Mary explained competently to successive neighbours that she was staying for a couple of weeks while the painters and decorators were in. Calum trailed after her, wondering who she was going to insult next.

At last he managed to extract her, and they walked slowly

along the road to the house. 'What did you think of that, Mum?' he asked.

'What did I think of what?'

'The meeting we've just been at.'

'It was awfully long and I was needing the toilet. I may have wet myself a little bit.'

'Oh you didn't, did you?' He glanced down at her backside. She was wearing black trousers and nothing showed. 'Why didn't you just go?'

'It's rude just to get up. I was embarrassed to put my hand up.'

'Mum, it's not school, you don't have to put your hand up. What did you think of the debate, though? The discussion.'

'I didn't understand a word of it. These are things that have nothing to do with us.'

'They have everything to do with us.'

'Well it's not right, spouting opinions in public like that. You're asking for trouble.'

He smiled. 'Dad wouldn't have liked to hear you say that. I wish he could be here now. He'd be in his element, he'd have nailed old Angus to the wall. You've got to vote yes for him, don't you think?'

'I don't see what it's got to do with me. What am I meant to be saying yes to?'

'It's about Scottish independence, Mum. We're being asked to vote whether Scotland should be an independent country. Has this passed you by completely?'

'Independent from what?'

'Jesus.' He stopped walking and stared at the water for a minute, sucked in a deep breath, counted to five.

'Is there going to be a war, Calum?'

'A war?' He stared at her. She was so small, with her hands knotting and releasing and knotting again. As irrationally frightened as a child in the dark. 'No, of course there isn't going to be a war.' He placed his fingers lightly on her arm. 'I promise, there isn't going to be a war. It's a peaceful democratic process. We're voting about whether to become independent from the United Kingdom.'

'I was never a nationalist. Neither was your father. He didn't believe in putting up walls between people.'

'Nobody's talking about putting up a wall. It's about democracy. I think Dad would understand that.'

Mary then moved on as if what he'd said had no meaning. 'They're spying on us. I've heard them.'

'Who? Who's spying on us?'

'Those voices that ring the telephone every day.'

'What voices? What are you talking about?'

'The robots. Spies. Whatever they are. They ring the phone every day at teatime. They say they've got my name on some list. They want to get inside my walls.'

'Oh ... ' His palms came up to his eyes. 'Mum, they're just sales calls. They're trying to sell you cavity wall insulation. It's just a recorded message. All you have to do is hang up.'

She raised her index finger. 'Either you think I'm stupid or you're one of them, Calum. I think you are. Don't think just because you're my son you'll get away with it. You won't find anything on me, I've burnt it all.'

'Aye, too right you've burnt it all.' Anger like a missile seeking a bigger target than her. He got the recorded calls too, but had never bothered to listen to the details. There had to be some way of making a complaint, of letting them know what they had caused her to do.

Who *were* they?

He was in danger of sounding like her.

His mind tumbled into one of its familiar monologues:

I can't do this. I can't look after her. I can't do this. Somebody take her away, I can't do this.

I have to. There's no one else.

Damn you, Finn, you never took responsibility for anything.

It's up to me. This is my mum. This is my bloody mother.

BACKPACKING

Catriona stepped off the bus in Fort William, swung her rucksack onto her shoulders and followed a group of back-packers onto the ugly precinct that passed as the high street. It had taken her all day to get here, a bus from Aberdeen to Inverness and another from Inverness to here, watching the Scotland she knew, the east coast with its sweeping expanses of sky and field, become mountainous and unfamiliar. The hills sat above the town like the haunches of great brooding beasts, mist hanging around the tops, veils of rain passing over, clearing and coming again. To the west, the sky was dark purple-grey, rumbling with electricity, promising a deluge.

She had no idea how to continue her journey from here, or quite what she would do when she reached her destination, but now she was tired and it was going to rain. This place felt alien, almost like another country, and so for the first time in weeks, she felt safe. Safe enough, anyway, to stop overnight and figure out the rest tomorrow.

She overheard the group of young backpackers talking about a hostel, so she continued to follow them, away from the high street and up a steep residential street, to a shabby bunkhouse overlooking the town. The place smelled of old food but it was cheap enough and there was a bed available for the night, a top bunk in a room with five other women. Catriona climbed up onto the bed and pulled the duvet over herself, listening to her room-mates chatting and rummaging. Two of the girls poured torrents of Spanish as they organised the contents of their luggage. There were two Americans who lay on their bunks, their thumbs twiddling on their phones, and one older woman who sat cross-legged on her bed, writing in a journal. Comforted by the presence of the other women, most of whom ignored her completely, she dozed as the sky outside blackened and the rain lashed into the window.

When she woke it was brighter again, and the room was quiet. The Americans and the Spaniards had gone out, and the older woman was wrapped in a towel, rubbing apricot-scented skin cream onto her wiry arms. Without modesty, she let the towel fall and stood naked as she removed meticulously rolled items from a bicycle pannier and selected clean clothes. She looked about the same age as Cat's mother, but had a knotty, angular body, tiny pert breasts, short blonde hair that stood out in spikes. Dressed, she turned and approached Catriona's bed.

'I'm Anna,' she said, a musical accent that pointed towards Scandinavia.

Catriona sat up, rubbing her cheek and pretending to be sleepier than she was. 'I'm Cat.'

'I am going down to the town to have something to eat. Would you like to come with me?'

'Oh, I . . . ' Cat's appetite had been strange lately and food didn't taste like it used to, but she supposed she would feel better with something inside her. 'All right. Thank you.'

As they walked down the hill, Anna told her that she was cycling the coast of Scotland, from Glasgow to the north coast, then across and down the east side from John O'Groats to Edinburgh. She was from Denmark where it was very flat, she said and laughed, and then embarked on an enthusiastic account of her exploits, including a near miss with a Glasgow bus that nearly ended the journey before it began. Catriona wanted to ask Anna why she would bother but the question felt juvenile. Instead she tried to imagine Jenny undertaking such a trip for fun. The idea was almost ridiculous. Jenny's idea of a holiday was a sun lounger and an all-inclusive drinks package.

They bought fish and chips and sat on a bench over-looking the coal-black water of Loch Linnhe. Anna was uncomplaining, effusive about Scotland, curious about Cat's opinion on the referendum.

'I'm voting yes,' Cat said. 'To me, voting no is like saying you don't ever want to grow up and leave your parents' house. You have to, even if you ... ' she paused as a terrible pressure grew inside her. She closed her eyes and hot tears formed behind her eyelids.

'Are you all right?' Anna asked.

'Yeah, I ... ' she blinked a couple of times, stuffed a chip into her mouth and focused on its comforting saltiness. 'I was going to say, you have to leave home even if you really screw up along the way.'

'This is the truth. Are you leaving home now, Cat? Is that why you're upset?'

'I've been away at university for the last year.'

'And it's been hard for you?'

'No ... not really. Just ... something happened there and it's changed things for me. I'm on my way to see my dad. He lives in a village, west of here. I'll go there tomorrow. I think there's a bus.'

'He doesn't live with your mother?'

'No, he never has. They were never married. I haven't seen him for a long time.' She pulled her phone from her bag and brought up a photo she'd found online. Calum was in a pub, playing his fiddle, face alight with laughter. 'This is him.'

Anna took the phone. 'So he is a musician,' she said, and there was some kind of ominous wisdom in her tone.

'He's an amazing musician.'

'Musicians are a special breed of people. Very beautiful and very passionate, but often they have ... troubled minds. You know?'

'Yeah, that's what my mother says about him.' Those weren't exactly the words Jenny used about Calum, though there was a list of other terms that possibly added up to the same thing: unreliable, argumentative, irresponsible, thinks-he's-cleverer-than-everyone-else, heid-up-his-ain-arse. And crazy. That was her favourite.

Anna nodded and continued to gaze at the photo for a moment, before handing the phone back. 'He is very hand-some,' she said.

TELEPHONE

There was that blasted telephone again.

It was them.

Mary let it ring out but her heart was going like a bass drum. Why was her heart going? She was being daft. It was only the telephone. It would be Jack. He'd be late home again. Always stuck late on jobs and not taking the money for them. It was his way. Too kind for his own good. It would be nice to sit down to tea together for once.

No.

Not Jack. She kept imagining he'd walk through the door. He'd see her. His eyes would see her and he would smile and kiss her, and she'd wake from this dream. Why him? Why both of them? Why Finn? So long ago. Why did she keep forgetting?

She was left with the one that didn't care. Calum couldn't get away soon enough.

She didn't know where he was. He never told her anything.

What if he didn't come back?

Who could be phoning at this time? What did they want? They were trying to get in.

No, they weren't. They didn't exist. Calum told her that.

But Calum could be lying. He did that. He lied. He had lied about Finn.

How else would they know she was here, if Calum hadn't told them?

It would be Iain. He often rang about this time. He'd want feeding, the lazy old bugger. He'd be after a free meal. If ever a man needed a woman. She supposed she'd have to call round. She'd bring him a tin of tomato soup. He'd grumble and say it should have been home-made. Lazy old arse. Beggars shouldn't be choosers.

She searched the cupboards for soup and eventually located a tin of Heinz. She tucked it into the pocket of her coat, stepped out the front door and walked up the road, into the woods.

WHAT TO EXPECT WHEN YOUR LOVED ONE HAS DEMENTIA

'Here he is, Mary,' Bert Richardson called into the living room, stepping aside to let Calum in. 'See I told you, didn't I, they always turn up when they get hungry.' He patted Calum's elbow. 'She's fine. We'd have brought her back up the road for you.'

'No, it's fine, Bert.' Calum let out a shaky breath. 'How long has she been here?'

'About half an hour. She's in good hands, she's just scoffed two of Georgie's scones in rapid succession. Come in, man.' He brought Calum into the living room. In his Uncle Iain's day, it had been a gloomy bachelor-cave, thick with old cigarette and wet dog smells. Now it was clean, white-walled with sliding glass doors leading onto a deck, gathering sunlight and shimmering reflections.

'Take a load off,' Bert said, motioning Calum towards the sofa where Mary sat with a mug between her hands. Her cheeks were very red but she appeared to have come to no harm.

'You gave me a wee fright, Mum,' he said, trying to keep his voice calm. 'I came home and you were gone.'

'You gave me a fright,' she replied. 'You just abandoned me in the house all day, with no idea where you were.'

'I was in Acharacle, working.'

'Well, you should have told me.'

'I did.'

'You never tell me anything.' Then she switched to Gaelic. '*English* settlers in Iain's house. Who decided to sell to them? I should have been consulted. It isn't what he would have wanted.'

'It was years ago already,' he replied, in English. It wasn't beyond the realm of possibility that Bert and Georgie had learned some Gaelic.

'A dram, Calum?' Georgie said, coming in from the kitchen with a buttered scone on a plate.

'Tea's fine. Thanks, Georgie.'

'Get him a dram, George,' Bert said. 'And tea. And while you're waiting, you should come out and have a look at our brood. They're doing beautifully.'

Calum put his plate onto the coffee table and followed Bert onto the deck, where a telescope was trained on the top of a pine across the tiny inlet. The eagles' nest was an imposing construction, which the scope brought into such sharp focus that it felt invasive. The two chicks had grown nearly to adult size and had traded their downy fluff for sleek dark feathers. Their heads bobbed around as they kept watch for their parents.

'They've been spreading their wings,' Bert said companionably, 'Ready to fledge soon. Ah ... here's a parent.' He raised his binoculars. 'Mum, with a fish. She's a good mother, a better hunter than that mate of hers.'

Calum watched the adult eagle swoop into the nest and the voracious youths hop onto the fish, bumping each other out of the way and tussling. The mother stood on the edge of the nest and watched.

'There won't be much left for her when those two are finished with it.'

'Always the way,' Bert said beneath his binoculars, allowing Calum another quiet minute on the scope. He dropped his voice when he spoke again. 'Mary said she was looking for your Uncle Iain. She got a bit upset when we told her.'

'I know . . . I'm sorry about this, Bert. She's had early-stage Alzheimer's for a while, but it's . . . moving on, I think. She seems to be forgetting that most of her relatives have died.'

Bert moved his fingers through his beard. 'We wondered.' He was silent for a moment. 'My dad had it. The middle stages were the worst. Once he lost everything it was a blessing in a way, awful as that sounds. You're in for a rough ride, I'm afraid.'

'Aye.' Calum leaned his forearms on the railing, stared down at the water and thought again about the faulty batch of brains his family had been given, terminal glitches hard-wired to kick in without warning. Maybe it was some kind of twisted proof that God existed after all, that he was actually just a hack programmer with a sick sense of humour. All you could do was hope that your own glitch would be catastrophic, a haemorrhage or aneurysm that took you out so fast you wouldn't even know it had happened.

'Are you thinking of keeping her at home with you for good now?' Bert asked.

'She had a fire in her flat. I'm hoping she can go back, but she was in hospital for a little while and I think it's made her worse.'

'It always does. Look, Georgie and I are happy to help, call in on her from time to time, take her for a walk or a drive if we're going over to town, that sort of thing. Don't be afraid to ask, Calum.'

'I hope this is going to be short-term, but . . . thanks.'

'Take it from me, Son, you don't want to deal with this alone. Come and have your dram, and don't tell me you don't need it.'

'What happened, Mum?' he quizzed her when they got home.

'The telephone rang. I didn't reach it in time, but I thought...' she paused, lips working, 'I was sure it would be Iain. He used to do that, you know...ring and then hang up. When he was lonely.'

'You remember Iain's dead, right?'

Mary nodded slowly. 'Everyone's dead. I suppose I'll just have to get used to the fact that the village is full of strangers.'

'Bert and Georgie aren't strangers. You've met them before.' But they would be strangers to her soon enough, he thought, along with everyone else.

'They were nice enough people in their way, but not really the sort to fit in here.'

'They fit in fine.'

'Iain wouldn't have liked what they've done with the house. It's so modern.'

'I don't suppose Iain will be caring what it looks like now, and it was an utter tip when he lived in it.'

She tutted. 'Well what do you expect of a man on his own, Calum? You were no better when you were young.'

'I think the fact he was pissed most of the time had something to do with it.'

'He was fond of a dram, but I never saw him drunk.'

'Oh Jesus Christ, you never saw him sober!'

'Language!' she crossed herself, then sighed. 'You're so coarse. I never raised you to be so coarse. You'll have learned that from the roughnecks.' Her lips were pursed, her brows drawn together, deep lines scored into her forehead. 'I'd like

117

to go to Mass on Sunday. Maybe you'll come with me for once?'

'I'll take you, but you know I won't go to Mass.'

'Will you ever explain to me why, Calum?'

At last, and where he least wanted to find one, a thread of continuity. They'd been having this same argument since he was fourteen. His refusal to be confirmed had caused an argument of Biblical proportions between his parents, and from then on, he'd quietly decided that his dad had been on his side and his mother on Finn's. He decided that the conversation was finished and stood up. 'I have tried, Mum, many times. I'm going out in the kayak for an hour. Please promise me you won't go anywhere.'

She gave him a blank stare, as though her excursion was already forgotten. 'Where would I go?'

Waking the next morning, he felt ambivalence lying over him like damp wool. From the pillow he could see heavy clouds, pending rain. The day would be easier if he could simply pull the covers over his head and go back to sleep. But his brain was rattling to work, churning out anxieties on a relentless assembly line. There wasn't a snowball's chance in hell of switching it off without chemical help.

The community nurse had given him a stack of leaflets, which he found on his bedside table beneath an empty whisky tumbler, a packet of ibuprofen tablets and a pair of off-the-shelf reading glasses. He turned onto his side and stared at this collection as the morning litany of bad news gurgled out of the radio, extracted his arm from beneath his pillow, reached for a leaflet and squinted at it. *What to Expect When Your Loved One Has Dementia*. He put on the glasses and read a page or two. The language was gentle, reassuring, patronising in the extreme. Advice tidily presented with bullet points:

- Dementia is an illness, for which there is currently no cure. However, with appropriate support and sometimes medication, a person with dementia can maintain a fulfilling life.

- Be patient and accept your loved one's condition. Try not to subject them to additional stress or frustration by asking them to 'snap out of it' or 'pull themselves together'.

- Encourage them to maintain an active lifestyle. Even small activities, such as taking a walk or tidying the house can help maintain mental function.

Soft-focus photographs of a smiling white-haired lady reading to a blue-eyed child. Calum crumpled the paper in his fist and chucked it across the room. The next leaflet informed him about a lunch club for vulnerable elderly individuals and the third invited him to join a self-help support group for carers in the Lochaber area: a fifty-mile round trip for an hour-long meeting. The nurse had called this wastage of trees *literature*. Literature was art. It was poetry, it was the human condition unwrapped and delivered on a bed of beautiful words. This was only instruction about how to make the withering of a life slightly less unbearable.

Just like that, his mother had become a patient or worse, a *service user*, and he had become a carer. Their names and life stories were as dispensable as Mary's fading memories. They were to be labelled and pigeonholed, not particularly to be helped but to be categorised by some number cruncher in an office up in Inverness. And so he lay there reading his leaflets through the cheap glasses – because he refused to admit that he needed them enough to pay for a proper prescription

– with a sore head, a list of aches in various parts of his body and what felt like rats gnawing at his gut.

Mary was up and about already; she rose early and had a surprising store of energy in the morning. He could hear her shuffling between her bedroom and the bathroom, the water going on and off, cupboard doors creaking open and bumping closed again. She seemed happier and less paranoid now that she was back in the home of her child-hood, but also more confused than ever. Time seemed to have collapsed in on itself and people long dead walked in and out of her consciousness without causing her much distress. Your da will help you mend the wall in the back field, she would say, or I really ought to bring some soup round to Iain. I haven't seen him in days. Mostly she pottered and made work for herself, reorganising drawers in his kitchen so that neither of them could find anything afterwards, deadheading flowers and clipping newspaper articles about obscure events that captured her interest. Sometimes she called Finn's name and looked displeased to see the other son appear, or called him Finn directly and tutted when Calum corrected her. Sometimes he didn't have the heart to correct her. Nobody could predict how long it could go on this way; she could remain relatively stable for quite a while or she could deteriorate quickly. Medication might keep her lucid for a period of time, or it might not.

He took off his glasses and lay there for another couple of minutes, his palms pressed into his eyes. His skull felt just a little too tight. Too much whisky before bed, to quiet his nerves after Mary's jaunt up the road.

He waited until he heard her descend the stairs before getting up and going into the bathroom himself. It was her lifelong habit to leave it immaculate after her morning ablu-tions, and she still did so with competence. So there were some small perks to her being here, he supposed, as he ran hot water into the sink and lathered shaving foam onto his face.

Shaved and dressed, he started down the stairs and paused halfway, distracted by the unexpected sound of singing. His left foot swung out into the air and threatened to pull him forward face first. Blood rushed in his ears as he caught himself and descended the rest of the way more slowly. At the bottom he stopped and glanced back up the stairs, which from below looked normal and unthreatening, and then stood and listened for a moment.

Mary was singing. He walked softly along the corridor and leaned in the kitchen door behind her. She stood at the stove with her back to him, stirring porridge. As a young woman, she had supplemented her schoolteacher's salary by performing at folk clubs, festivals and weddings. Mostly now she hummed wordless melodies, and it was rare to hear her sing like this anymore, fully articulating a set of lyrics. It surprised him that she could still remember them, and he supposed the knowledge must reside somewhere in the deepest core of her brain, where the disease had not yet penetrated. It would be the same reason he could still play the fiddle when he was too drunk to walk.

'That was bonny, Mum.' He stepped up beside her and took two bowls down from the cupboard.

She faced him, unsmiling, and replied in Gaelic. 'You were eavesdropping.'

'Is that a bad thing?'

'Can a person not have a little privacy in her own kitchen? What time did you arrive? Isn't it a bit early for a visit?'

He felt his eyebrows lift. 'I live here. You know this is my house now, Mum, don't you?'

She pointed the porridge spoon at him, her face colouring abruptly. The anger came so quickly, from nowhere. 'My father built this house with his own hands, and I'll not have you displace me from my own home.'

So the Fort William flat, which she had insisted on buying after Dad died, had already fallen by the wayside. It was beginning to feel like he'd be stuck with her for the duration, and he silently cursed Johnny and Abby for talking him into having her at all.

He patted her arm and she swung it away. Since her stay in hospital, she had acquired a dislike of being touched. Another development he had to accommodate.

'Nobody's displacing you, don't worry. Please just try to remember that I live here too. You've still got your flat, but this is the only home I've got. And can you please speak English?'

She still looked doubtful, but obliged and changed languages. 'When did you leave Texas?'

'California.'

'You were in Texas, Calum.'

'Aye, before California. And I've been back here five years, Ma.'

'You told me you were only taking a break.'

'Well it turned out to be a permanent break.'

'And you just ... walked away from that lovely girl. What was her name again?'

'Michelle.'

'Oh, yes. Such a beautiful figure she had. Whatever possessed you to leave her?'

'She was the one who ... '

'I had a figure like that when I was young, you know. But I did always wonder, Calum, were her breasts real? I've never seen breasts as firm as that.'

She was not laughing, and he tried not to. 'Ehm ... they might have had some help. *Before* she met me, I hasten to add. Bloody hell, Mum.'

122

'Language, please.'

'Sorry.' He drew his fingers over his lips. 'I'm working down in Acharacle again today. I'll be finished up by the middle of the afternoon.'

'That's fine, dear. I've only made enough porridge for myself, I wasn't expecting you.'

'You have it.'

'No, you have this. I'll make more.' She tasted the porridge and switched off the hob, dished out his bowl and carried it to the table, then came back with brown sugar and milk in a warmed jug. Another of her ingrained routines. *Never underestimate the importance of table manners*, she used to say to him and Finn as they threw toast down their throats or drank milk from the bottle on their way out the door. Calum ate and ran through a mental list of tasks to finish off the Acharacle job.

'Before you go, would you get out a set of steps and a long-handled brush?'

He paused with his spoon halfway to his mouth and looked up at her. 'What for?'

'I want to make a start on the cobwebs in the byre.'

'Mum . . . '

'They're terribly inflammatory, Calum, you really shouldn't let them accumulate like that.'

'Inflammable.'

'Yes, that's what I'm telling you. You've let that byre get into a terrible state.'

'You said inflammatory.'

'I know the difference between inflammable and inflammatory.' She shook her head and huffed. 'I don't believe your hearing is as good as it used to be, Son.'

I don't believe your mind is as good as it used to be, Mother. 'I need the steps, and I'd rather the spiders stayed where they are, eating midges. Honestly Mum, you don't have to work for your keep, right? Put your feet up and relax.'

She didn't offer a reply to this, but sipped her tea and fixed him with an accusatory stare. As soon as he finished his porridge, she took his empty bowl from his hand, scrubbed it in the basin she'd already filled with soapy water, wiped it dry. 'Can I make you a bit of bacon?'

'No thanks.' He refilled his coffee, made a cheese and pickle sandwich for his lunch and put the kettle on again to make tea for his flask. Mary buzzed around behind him, wiping up crumbs and washing up.

'There's a woman in Donald's back garden,' she said from the sink. 'I've never seen her before.

He glanced out. Julie was outside, digging a new bed at the side of the house, driving the spade deep into the earth with the heel of her purple welly. How very like her not to tell him she was coming back.

'It's Julie. She moved in a few years ago.'

'No, I've never seen her. Who is she?'

'Julie Morrison. She's . . . a friend of mine.'

'English. Another incomer.'

'She's from Glasgow.'

'The Highlands have become a holiday theme park. Overrun with tourists.'

'We need them. Julie isn't a tourist anyway. She lives here, most of the time. Sometimes she goes back down for work. She's a sculptor.' He turned away before she could argue, screwed the flask closed and shoved it into a rucksack along with his sandwich box. 'I've got to go, Mum. You'll be okay? I've left Bert and Georgie's number by the phone. If there's any problem, call them.'

She stood there winding her hands in a tea towel as he tied up his boots. 'Your Da's Cousin Seumas was killed on the road home from Acharacle. His brakes went out on the brae at Ardmolich.'

Calum straightened and looked at her. Like Cousin Seumas,

Finn went out the door to go climbing another day, not so very many years later, and never came home. Was she thinking of him too, or was it just a shapeless fear that she couldn't name?

'I'll drive carefully,' he said and kissed her cheek.

'Stop that.' She swiped her hand over her face. 'I don't like that.'

It was a shameful relief to close the door on her.

WATER

There was so much water. It spilled from a saturated sky, overflowed the small burns that cut the hillsides, gathered into larger streams and then into torrents; it raged over rocks, pooled in ruts at the side of the road. The rain came on as Catriona waited for the bus in Fort William and showed no sign of stopping as they travelled west. The window steamed until the landscape outside dissolved into a wash of green and grey, and the tears that she had been spilling for weeks now were indistinguishable from the rest.

The bus trundled on through the rain, through a country she had lived in all her life but couldn't claim to know. Holidays with her Mum had mostly been Spanish packages, and although her Dad's family were all West Highlanders, she'd never been out here before. She'd never seen the place where he was born and grew up. As they cleared Fort William and its outlying villages, the hills became steeper, the cottages more remote. The soggy greenness was oppressive. What did everyone do out here for fun? Maybe they all died young of extreme boredom. Maybe that was why there were so few houses.

There were worse things than boredom. She had to remind herself of that. Maybe some time away from people was what she needed. Maybe being out here where she didn't have to talk to anyone would help reduce the inflammation of her brain inside her skull. Lately it had been like a bowling ball in her head, rolling from one side to another, grinding everything else to powder. There was no structure left to hang her thoughts on so they swirled like dust around a fan, impossible to pin down.

They turned south at Lochailort and the rain thrummed onto the surface of the loch, pocking the grey-black water. Small boats listed drunkenly and gulls stood still on humps of kelp-swathed rock, waiting for better flying conditions. She cracked the window. The outside air suggested rotting seaweed and wet animals.

They followed the road south until the coast opened up, revealing a bay and a view to islands she couldn't name, blurry beyond the screen of rain. A sign announced their arrival in Glendarach. The bus pulled in and she stepped off alone into the rain, beside a ramshackle cabin that seemed to be a shop of some kind. It was closed now. She wondered if it ever opened. The bus rumbled off and she pulled the hood of her sweatshirt lower over her forehead.

The village, such as it was, spread along a single-track road at the head of the bay. Catriona walked up the road, past a pub, a community hall and a few dirty white cottages. A couple of boats sat on their hulls, waiting for the tide to float them again. There was a tiny church tucked into the woods. Sheep stood in a muddy field, accepting their miserable lot in life as sheep and too many people do. The rain soaked through her cotton sleeves, chilled her skin and dribbled down her back. Everything in the rucksack would be completely soaked.

His house had to be on this road, but she had no idea how far along. All she could do was keep going, getting colder by the minute. A forest of gnarled oaks and birches gathered around the road, trees made small and crippled by their exposed existence. They thinned again to reveal a tiny beach:

a crescent of pale sand fringed by a spill of sea-rounded rocks, a hummock of land further out with a channel of grey water in front of it. More grounded boats. To her left, opposite the beach, were two cottages. One was dark grey stone, with white-painted lintels. An upturned yellow kayak lay beside a separate outbuilding. The second cottage was smaller, the front wall decorated with shells in swirling wave patterns. Catriona lingered for a moment, trying to conjure some sense of familiarity. The grey house was Calum's, she was sure of it. She'd seen photographs of this beach, the yellow kayak, these cottages.

All she had to do was knock on the door, but her legs refused to carry her up the drive. Anyway, there were no cars around and it didn't look like anyone was home. She was shivering, drowning slowly but surely.

She walked back up the road and went into the pub. It was empty apart from the woman behind the bar and a couple at a table by the window.

'Can I have a cup of tea, please?' Catriona asked. She no longer trusted the promises of alcohol.

'Of course you can, darling,' said the bar woman. She seemed amused by Catriona's bedraggled appearance. 'It's a bit damp out there.'

Catriona wanted to cry. 'A bit.'

'Have a seat by the stove and dry off. I'll bring it over to you.'

'Thanks.' She wondered if she should ask the woman about Calum, but couldn't bring herself to speak anymore. Every time she opened her mouth, she was afraid of what might come out. She might vomit. She might scream. She might spill a gutful of snakes and beetles onto the bar.

Maybe once she'd warmed up a little.

She sat and held her hands towards the woodstove. A black and white collie padded towards her, sniffed at her, let

128

her bury her fingers in its hair for a moment, then wandered off. Catriona peeled off her hoodie and draped it over the end of the bench table nearest the fire, where it began to steam. She wondered how long the rain could go on.

FIVE YEARS

As he drove south, past Kinlochmoidart and up the steep hill where Cousin Seumas had crashed out of the game, Calum thought about the randomness of the things Mary remembered. Why, for example, did she remember Michelle at all, when they'd only met on a handful of occasions and never got to know each other well? To Calum, it felt like Michelle belonged to another man's past. He could go weeks without thinking of her. Occasionally he missed her, but it wasn't a sorrowful missing anymore, just a minor nostalgia for a phase of his life that was gone.

It was even funnier that Mary remembered her augmented breasts. *They* certainly didn't top the list of things he missed. They sat on Michelle's narrow body like pincushions on a board, and he'd always been a bit afraid of them. You didn't want to massage or manipulate too much; things might get pushed out of place. What he did miss was the vitality of her passions: sailing, skiing, dancing, travelling, eating, love-making. He missed her lust for sensation and novelty. He missed feeling like they could afford to buy as much adventure as they wanted. Living with Michelle had been a long hit of cocaine, an addiction with a bastard of a comedown.

*

Ventura, California, 2009

The house was dark, blinds drawn against the afternoon sun. He pushed the front door closed, let his bag flop onto the terracotta tiles and paused to tune in to the noises of an empty house. The air conditioning hummed even though Michelle was at work; the wall clock in the living room ticked. He went to the kitchen and pulled a bottle of Anchor Steam out of the fridge, twisted the cap off and sat at the breakfast bar. Outside, waves of heat radiated up from the bleached patio and the eucalyptus trees stirred in a dry wind. The air was murky with smoke from the wildfires in the hills out east. It stung his eyes, even indoors.

He drank the first bottle quickly because he was thirsty, then opened another and worked on it more slowly, trying not to worry about what had happened on the rig but unable really to think about anything else. It had been like a kind of paralysis: a fear so intense that it froze him and stopped his breath in his throat. If it had lasted a few minutes it might have been described as a panic attack, but it had lasted three days: three days in which he had been unable to leave the accommodation block. He'd had a few episodes before, seconds of dizziness or moments in which he had felt himself pulled towards the edge by some external force, but this was different. He knew this changed things.

There had been a suicide on the platform. For reasons as yet unexplained, a roughneck had climbed the drilling tower and thrown himself off, hitting the Pacific below with sufficient force to shatter his bones and fatally compress his internal organs. The questions and repercussions affected everyone on the rig; Jose was a hard worker, he had a young family, he sent money back to his parents in Mexico. Calum hadn't actually witnessed his fall, but when he closed his eyes, he could see it in vivid detail.

131

Then he dreamed of Finn falling, just falling down into space, falling but never disappearing from view, and he had to watch his brother fall forever: a death that couldn't be averted but never actually came. He was jolted awake by his own voice and the freaked-out face of his room-mate, shaking him back to life. Now there would be questions to answer, an evaluation of his physical and mental fitness to continue his work, and he already knew the outcome.

Michelle got home after ten, her breath pungent with alcohol, and found him half asleep in front of the television only a week into his usual two-week stint. There was no point asking her where she'd been. He often wondered what she got up to while he was offshore, but probing for details provoked such an aggressive response that he had stopped asking. There was no evidence that she was sleeping with anyone else; she simply didn't see any need to be answerable to him.

'You're late,' he said, pushing himself upright.

'You're early.' She didn't kiss him or even try to pretend it was a pleasant surprise. They'd been skirmishing these last few months, for reasons he hadn't yet tried to grapple with. Maybe all marriages went this way: the inevitable subsidence of familiarity into contempt. Her purse and keys clattered onto the counter and she pulled off her heels, unclasped her hair and let it fall down over her shoulders in a flaxen sheet. It was the only soft thing about her; the rest was sinew and attitude. 'You look like shit. Are you sick?'

'I don't know. Maybe.'

'What do you mean?'

'A guy killed himself, Shell. He jumped.'

'Oh crap,' she said, hearing but barely registering as she rifled through the stack of mail he'd left beside the telephone. 'That sucks.'

'I kind of ... freaked out. I had ... I don't know ... a

132

flashback about my brother, and I couldn't . . . ' he paused, pressed his fingers into his eyes and focused on her again. She wasn't looking at him. 'Are you even listening?'

She sighed. 'Yes.'

'Every time I went outside I could see him falling.'

'You're seeing things that aren't there? Oh my God, you are so fucked up.'

'Thanks.' His lungs felt like bagpipes squashed under somebody's elbow.

'You are. I keep telling you to go see someone.'

'I think it's past that now.'

'Uh . . . like . . . no shit. They could fire you tomorrow.'

'They're not going to fire me, Shell, I've been with the company a long time.'

'Then they'll manage you out the door. They can't have a psychotic chief engineer.'

'I'm not psychotic. Jesus. I know it's not real.'

'Well, what do you call it, Cal? You're *seeing* things.' She sat down at the breakfast bar and visibly processed the implications. He knew she'd be thinking about the money before anything else, but then it felt like a cruel assumption and he had a quiet argument with himself because he was too weak to argue properly with her.

She's a materialistic cow.

What's wrong with that? She grew up in the age of Madonna.

Everything's wrong with that.

Okay, Saint Francis, prove it. Turn out your pockets and walk away.

'Maybe . . . ' he had to suck in a deep breath to finish a sentence. 'Maybe it's time to do something else. Maybe I can get an onshore job. It'd be nice to be home more.'

'You think so?'

'Do you not?'

133

She raised an eyebrow at him. 'Two weeks on, two weeks off works pretty good for me.'

'What are you saying, Michelle?'

They stared at each other from opposite sides of the room.

'I think you know what I'm saying,' she replied. Then she slid off the stool and picked up her shoes by their straps, staring at him for two or three long seconds. A look of pity crossed her face, but only for a moment. Then she sighed. 'It's been a day. Goodnight.'

Usually his first night off the rig was a mini-honeymoon, a celebratory reunion of bodies after a meal and a couple of bottles of wine, and it had always felt like what he thought love was supposed to feel like. Now he wondered how much of this had been a performance, however masterly, perfected and reserved for that single night per month when it most mattered. Was it her performance, or his, or both? Or maybe it was worse than that. Maybe it had never been what he thought it was. Maybe it was a semi-inebriated shag that she barely tolerated, and his misfiring brain had turned it into love. So much in California had proved to be illusory: imagined happiness made almost believable by sunshine and blue sky, a shimmering mirage over hot black asphalt.

He pulled off his trousers and slept on the couch.

He arrived back in Glendarach around two, just as a keen breeze from the sea blew the rain off to the east. The sun emerged and a swell billowed in with the tide. A stranger emerged from the pub as he drove past. It was a girl, well-built but not particularly tall, with short hair dyed cherry red. Enormous rucksack. She walked slowly, head down, thumbs working on the screen of a mobile phone. That would be fairly pointless. He wondered whether he should stop and offer her a lift somewhere, or if that would automatically be taken as creepy. She looked up as he drove by her. She was very like Catriona. His breath caught in his throat and he looked back. Then he hit the brakes, swerved onto the gravel verge and got out. He felt like he'd just draped himself over an electric fence.

'Cat?'

She approached hesitantly, lifted a hand in a shy greeting. 'Um . . . hi.'

'Hi,' he managed to stay, rooted to the spot and rubbing his hands on his jeans. He hoped his sunglasses hid the fact that his inner workings were going into meltdown. Panicky questions came in quick succession, followed by inadequate answers:

This is my daughter.

Five years of nothing and here she is.

She's got so much gear she's obviously fixing to stay a while.

What do I do? What do I do, what do I do?

Don't fuck it up like you did last time.

How?

She'd been a child last time, small, late in developing. Her shape was presently obscured by an oversized lumberjack shirt, but she was quite visibly not a child anymore. Black eyeliner extended beyond the corners of her eyes, and her full lower lip was punctured by a silver hoop. She had prominent cheekbones in a broad, heart-shaped face, clear pale skin, very like her mother had been when he'd met her. So much like Jenny. Even from afar, he'd never been able to see himself in her. But even so, she was his daughter.

It was shameful that he had to remind himself of this. There had been so many times he'd almost forgotten her existence. This is your daughter, he bellowed at himself. You haven't seen her in five years, you useless prick.

He'd been ill then, needy and drugged and hurting,

embarrassing to a fourteen-year-old who hadn't seen more than photographs of him for longer than he cared to quantify.

Don't fuck this up, don't fuck this up, don't fuck this ... 'What the hell are you doing here?' Perfect. Good start. Idiot. Close your mouth. Breathe.

She looked him in the eye for the first time. 'I've come to see you, stupid.'

'Okay.'

'Is it?'

'What?'

'Okay that I've come to see you.'

Another rapid-fire volley of thoughts. For how long? You might have called first. And now I've got two of them to look after. What's Mary going to say? Will Mary even remember who you are? It was a minor victory that he managed to think all of these things without saying them.

'I'm glad to see you,' he said instead, and reached towards her hand.

She swallowed, looked like she was trying to hide her relief and allowed her fingers to twine with his. 'Thanks.'

He held onto her hand for a moment. 'You got a hug for your old dad?'

She nodded and stepped toward him. They embraced and she burst into tears.

SEVENTY-SIX
PER CENT

'All right now?'

Catriona nodded, mortified by her display. He would think she was a pathetic snivelling child. 'I don't know what that was about. I'm not usually a crier. Sorry.'

'It's okay.'

She'd been afraid that he might look even worse than last time she'd seen him, if that was possible. Now, as she dared to focus on him, she saw a man she recognised. It was as if the person who had appeared at the door five years ago had been some kind of imposter. His hair was shorter and greyer, and he looked older but seemed a million years younger. He was fit again, robust in dirty work clothes, with arms most of the boys her age would envy. She couldn't remember what age he was. Forty-six or forty-seven, a fair bit older than Mum, anyway. Mum had only just turned forty, but he'd recovered and she'd withered, forever complaining about her sore back and her headaches. Calum *was* handsome for someone his age, she supposed, like Anna said. So did her mum. It was the only nice thing she ever said about him. Be careful around the good-looking ones, she would say. Catriona understood that now.

They sat in the pub again and he ordered them burgers and pints from the bar, and she mopped her smudged eyeliner with the tissue he'd given her, feeling babyish and embarrassed. He didn't seem angry that she'd turned up, but he could be saving it. Mum would have hit her with a million questions already, but he held back, drank his pint slowly and offered a few relevant pieces of information.

'Your Granny Mary's staying with me just now. You remember her, don't you?'

Cat felt a weight of disappointment form in her gut. She didn't want to share him with some old lady she barely knew. 'I remember her singing. She used to sing all the time. She tried to teach me Gaelic.'

'Oh aye, she's still at it.'

'She must be so old now.'

'Not so old, but she's not that well. She's got Alzheimer's disease.'

'So she can't remember anything?'

'She remembers a lot of things. And she forgets a lot of things. I don't know if she'll remember you. Some days I think she barely remembers me, and then other days she's fine. She can be argumentative. Sometimes she's paranoid. She thinks people are stealing from her, that sort of thing.'

Cat considered the implications of this. She should have called him first. It was selfish to assume he could automatically make space in his life for her. 'So you're saying it's not a good time for me to be here.'

'No, it's fine. You just need to know.'

'I can leave. I could stay a day or two and then ... ' And then what? Home again, like the four-year-old runaway. 'Just, you know ... tell me straight.'

'Aye, straight up. I'm just ... surprised, Cat. After all this time you've refused to speak to me and now here you are.'

'Sorry. I should have called. I was going to call you, I just ... ' She was on the verge of panic. 'I needed to get away from Aberdeen.'

'Why? What's happened?'

Not yet, she thought. Not here, in a pub, in this tiny place where everybody would know him. 'It's a long story.' He was looking at her strangely, like he could see the strain on her. She needed a quick diversion. 'What about Granny Mary? Will she be okay with me?'

He shrugged. 'I hope so. We're on new ground every single day. She's completely freaked out by this whole referendum thing, so it's probably best not to mention it around her. She thinks there's going to be a war.'

'Why?'

'God knows.' He drank some beer and gave her that look again. He could see straight through her. Or maybe he was just shocked by her style but was politely keeping quiet about it. Probably he was having a hard time matching her with his memory of her.

'Don't say it,' she muttered.

'What?'

'You hate the way I look.'

'No, it suits you.'

'So why are you staring at me?'

'I was trying to work out what side you're on. Are you an Aye or a Naw?'

'Aye. *Obviously*.'

He sat back. 'Well thank God for that. The lip ring I can live with.'

A giggle rose like a gas bubble in her chest. At least they had that in common. 'So ehm . . . are you like . . . remarried or anything?'

'No. You think I'd get married without telling you?'

She shrugged. 'You could be doing all kinds of things without telling me.'

'My life is pretty quiet, Cat. Boring, probably, compared to whatever you've been up to at uni.'

She sipped her lager and looked out the window, watching the sheep grazing on the seaweed-strewn peat at the edge of the bay. They were the only people sitting in this end of the pub and she was grateful for the relative privacy. 'Uni's not that good. It's completely shite, actually.'

'How's that?'

'It just is.' She felt the tears gathering again. 'So's home. I just ... don't want to be there right now.'

'Do you want to tell me what's going on?'

'I ... ' She couldn't look at him. 'No. I don't.'

He accepted this, but narrowed his eyes and chewed his lip. 'Does Jenny know you're here?'

'Yeah, I told her. I lied and said I'd spoken to you. She's not happy about it. She thinks you're ... ' she paused, wished she could call her words back.

Calum sighed. 'Jenny thinks I'm a lot of things, some of which are true. You don't have to drop her in it.'

'She thinks you're a bit ... you know ... unstable.'

He cleared his throat and looked away, his mouth forming some kind of silent response. It looked like a curse. 'I had a bad time for a couple of years. You know that, right? Well, you remember. Call it what you want, a breakdown or something. I'm better now. Your mother can say what she likes but I hope you'll take me as you find me now.'

I have his eyes, Catriona thought as she looked at him. It was hard to see any more similarity than that. He'd blown in and out of her life, felt more like a distant uncle than a father. Their little holidays without Michelle had been good: three or four days each, to London or Rome or Copenhagen. Sometimes all they would do was walk and talk, pausing here or there to look at an old bridge or church, and he would point out tiny features of the engineering and describe the ingenuity of the design in a way that made her forget she'd rather be at a theme park. They would stop to listen to a street musician or sit in a cafe and eat some delicious thing. And then long periods, months running into years, when he was away. She never knew why his promises to bring her to America came to nothing, but there were always Christmas and birthday parcels: cuddly toys and trendy American clothes, books, CDs of bands he wanted her to like. Phone calls and emails came regularly, postcards, photos, grinning pictures from the back of his motorbike or on oil rigs, in bright orange waterproofs with crazy big waves crashing behind him.

Mum would go all sour-faced, stare over her shoulder at the pictures and vent: 'If he thinks that's being a father, he's completely delusional. He was never here when you were screaming in the middle of the night, or to stay home with you when you were ill. Remember when you had appendicitis? I had to take two weeks off work, unpaid. He wants to be your pal, but he's not interested in the hard part. I don't think he's capable. He's completely detached from reality.'

He seemed as well anchored to reality as anyone, but she decided to test him. 'How did you get better?'

A girl brought out their plates of food. Calum thanked her and waited until she'd gone away again before replying. 'Medicine. Counselling. Lots of exercise. A career change . . . a divorce. Moving back here.'

'Are you completely okay now?'

He raised his eyebrows as he bit into his burger. He chewed deliberately slowly and wiped the paper napkin over his mouth. Maybe he thought she wouldn't like the answer.

'Is this why you haven't wanted to see me up till now?'

'No. Well . . . not really. I just want to know.'

'All right . . . ehm . . . I guess I would say that I don't know if that's possible. We all have our hard days, right? I'm . . . seventy-six per cent okay.'

She laughed softly. 'Seventy-six?'

141

'Aye. I did the sums in my head just now. It's a complicated equation with a lot of variables. What about you?'

'Less than that.'

'Right.' He paused for a drink, eyes not leaving her.

She stared at her nails. Bitten. Dark blue varnish, flaking, showing white beneath. Ask me about music, she wanted to say. Or telly, or my favourite book. Anything that doesn't mean anything. Give me some chat about the weather. That's the stuff most people talk about. You know, point-less blethers? Don't you do that, Calum? Let's talk about the referendum. That's important, right?

Just don't ask me how I am.

That was from a song. That singer Mum likes. Suzanne Vega.

Stop now. Don't go there.

I'm here. Wherever here is. Tell him what he needs to know.

'Calum, just . . . to save you asking, I'm not ill and I'm not on drugs. All right? Trust me on that.'

'That's a start, at least.' He smiled at this and watched her tear a chunk from her burger with her fingers and nibble at it.

She wished she hadn't let him buy her beer. Even after half a pint she felt light-headed. The world was soft and broken around the edges, filtered through a pale green haze. It was a milder version of the wooziness she last felt when she was with Kyle, that same feeling of falling, less a memory in her head than in her body. There were images of what had happened that night floating behind her eyelids, as if she had seen the event from outside herself, and now she had started to wonder if it had happened the way she now saw it, or if it had happened at all.

She *was* going to tell her dad. That had been the brave plan. Tell him, so he'd know and her mum wouldn't. All the way here on the bus, she had rehearsed how she was going to say it. But it could go wrong. Very badly wrong. You couldn't know how he'd respond. He might not believe her. He might think it was her fault.

What did Calum need to know for, anyway? If it was talked about, it would just stay around, a real thing, an event that dominated her life. She had to forget about it. Pretend it was a bad dream.

'I was hoping you'd let me stay for the summer,' she said. 'I'll pay my way. I'll get a job.'

'That's easier said than done around here. Cat, it's . . .' he paused and looked away.

'No . . . look, forget I said that. It's fine. I'll just stay a day or two and . . .'

'You can stay, it's just . . . I've got my bloody mother and she's a nightmare.'

'Your bloody mother and now your bloody daughter.' She laughed bitterly. 'I know you've always hated it when your family get in your way.'

'Oh come on, that's a bit low.'

'True though.'

'So why did you come?'

She shrugged. Why *did* she come? 'Maybe I shouldn't have bothered. When's the next bus back to Fort William?'

'Stay, Catriona,' he said. A grizzled dog backing down in the face of tougher opposition. 'I'm sorry, I'm just bad at this. I do want you to stay, but . . . why don't we just take it a day at a time, all right?'

She lifted a shoulder and tried to show him that she didn't care one way or the other. 'If you're sure. I didn't even know if you'd be nice to me.'

'Cat . . . if you thought I was going to be awful, I've got to ask again what you're doing here.'

'Dunno. To get at Mum, maybe.'

'For what?'

143

'She says you don't give a monkey's about me.'

'She is absolutely wrong about that.'

'Why does she hate you so much?'

'I got her pregnant when she was younger than you are now and wouldn't marry her. I was an arsehole about it.'

His bluntness jarred her. 'Why wouldn't you marry her?'

'I got offered the chance to manage a project out in the Gulf, and it would have meant living apart most of the time. You're probably right, I was selfish that way.'

'So why did she keep me?'

'She wanted to.'

'Did you want her to?'

'She made it very clear it wasn't up to me.'

'That's a no, then.'

'For fuck's sake, Catriona, what do you want me to say? I felt differently about a lot of things after you arrived.'

'I think Mum wishes I'd never been born.'

'I can't imagine that's the case.'

'I can.' She couldn't imagine it was anything other than the case.

Calum looked away and was silent for a period of time. Men were strange, hard beings, with their bristles and straight angles. Skin that looked thick, almost impenetrable, like you couldn't cut through it, almost like they were another species altogether. Like you could say things to them, cruel honest things, and it would hardly touch them because they didn't speak the same language as you.

'You've hardly touched your lunch,' he said.

'The burger tastes funny.'

'It's venison.'

'Oh.'

'We'll take it home. Your granny'll be glad of it.'

'Sorry.'

'It's fine.' He took the plate and carried it to the bar, came

144

back a couple of minutes later with a polystyrene box. 'You ready?'

'Yep.' She followed him back to the Land Rover and climbed onto the sticky seat beside him. 'Don't you ever clean this thing?'

'Not often.'

'Is your house this dirty?'

'It isn't.' He glanced at her. 'Cat, whatever's going on, I'll do my best to help you, if you let me.'

So much for pointless blethers. She should have known. Jenny always said, didn't she? He was a conversational oddity. It was like his big hand had just gone straight through her sternum and grabbed hold of her heart. Her eyes burned. 'There isn't anything you can do, so don't worry.'

'Whatever it is, honestly, I promise I won't think less of you. I've been there myself, right?'

'No, you haven't.' She crossed her arms over her chest and stared out the window. 'I am one hundred per cent certain you have never been where I am, Calum.'

HOTEL CALIFORNIA

I've been there myself, right?

Still a bloody hard thing to say. He knew how awful he must have looked the last time she'd seen him, but he'd come through the worst of it by that point. *It*. He had never been able to name the thing that had happened to him. Once upon a time you would have called it a nervous breakdown, but you weren't supposed to say that anymore. The psychiatrist made a pronouncement and treatments followed, including medication that muffled the panic and boiling anger but made him feel like all he'd done was lock the devil in a room somewhere at the back of his head. It felt wrong. The whole process felt wrong, like it was doing him more damage than good: psychiatric treatments that focused down on him – his inner conflicts, his triggers, his responses – as though he alone was responsible for his crash.

But it wasn't like that. He knew it wasn't like that even though he couldn't explain it at the time. Now he could imagine himself like an eighteen-wheeler on a Californian highway, blowing tyres, throwing shredded rubber across the overheated tarmac but still travelling at seventy, terrified of stopping because he might damage his reputation or lose his job. Dad got cancer and died: bang went a tyre. Finn went off the rails: bang went another. Finn fell in front of his eyes: bang went three more. His relationship with Mum disintegrated: bang and boom. He abandoned Catriona in pursuit of black gold, sucking the earth dry and choking the atmosphere; he got caught up in the greed and heat and sex of capitalism; he let himself be dazzled by the American wet-dream. He's grinding on his rims. There's only so long you can keep going. Some things were not his fault and some things were, but the disorder was not just his. It was far bigger than him. The whole world was disordered. You couldn't just change yourself, you had to change your world.

CARMEL, CALIFORNIA, 2009

Michelle's foot was heavy on the gas as they entered a wide right-hander, heading north up Route One toward Big Sur. Steep hillsides rose to their right, bare earth showing through parched grasses and coastal shrubs. To their left, unstable cliffs tumbled down into the ocean. Tufts of fog sat over blue water, lower than the height of the road, reaching inland along the arroyos that cut between the hills. Above the fog, the sky was undiluted azure.

Calum hid behind dark glasses and stared straight ahead, not allowing his eyes to shift right or left from the road's centreline. Around every bend, he felt the wheels lift from the road. The release of gravity, the moment of lightness before it recaptured its hold. The black certainty of death. His fingers dug into the leather seat.

'Slow down a bit, Shell.'

'I'm going the speed limit.' She glanced at him. 'You all right?'

He didn't answer. With the top down, the wind made conversation next to impossible. Most likely, Michelle preferred it that way. Not that he could blame her; he was almost incapable of stringing a coherent sentence together. He'd also gained close to thirty pounds and his body poured acrid sweat without any physical effort. Even now, with the Pacific blow dryer in his face, his back was wet against the seat. No wonder she insisted on having the top down.

The car shimmied as she came up behind a slower vehicle. She drifted over the line, trying to get a view around it.

'Jesus.' Calum closed his eyes, fought nausea. 'Don't overtake him, for fuck's sake.'

'Do you want to drive?' A venomous question. She knew he couldn't.

'No.'

'No. You don't want to do anything. You just want to sit there.'

'Sorry,' he muttered, but the wind blew the sound away. There were words in his head – arguments, apologies, explanations – but his dry tongue wouldn't manage them. He leaned back and looked at nothing. A thought materialised: he was in a convertible sports car on the Pacific Coast Highway with his beautiful blonde wife, and he didn't give a toss about any of it. He had achieved every man's fantasy and it was as meaningless as an aftershave commercial. This was what he'd been breaking his back for all these years. What a joke.

Eyes closed, he laughed and felt his new belly wobbling under his shirt.

'What's so funny?' Michelle asked, eyes flicking from the road again.

'Nothing.'

'You never laugh anymore. I'm glad you're still capable.'

'I'm not, Michelle. This isn't laughing.'

'What is it then?'

'I don't know.' The effort had exhausted him. 'Dying, maybe. I think I'm dying.'

'This is going to be a fun weekend,' she said.

She checked them into the boutique hotel outside of Carmel and he lay down while she unpacked her weekend bag: sundress, shorts, swimsuit, gossamer black underwear. Full marks for optimism, anyway. It was a last-ditch Hail Mary, this trip. She had been trying so hard to help him through these last few months, but maybe only because her conscience wouldn't let her move out while he was ill. This marriage was going nowhere but down. Even in his doped befuddlement, he knew that much. It wasn't Michelle's fault.

She managed to prise him off the bed and out for a walk along the beach. She gripped his hand as they walked, pulling him along so briskly that he tripped repeatedly. His feet seemed to have got too big, his legs too heavy, his lungs ineffective. He felt elderly and broken. After a short distance, he stopped and faced the pristine green tubes of surf. Sweat dampened his armpits. Breathing heavily, he sat down on the warm yellow sand.

'I'm puffed out.'

Michelle sat beside him, her arms wrapped around her knees. 'You just need to build your fitness up again.'

'I'm gonna come off the drugs. I can't stand this.'

'Cal, you can't stop.'

'Yeah, I can. I have, starting now.'

'You can't just come off them like that. You were suicidal three months ago. You were out of control. You remember that? You remember punching your fist through our back door? You want to go back to that? If it's not working for you, we'll go back to Dr Rosen and try something else.'

'I don't get where the *we* comes into it. I'm the one

149

swallowing this shit. I'm the one turning into a fucking sea cucumber.'

She stared at him. 'You have to.'

'I don't have to do anything.' He lay back in the sand and thought, I get it, Finn. I get it now. I understand. I'm sorry.

Michelle lay on her side and ran her hand up his arm. Golden hair blew across her eyes. He was surprised she even wanted to touch him. 'You don't want to get well?'

'I don't know what you call this, but it isn't getting well.'

'But you *will*.'

'Will I?'

'Of course.' She moved her body partly over his and kissed him, sliding her fingers through his hair. 'I know you will.'

'With or without the little pink pills?'

'Plenty of people take antidepressants for years, Cal. Maybe all their lives. If it helps, then what's the problem? You've gained weight because you've stopped working.'

She acted the part well when she wanted to, but she wouldn't want to much longer. He looked up at her and was sure he could see the impatience there, behind the smile. The glint of disgust in the corners of those dutiful wifely blues.

'Maybe,' he murmured. She was right about one thing. Three months ago, he'd have shoved her into the sand and set into her. Now he didn't care enough to respond one way or the other. It was easier by far just to lie on the beach and let her think he was listening.

'You want to go to dinner?' she asked.

He sat up, brushing sand out of his hair. 'Yep. Best idea you've had all day.'

'I knew that would wake you up.'

He put his hands on his belly. It felt like an overstuffed haggis. 'Clam chowder. In a sourdough bowl. Chips. A big ol' steak.'

Michelle shuddered. 'Maybe you shouldn't eat that kind of stuff right now.'

'My taste buds are the only part of me that are still alive, Michelle. Don't deny me.'

Michelle ate a spinach salad with chicken breast and mango. She cut the green leaves into small pieces, chewed meticulously, and sipped white wine. He tried to eat slowly so he didn't finish his steak before she'd made a dent in her pile of foliage. He needed the taste of the meat on his tongue. Little bursts of sensation, reminders of what it was like to feel anything other than exhaustion. If he could just keep eating, he'd be okay.

Calum imagined what the other diners would see: athletic brown woman with fat white ogre. Beauty and the beast. Must be loaded, what else would she see in him?

'What do we do now?' he asked between mouthfuls. It came out unintentionally, a question which announced itself to the world because it couldn't be contained any longer.

'Well the spa looks amazing.'

'No, I meant ... ' He swallowed hard. 'I don't mean tonight.'

'We don't have to talk about this right now.'

'Yeah we do. I want to go home.'

Her face drooped and she closed her eyes. 'Cal ... '

'I know you hate it, I'm sorry.'

'I don't *hate* it. It's just ... cold and grey, and ... foreign. It's great for a visit, but it's ... '

'It's where I come from, Michelle. My daughter's growing up without me. I think I'd be better there. I like to feel the rain sometimes. It reminds me to appreciate the sun.'

'It didn't do your brother very much good, did it?'

'I don't see how California's doing *me* any good. I'm not going back offshore, I've decided that.'

'Since when?'

'Since about five minutes ago.'

'You can't just say these things, Cal. I mean, you need a plan. We need to talk about this with Dr Rosen.'

'Dr Rosen isn't the master of my fate.'

'And you *are*?' She snorted softly.

'I used to be.' He pushed his plate away and wondered about the dessert menu. The ever-expanding waistline could always accommodate something sweet. Soon it would be an unrecoverable situation. 'Will you come with me?'

'For how long? I don't know if work will let me go.'

'You could get something over there.'

Michelle raised her napkin and drew it down very slowly over her mouth. 'I don't want to move to Scotland.'

'Think about it. Please. You'd like it if you gave yourself the chance.'

'Okay.' She took a deep breath and looked for the waiter. 'I'll think about it. Let's get out of here.'

'I might need some cheesecake.'

'You do not need cheesecake.' She stood up and put on her cardigan.

They made love after a fashion: he lay on his back and tried to remember what it was supposed to feel like while Michelle bounced on his gelatinous gut like a trampoline champion. This is a ridiculous thing to be doing, he thought. All this slavering and shoogling to achieve a few seconds of pleasure. Creaking beds and embarrassing expressions. He was sure he used to enjoy it. He could remember a version of himself that loved the feel of her skin, the brush of her hair over his chest, the warm must of her private places. That old version of himself could be aroused just looking at her, even with her clothes on. Other men were too; she was that kind of woman. Other men used to envy him.

152

'I want a shower,' he said when she'd finished with him. He pulled his boxers and shirt on, embarrassed to let her see his profile silhouetted in the moonlight, and shuffled into the bathroom. He ran a bath because his legs were wilting stalks, folded himself into the tub and looked down at the convex curve of his belly: a great white moon of flesh. It still shocked him to see it. So did the baggy face in the mirror, which surely had to belong to somebody else.

He closed his eyes.

He opened them to Michelle banging on the door, practically screaming his name. His heart did a little dance. The water was cold.

He heaved himself out of the bath, grabbed a towel and opened the door.

Michelle was sobbing. 'Oh my God, Cal. Are you all right?'

'Of course I'm all right. What's wrong with you?'

'What's *wrong* with me? I wake up and it's two in the morning and you're still in the bath? I thought you were dead in there. I thought you slit your goddamn wrists.'

'I fell asleep, Shell. Calm down.'

'You could have slipped down and drowned.' Her body was shaking.

He laughed softly and reached for her arm. 'I'm fine. I was wedged in there so tight I wasn't slipping anywhere.'

'That's not even funny.' She yanked down a fresh towel and scrubbed at her face. 'You don't know what this is doing to me. You're completely oblivious.'

'Feel free to join the party.' He snatched the brown plastic vial of pills and threw it at her.

She caught it neatly and returned it to the shelf. 'I've thought about it. I'm not moving to Scotland. You do what you have to do.'

'Aye.' He felt cold and raw, and awake for the first time in months. 'I will.'

Maybe you would call it an existential crisis, only to be solved by remaking yourself completely. You had to do that with your eyes open and your skin exposed. If he'd still been a Catholic, maybe he would have walked barefoot over stones and cacti to some holy place, fallen to his knees and been refilled by the Holy Spirit. He'd stopped believing in God by the time he was ten, but his mind still turned to the darkness and blood of those early foundations. He still instinctively reached for some kind of redemption.

They pulled into the drive in front of the house and he turned off the engine. Catriona sat still for a minute, arms folded over her chest, eyes looking at anything but him. He remembered that need to withdraw, to be invisible and untouchable, to find a place where other people couldn't reach you. She was a little girl hiding at the back of the wardrobe. She'd come all the way here to hide from Jenny.

The question was, why?

MOUTH MUSIC

The hens were an unexpected delight. Calum had appointed her keeper of the hens and Mary took her duties seriously. Each morning she opened the door of their house and they looked at her with dozy eyes, making soft throaty noises and shaking out feathers before stepping out into the garden. Like four noble ladies, they strutted across the grass, breakfasting on slugs and snails while Mary gathered their eggs. Sometimes she sat with them and their conversations reminded her of old women telling stories or singing while they knitted.

An insurgent sun had emerged after the morning's torrent, bringing heat, lifting steam from the earth. The water in the shallows brightened, glowed translucent turquoise over the white sand. There was sufficient breeze to keep the midges down, so she sat out with her pot of tea and the last of the cake Calum's friends had brought. Mary couldn't recall the name of the English girl with the childish plaits and the accordion, but she made a decent sponge. The raspberry jam in the middle tasted home-made. It was a taste of summer, of childhood, of a time before worry or loss. She turned her face to the sun, absorbing its goodness. Her skin burned easily, peeled and freckled, but she didn't suppose it mattered that much anymore. She wasn't saving her looks for anyone.

Accompanied by quiet, satisfied clucking, she let a song rise from her throat: the Gaelic mouth music mother and aunties used to sing. Most of the syllables were meaningless, simply there to give voice to rhythm, and so it was fine to sing along with hens. They seemed to like it, their little bird heads twitching and tilting towards her, their coal-black eyes glinting. *Sing another one, Mary*, they seemed to say. *Sing a naughty one.*

Out front, tyres ground over the gravel. The engine of Calum's Land Rover shuddered then turned off. She sat up, hastily rearranged her blouse and gathered her dishes, not wanting him to catch her resting. From the kitchen, she heard the front door open and his voice in the hallway. A young girl followed a few steps behind him, crowned by a pincushion of shocking red hair.

'Mum, we've got a surprise visitor,' Calum said. 'You remember Catriona?'

Mary gave enough smile to be polite and no more. 'Are you one of his fiddle students, dear?'

'Eh...no...'

'Mum, Catriona's my *daughter*. Your granddaughter.'

'Oh...' Mary brought her fingers to her lips. She remembered a toddler with dirty blonde hair and a stubborn set to her jaw. 'Goodness me.'

The girl's eyes flicked to Calum. She looked like a punk, her ears and lip studded with metal. 'Hi Gran.'

'Let me look at you.' Mary moved towards her. She could see no family resemblance at all. This girl was an alien creature: short, pale and busty. She was so dark under the eyes she looked like she took drugs. 'Are you sure, Calum?'

'Pretty sure.'

The poor girl stood like a lamb waiting for the slaughter. 'You must have been just a wee baby last time I saw you, pet.'

'I think I was about twelve,' she replied.

Mary couldn't remember. She looked at Calum. 'You might have told me she was coming.'

'I didn't know. I found her outside the pub.'

'Ocht, Calum.' She shook her head. What could she say? He was always in a guddle, floating about in his own thoughts, pretending nobody else existed in the world. 'How old are you now then?' Mary asked. 'You must be sixteen at least.'

'Nineteen, Gran.'

'You never are.'

'Aye. I'm at uni. Just finished first year.'

'In Aberdeen?'

'No, Edinburgh.'

'What are you reading?'

'Sociology and politics.' She fidgeted from one foot to the other as though she needed the toilet.

'Oh, well. You must be a very clever young lady.'

'I was all right at school, if that's what you mean.'

'Mum, I'll show Catriona up to her room, all right?'

'Aye, on you go.' Mary waved her hand. The girl turned a shoulder on her without a backward glance and slouched up the stairs after Calum. Mary turned on the television and sat with an unsettled tummy. Something wrong with that one, she thought. His fault, partly at least. A child needed a father. She only had to remind herself what happened to Finn after Jack died.

Calum came downstairs after a few minutes. 'She's getting changed. Poor thing got soaked in that rain. I'll make up the bed in the study for her. What a surprise, huh?' He unpacked his workbag and handed her a polystyrene box. 'It's most of a burger she didn't eat. I thought you might like it.'

Mary opened the box and sniffed at the burger. 'I don't think it's a good idea to eat her food. She might be unwell.'

157

'For goodness sake, Mum, she's not carrying diseases. Here, I'll put it in the fridge.'

Mary handed him the box. 'What's she doing here? I must say, it's strange for her just to turn up unannounced.'

'She is allowed to visit.'

'Is she in trouble?'

'What, you mean pregnant? I don't think so.'

'Well, she might be.'

'Can't you just stop fretting over ridiculous possibilities?'

'It isn't ridiculous Calum, as you of all people should know.'

'Point made.' He set his jaw hard and turned away, emptied the remainder of the tea from his flask and rinsed it. Mary leaned in the doorway and watched the sun illuminate the silvery stubble on his cheeks. She wished he'd shave more. Jack shaved every day, sometimes twice if they were going out in the evening, and he always wore a shirt tucked in.

'I don't like the way she's dressed.'

He laughed. 'I'm not sure she'd appreciate your fashion sense either.'

'Oh stop it. It's unbecoming. All those studs are unhygienic. I wouldn't have allowed them in my classroom, I'll tell you that. You should make her take them out.'

'I'm not making her do anything,' he said sharply, 'and neither will you. Just let her be. She's upset about something and she needs some time to get over it.'

'Well what is it?'

'I don't know.'

'I'll speak to her.'

'Mum . . .'

'What?' She waited for him to finish but he stood there like a cat about to bring up a hairball. Infuriating and tongue-tied. No wonder he could never keep a woman. 'Do you think I'm a fool, Calum?'

158

'No.'

'You treat me like one.'

'I'm sorry.' He pulled off his filthy grey sweatshirt and draped it over the back of a chair. 'I heard you singing when we got back. Mind how Finn used to dance? The way he jumped around the place and jigged his wee feet? He couldn't contain himself.'

Mary lifted the jumper. It smelled of sawdust and turps. 'The kitchen isn't the place to leave your mucky clothes.'

'I was talking about Finn, Mum.'

'What about him?'

'How he used to dance? Remember?'

'Of course I do. I always said he could have been a dancer. He moved so gracefully, even when he was tiny.'

'He could have been a lot of things.'

'He might still have been, if he'd had more time.'

Calum stared at her. For two seconds, maybe less, there was a look of such black hatred on his face she thought he might attack her. Then it passed. 'I'm popping next door,' he said very quietly.

THINGS YOU CAN'T SAY
TO YOUR GRANNY

From the cupola window, Catriona watched Calum stride across the drive to the other cottage, his boots driving hard into the gravel. He knocked once and pushed the door open. Briefly she caught a glimpse of a woman in the hallway, slender and pale. They kissed briefly on the lips and then he stepped inside and the door closed. So already he was hiding things from her.

Fine, she thought. Permission granted not to tell him everything.

She emptied her rucksack onto the threadbare red sofa bed in Calum's study and draped the damp clothes over the radiator. Her stomach felt empty and nervous. She wished now she'd eaten the burger but was too embarrassed to go down and ask for it. Her own grandmother hadn't even recognised her. It was possible that Mary had forgotten her existence entirely. Was she so low down in their priorities that they never even talked about her?

The old lady had dementia, she reminded herself. You wouldn't necessarily know it to speak to her, except that she'd behaved like they were complete strangers. Catriona wondered if she'd have to introduce herself all over again when she went downstairs.

To postpone that embarrassing prospect, she scouted around her new digs. It was a small room, wooden-floored, the computer desk and shelves cluttered with dusty files and boxes of paperwork. She looked around, not touching anything but gathering clues about his life: a poster for a music festival in some place called Telluride, an ice axe and a pair of crampons on a hook, old textbooks about engineering and geology, other books of poetry. CDs of his band took up a whole shelf. She took one down and looked at the cover art: swirly, stylised line drawings of two men and a woman in a rowing boat surrounded by mountainous waves, the woman's hair streaming loose and flowing into the water. The only CD player in the room was the computer, so she switched it on and hoped it wouldn't ask for a password. It didn't.

She slipped the disk into the slot, expecting the usual snap and jerk of fiddle and accordion ceilidh music. What emerged was something else entirely: a long, haunting wail on the fiddle, a single note splitting into a chord, almost like a train heard far in the distance. It gave rise to a melody in some dark key. Spartan, primitive, nothing you could dance to. Catriona sat down amidst her few possessions and listened. The next tune was brighter and sweeter, a happy turn after a bleak opening. She lifted her feet up onto the sofa and let herself drift into a doze for a little while.

Her mobile phone woke her and sent her scrabbling around in the pile of stuff she'd unloaded. The screen said *Mum*. She swiped it. 'Hi.'

'Hi Love. How are you?'

She was *Love* from a distance. 'Fine. I'm at Dad's.'

'Okay ... how is it?'

'All right. His mother's here. Granny Mary. She has Alzheimer's. She didn't recognise me.'

'Oh ... ' Jenny paused. 'I'm sorry to hear that. How's Calum?'

'He's ... yeah ... okay I think. He looks good.'

'He's all right with you?'

'Aye, sure.'

'I was worried. I tried to call you a few times earlier, but ... '

'There's not always a signal here.'

'I'll call the landline then, if I need to reach you. Cat, there was a boy on the phone for you last night. From Edinburgh, he said, and ... '

Catriona's chest tightened. Clutching the phone to her ear, she went to the window and peered out. 'Who? What was his name?'

'Kyle. He was upset, Cat. He said he's been trying to reach you for weeks. He said you finished things on bad terms and he wanted to apologise ... '

'What did he tell you, Mum?' Catriona almost barked down the phone. 'How did he get our home number?'

'I assumed you gave it to him. He didn't say anything more than that.'

'Mum, don't speak to him. If he phones again, don't answer it. And don't tell him where I am. You didn't, did you?'

'No, of course not. Catriona, I don't like this. This isn't something that needs to be dealt with by the police, is it? You're not in some kind of trouble?'

'No, I'm not in any kind of trouble, Mum, I swear. Kyle's just a loser who got a bit obsessed. A posh creep who needs to get over me, that's all. *Promise* me you won't tell him I'm here.'

'I won't. Of course I won't. Is this why you've been so strange? Is this why you've run away?'

'No!' she blurted, hoping if she said it forcefully enough Jenny would believe it. 'I haven't *run away*. God, Mum. Kyle's just an asshole I met at a club. I don't want anything to do with him.'

'He sounded genuine.'

'Well he isn't.' She felt sick. She rubbed a sweaty palm on her leggings, her pulse racing. The safety she'd felt since getting off the bus in Fort William yesterday crumbled. If her mum had mentioned anything at all about her coming to stay with her dad, Kyle could trace her. She'd told him too much about Calum. If he could track down her mum's landline in Aberdeen, he could sniff her out here.

What if that really *had* been him in the shops that day?

She'd have to tell Calum, soon.

'Mum, I have to go.'

'Catriona, are you all right?'

'Yeah, but I have to go, okay? I'll ... call you.'

She ended the call before Jenny could ask any more questions and sat for a moment, struggling to breathe. It was like someone was holding a pillow over her face and she couldn't make a sound.

Sitting still made her feel vulnerable, as if Kyle was on his way here already. She went downstairs. Mary was watching the news, perched on the edge of the brown leather sofa, her hands knotting and unknotting against her belly. She looked as anxious as Catriona felt.

'Did my dad come back?'

Mary looked at her, chewing her lower lip.

'Calum, I mean,' Catriona added, just in case.

'No, dear.' Mary's hands continued to twitch, and to that she added what looked like an involuntary head shake. 'No ... Calum's not here. Can I make you something? Some tea? There was cake earlier but I'm afraid I've finished it.' She started to stand up.

'No ... no thank you, Gran. I'm ... fine, I can help myself. Can I watch with you?'

'If you like.' Mary shifted towards the end of the sofa.

Catriona sat, leaned back, tried to breathe calmly. The

Scottish news was all referendum: Salmond asserting that an independent Scotland would keep the pound, Osborne asserting that it wouldn't. The House of Commons bleating like sheep. Young people campaigning for independence in the Meadows. Her stomach clenched all over again: Kyle might be there. But if Kyle was there, at least he couldn't be here. She looked for him in the brief images but they soon disappeared.

Keep the heid, she thought.

He'd phoned her house. *He'd phoned her fucking house.*

She tried to distract herself with her phone. She scanned her friends' Facebook updates. There were the usual holiday snaps, boyfriends met or broken up with, tiffs and reconciliations, summer jobs with hateful managers, gigs and nights out. Melanie Goodwin had an enviable new pair of Docs. Leah Mathers was fundraising for a trip to Swaziland. In addition to all of this, there was now a backdrop of political anticipation, as if they were collectively about to embark for a new world. Maybe they were, and most likely they wouldn't get there. Even if they did, she couldn't help wondering if anything would change that much. Life would probably still rumble on in ignorance of other people's pain, just like it always did.

She had unfriended Kyle and had posted nothing about her present location. She offered a couple of YouTube videos so that people didn't forget her existence entirely, but nothing personal. They didn't need to know; she didn't want anyone to know. A thing had happened and it needed to be left in a dark cave somewhere and forgotten about.

'Flabby, over-fed men arguing about money,' Mary said.

'Pardon, Gran?'

'These politicians, bickering like children. They never tell the full story.'

'No, they don't.'

'You should be careful with that.' Mary pointed at the phone. 'They spy on you with those.'

'Who?'

'The government.'

Catriona let out a little laugh. 'Do they? They won't see very much here. I'm the most boring person in Scotland.'

Mary turned off the television, turned and looked at Catriona, tilting her head the way a puppy would.

'I hope you don't think I'm being critical, dear.' The way she said *dear* made Catriona wonder if Mary had forgotten her name as well. 'You're a very nice looking young lady. I don't know why you want to poke holes in your face and hide yourself under men's clothing.'

'Dunno. It's just my style.'

'It's not becoming. You could do better. Boys won't look at you like you are now.'

'I don't want boys to look at me.'

'Why not?'

A dozen possible answers crashed around in her brain. Because looking is never just looking. Because whatever you wear, all they ever see is tits and a cunt. Because I'm spoiled, like meat left out in the sun. Because I'm never letting anybody get me unwrapped again. Because I can't go around wearing a shark cage for the rest of my life, but if I could, I would. There was a potentially endless list that could be labelled: *Hashtag: Things You Can't Say To Your Granny*. But right now, all she could manage was a shrug.

'At your age, I had my pick of men. My Jack always came back from London with a dress or a blouse or a pair of stockings. Maybe you should ask your father to take you up to Inverness for some new things.'

'I don't want anything new.'

165

More head quivering, indicating displeasure or lack of comprehension. 'What girl doesn't want new clothes?'

Catriona exhaled sharply and got off the sofa. 'Me. I don't. I'm tired, I think I'll just lie down for a bit. I'll be upstairs, okay?'

WHAT THIS IS

Strong evening sun and thoughts of his mother and daughter next door stopped Calum from drifting off again. It was always strange to wake up in Julie's bed in the daytime, blades of light hitting the prints on the walls: female nudes, disjointed and cut through with lines and blurs of colour. Like victims of a magician whose tricks kept going wrong. There were no angels in here, just women who had been broken and discarded. Disturbing sort of an allegory for the bedroom, he thought. It was just the kind of thing Julie would do to confront herself – and anyone else who might be in her bedroom – with the realities of the world as she saw them.

He raised himself on one elbow and looked at Julie. She was lying on her stomach, face turned away from him, her hair falling to the sides revealing a few sweaty curls at the base of her neck, darker hair at the roots, strands of silver. He kissed the place where her hair parted, then lower down her neck towards the top of her vest, and she made a little noise into the pillow and turned over, rubbing her eyes with her fingertips, drawing away sleep and remnants of her make-up.

'You feel better now?' she asked.

'A little.'

She gave him a lazy smile and sang, '*When I get that feeling, I need ...*' Her voice trailed off and her hand slipped down his chest and under the covers. 'You know pygmy chimpanzees? Bonobos? They make love to make themselves feel better after fights. It's not for mating. Sometimes they just do this ... ' Her hand moved lower.

Calum shifted. 'Julie, I should go home. I've been here too long as it is.'

She nuzzled her lips into his neck, her breath tickling the little hairs. 'Sometimes they do boy on boy or girl on girl. They don't care as long as it feels good.'

'How do you know so much about the sexual habits of pygmy chimpanzees?'

'I had a girlfriend in London who was a primate biologist.' Her hand crept down towards his groin again. 'Pygmy chimps understand the importance of sensual contact for their emotional wellbeing. They never suffer from depression, so it must work.'

She was definitely trying to distract him from conversation about that bloody statue, and everything else. He rolled away from her and sat up. 'It kicks in quicker than Prozac but stops you getting anything done.' He laughed. 'How would you know if a chimpanzee was depressed?'

'Because they turn into gruff, sulky buggers with saggy eyes and lines across their wee furry foreheads.' She placed her fingertips at the corners of his eyes and pulled them gently upwards. 'Just like someone else I know.'

'I'm not depressed.'

'Aye, pull the other one, Calum.'

He reached for his pants. 'I'm teetering, Julie. When I used to climb, sometimes I'd get the shakes. I'd hit a point where I didn't think I could go on and I'd just ... hang there, on the brink of letting go. That's how I feel right now.'

'It's okay to feel that.'

'No, it isn't. I can't afford to let go at this particular point in time.'

She got up and took her silk dressing gown from the hook behind the door. Just before she slipped her arms into the sleeves, the sun caught the thin white scar on the outside of her left upper arm. She would deny that she was self-conscious about it, but she rarely wore short sleeves. *My boyfriend beat me up. I kicked him in the balls and the bastard broke my arm.*

She'd told him the first night they slept together, when he was too drunk not to ask about it. *That's not all he broke.* So he'd showed her the scar on his knee and told her about Finn. These ugly souvenirs brought them together and kept them apart: Julie didn't do monogamy and Calum didn't do responsibility.

'You can go in a minute. I have something for you.' She went barefoot down the hallway and came back with a little blue plastic bag. 'Here. Courtesy of my pal Matthew, guaranteed to get you over the crux.'

He opened the baggy, looked at the dried green leaves and buds, took a sniff. Mary would go off her trolley if she caught a whiff of this in the house, and he had no idea about Catriona.

'A wee walk in the woods may be in order later. Thank you. This is a timely gift.'

'I thought it might be. And I wanted to say sorry. I should have told you about the angel. Still though, you shouldn't have been snooping in my studio.'

'I wasn't snooping, I was checking, and I got curious.' He sighed and lifted his fingers to her cheek. Her skin was so thin and clear, sometimes it seemed almost translucent. She was only a few months younger than he was, but her face was barely lined and she seemed as ageless and ephemeral as one of the fair folk his Granny Ina used to tell stories about. But he was reasonably certain the fairies wouldn't have Glasgow accents.

'What is this, Julie? What are we doing?'

She turned her head and kissed the inside of his hand. 'It is what it is. Why do we have to name it?'

'You know me. I like to call a spade a spade.'

'Mmm. What if it only looks like a spade and it turns out to be something else?'

'Until it's empirically demonstrated to be something other than a spade, it's a spade in my book.'

'Okay . . . so . . . how do you feel about that?'

'If you want to dig a hole, a spade is exactly what you need.'

'Enough.' She sighed and folded his hands around the bag of weed. 'I'll see you at the ceilidh on Saturday, if not before.'

He groaned. 'I forgot the ceilidh.'

'You're kind of the main attraction.'

Sometimes the idea of being on stage made him want to dissolve. 'My brain hurts. I'm fed up with the politics. I know my mind, I can't be bothered trying to change anybody else's.' He pulled his crusty work trousers up and slipped his shirt over his head.

'Abby told me what you said at the meeting. She said you made the best point of the night.'

'It was nothing compared to my mother calling Angus MacBride a fat bastard.'

'Aye, I heard about that too.'

'The thing is, we can write a new constitution, we can call ourselves the People's Republic of Scotia and get rid of this big old chip we have on our shoulders, and that's all fine and good. I'll still have a mother with Alzheimer's and a daughter who looks like she's on the brink of a meltdown.'

'She might not be.'

'I know what it looks like, Julie. I'll still have days when I wake up and feel like it's too daunting to even get out of bed. None of that is going to change. I know you understand

170

this.' He thumped his fist against his forehead. 'Yes or No, none of this in here is going to go away on the nineteenth of September.'

'No it isn't.' She kissed his lips. 'Go home and see your family. I'll see you later. Let me know if you fancy company on that walk you mentioned.'

It was after eleven when he slipped on his trainers and jogged silently into the woods. He took the little path that led up over the headland, bypassing Julie's house and only turning on his head torch when he was well hidden from view. Catriona and Mary were both in bed but he didn't want to cause any kind of panic by being seen. He moved as fast as he could. Lately his knee hurt when he ran, but the midges were thick in the woods, biting his forehead whenever he slowed his pace.

When he reached the beach below Georgie and Bert's house, he climbed right out onto the long spill of rounded stones at one end of the crescent and sat in the breeze, the waves lapping below him. The sky to the north-west was a dark teal blue, laced with silver and pink. He lit the joint he'd rolled in his bedroom, sucked in deeply and looked across to Skye. The profile of the Cuillin ridge was still just visible. He thought about that trip with Finn and Andy. Then, as the dope worked its way into his blood, he thought about Dougie and Alison.

BEN ALDER, JULY, 1994

MacCaig got it right in that poem about the Green Corrie, it was the descent that killed you. His knee had carried him up Ben Alder, slower than any of them would have liked, but painlessly enough. Now, as afternoon tipped into evening, he hobbled downhill, leaning on boulders and peaty embankments whenever he could, wishing he'd had the sense to buy himself a pair of trekking poles. The scramble down to the bealach was hairy; he slipped and stumbled, his balance gone along with his confidence. If he looked more than two feet beyond the toes of his boots, he felt himself falling forward. Dougie and Alison could have been halfway home by now but they went at his pace, chatting politics to keep his mind occupied, never rushing him.

Calum hadn't been sure about this trip, but they'd threatened to drive to Aberdeen and kidnap him if he didn't agree to come. It was a year to the day since Finn died, and this was his first big hill walk on his reconstructed knee. Dougie and Alison were down to their last few Munros, picking off the ones that required long treks in and overnights. They'd hiked in from Dalwhinnie yesterday and stayed in the Culra bothy, songs and bottles to keep themselves cheery, a pot of bean and chorizo chilli on the stove, recitations of Dougie's latest poems as hail clattered against the windows.

'Your poetry's worse than the bloody weather, man,' Alison told him.

'For better or worse means nurturing my creative efforts, *woman*.'

'Well thank almighty God you didn't bring the banjo, that's all I can say.'

'Who in their right mind would carry a banjo out here?'

'You would, Doug.'

The banter continued all night, and by the wee hours Calum had laughed so much his stomach hurt. He couldn't remember the last time he'd laughed like that. Not since he was a kid, probably. Some people kindled a happy fire in your belly even though you'd known them only a short time. They were Geordies, a decade older than him, childless by circumstance rather than choice. He was a printer and she was a social worker, but they were headlong in their passions: socialism, mountaineering, poetry. Alison would shrug and say that without bairns to look after, they could afford to invest in their hobbies and their friends. She wasn't bitter but it was obvious that she wished it could be different.

Calum had known them for a year, to the day.

This morning the mist had been thick as wildfire smoke, but by the time they'd paused for lunch it had started to lift. They had reached the summit under a baby blue sky and a sharp, cold northerly breeze. A stolid lump bang in the middle of Scotland, Ben Alder looked west across the expanse of Rannoch Moor towards the familiar profiles of Glencoe, the Mamores and Nevis. This time of year, the land was a lush palate of greens, yellows and purples, although there were still dirty patches of snow on the highest tops. To the east, the glacier-rounded humps above Drumochter, and beyond that the Cairngorm plateau. From this distance it looked blue-grey and innocuous. Dougie and Alison hadn't been back either. They'd asked him if he wanted to go with them, to hike into the corrie together, but he couldn't. Not yet.

After surveying the panorama, he sat in the lea of the cairn and wept for Finn. Alison and Dougie left him alone for a while, drinking tea and turning over their own memories of that afternoon. They'd seen more of it than he had.

Walking back to the bothy, Calum's knee felt like broken glass but he refused to let Dougie carry his pack. He told them the history they didn't yet know: about Finn's hallucinations, his conversations with non-existent characters, his angel. He told them about the drugs, the self-harming, the suicide attempts. He told them what he had only told one other person about Finn's death.

'I wish he was still here, but not the way he was. He didn't want to be here the way he was, and he knew he was never

173

going to get better. He wanted to die. It's a relief, in a way. He *believed* . . . I don't, but he did. He knew where he was going.'

Alison slipped her arm around his waist and they walked like that for a couple of minutes.

'Does that sound awful?' Calum asked her.

'No.'

He turned to look at her face. She only shrugged.

'There are worse places to die than the Corrie of the Snow,' she said, afraid to mangle the Gaelic pronunciation in front of him. 'Believe me, pet, I've seen them.'

The dope wakened his senses and dulled his thoughts. He lay back and let himself feel: the cold, solid stone under his back, the briny night on his tongue, the wind pushing his hair back from his forehead, touching his scalp. He had to be open to the elements and allow them to touch him, even if they were uncomfortable. He listened to his breath, thought about the molecules of air entering his nose and lungs. Dr Rosen, the shrink who came so highly recommended by Michelle's friends, tried to make him believe that loss and trauma had reprogrammed his brain. He couldn't fathom it. If that was true, he was broken, well and truly, forever. It only depressed him even more.

Back in Scotland, free of Dr Rosen and his medicine chest, free of California and its film-set realities, free of Michelle, free of the corporate overlords he'd worked for since he was twenty-three, he'd learned slowly to earth himself. He was alive because he could feel. He was alive because he could pull horsehair over fiddle strings and make that wooden box sing. He learned to check himself when his thoughts began to take over, to return to what he could see and touch and hear. He had set to work refurbishing the house that his grandfather

174

had built, ripping the walls back to the stonework, pulling up floorboards, putting in insulation and new windows, and it was like he was rebuilding himself. It took a full two years before he was ready to welcome anyone in to the house or his life, but he was proud of the outcome.

Right now the house felt a lot more solid than he was. He didn't want to share it with Mary and let her reassume her matriarchal position above him. He wasn't even sure he wanted to share it with Catriona. Maybe they were right about him, maybe he *was* selfish. Maybe it went all the way back to his decision to leave for university right after his dad died. Maybe he should have stayed home with Mum and Finn. He could have worked the croft, driven the post van, gone onto the fishing boats, made ends meet and put thoughts of bigger achievements out of his mind. Maybe if he'd stayed home, a whole chain of other things would never have happened. Maybe.

Maybe.

There were always maybes, and they were pointless.

He took a final drag and flicked the roach into the sea.

CEILIDH

Calum, Johnny and Abby seemed to have captured the rhythms of the land and shaped them into melodies: the bubble of water over stones, the rush of waves onto the shore, the wind moving through tall grass. Just three people produced a sound as immense and changing as the sky. They played with eyes locked together, improvising, sometimes laughing at each other's efforts or exchanging brief words and cues. Catriona possessed no musical expertise at all but understood that this was a display of virtuosity. She watched the muscles of Calum's arms and broad shoulders flex and his face shift from concentration to joy as the music moved in ways that seemed to surprise him, as though it came from the instrument almost without his input.

They played a few tunes from their record in the break between dance sets, while people queued up for stovies and drinks. Catriona backed her chair further into the corner, positioning herself a little behind Mary, and tried to avoid eye contact with anyone. A guy with a big mouth planted himself when Mary got up to chat with neighbours. The smell of beer off him threatened to make her ill, but he didn't even take the hint when she brought her hand over mouth and nose.

'Who are you, then?' he asked, leaning in closer. 'I've never seen you before.'

'I'm staying with my dad,' she said, then regretted it.

'Who's your dad?'

'It doesn't matter.'

'Come on, who's your dad?'

'Calum.'

'Calum who?'

'Calum Macdonald. *Him*.' She nodded toward the stage. 'The fiddle player.'

'Oh aye.' The guy watched Calum for a minute. 'He's no bad. Got a high opinion of himself, though, eh?'

'Not unlike you, then,' she said, crossing her arms over her chest and leaning as far back as she could. 'I'm not interested, right?'

'Are you a dyke, aye? You look like a dyke.'

'I might be but you'll never get to know. And that's my granny's seat, so you don't get to sit there.'

He let out a laugh and a high pitched, 'Ooof,' and stood up. 'Shame,' he muttered and wandered off.

Catriona bolted out of her seat and went to the bathroom, locked herself in the cubicle and sat on the toilet until some woman knocked and asked if she was all right.

When she came back to the table, another woman sat down beside her: petite and funky in a tartan mini skirt and platforms. She wasn't young: on second glance, you could see the fine lines around her mouth and eyes. The outfit would have looked ridiculous on a bigger woman, but she was delicate as a songbird. Her curly hair was tied up on top of her head and fell around her face.

'Hey, I'm Julie. I live next door to your dad.'

'Oh ... hey.' She wasn't sure what to say. 'You're his girlfriend, right?'

Julie smiled, gave a soft laugh. 'Is that how he described me?'

'No, he hasn't mentioned you at all. I saw him go into your house.'

'Ah. Well . . . it's a casual thing. No strings. We're mostly just friends.'

'My dad doesn't like strings unless they're on a musical instrument.'

Julie almost spat a mouthful of red wine. '*That's* the truth. You're definitely his daughter. You say it as you see it.'

'Sometimes,' Catriona replied. 'There's too much bullshit in this world already.'

'Yeah there is. Pop over sometime, Cat. I go down to Glasgow a lot but I'm around the next couple of weeks.'

'Okay . . . thanks, that would be nice.' She said it to be polite, but Julie seemed all right. It would be a relief to have someone to talk to beside her Gran while her dad was out working. Someone who didn't need to know what Catriona didn't want to tell her.

Julie turned towards the stage and they both watched the band for a minute. Then she turned back and touched Catriona's arm. 'I bet you've never heard anything like that, eh?'

'I really haven't.' Catriona watched Calum as he picked up a pint glass and took four or five big swallows. Then he put it back down on the floor beside the mic and met her eyes across the room.

STRIP THE WILLOW

Some days, Calum woke up in the wrong place, as if his bed had fallen through a wormhole while he slept and brought him out into a parallel universe where he was a well-disguised alien, just slightly at odds with everything. It was a fact of his life, and mostly bearable. It might not have been. It might have been a one-way journey, like Finn's. He didn't like to think about how bad it had been in the months after the incident on the rig: bad enough that Michelle had driven him down to that posh hospital in the hills above San Diego, like a country club where they gave you electric shock treatments instead of massages, and left him at the mercy of shrinks and art therapists.

Music carried him through the worst days, and there weren't as many of those as there used to be. Ceilidh tunes were as easy to produce as breath, Virginia Reels and Dashing White Sergeants and Gay Gordons that had been imprinted into his psyche before he was old enough to hold a fiddle and repeated over nearly five decades. When he got bored he glanced at Johnny and went off on an improvised ride, driving the tempo with his boot and pushing the dancers into a blurred frenzy. Other times he played them straight and let his eyes wander through the hall, watching the interactions and groupings, the tensions, the drinking and posing.

For a while he watched Mary, who agreed to a Saint Margaret's Waltz with Angus MacBride and steered him like a shopping trolley with a rogue wheel, scolding him for the placing of his hands. Then he watched Catriona, who spent most of the night sitting at a table with her back to the wall and her arms crossed, drinking Coke, black-lined eyes flicking nervously, refusing to make eye contact with any of the younger men in the room. The young guy who had spoken up about oil at the referendum meeting made a move and she visibly cold-shouldered him, got up and disappeared into the toilets for several minutes.

Then Julie sat beside her and some meaningful words seemed to pass between them. Calum was almost afraid to wonder what they were. When he took his break, he bought them drinks and sat beside them, retreating into his pint and hoping they wouldn't notice that he was fading out. A few other people did floor spots: solo songs, self-penned poetry and pro-Indy speeches, which at the very least spared the need to make conversation.

'You should get up for a song, Gran,' Catriona said.

'Nobody understands Gaelic here anymore. I'd be singing to myself.'

'*I* apparently don't count but I'm sure Angus would appreciate you.'

'Ocht, Calum, away with you.' She pursed her lips and brooded, then leaned across him to inform Catriona, 'Angus courted me when we were young. He never forgave me for marrying Jack.' A fond smile played on her lips. She turned to Calum. 'You haven't forgotten you're taking me to Mass tomorrow morning, have you?'

He sighed. Of course she would remember church. 'No.'

'You should come for a change.'

'No, I shouldn't.'

'Catriona?'

'It's not really my thing, Gran.'

He glanced over the chin rest of his fiddle towards Johnny, then the other way at Abby and mouthed the words *last time*, his arm aching as he pulled his bow faster over the strings. He was slightly drunk, sweat dripped into his eyes and the dancers on the floor in front of him were a blur of flying hair and colours. They played the reel through a final time and he lifted his right boot from the floor to indicate its conclusion, and finished with a stomp and a final reverberating G chord.

'Thank you everybody. Mòran taing. See you next time. Good night.'

Dizzy people parted hands, laughed, clapped and stumbled off towards their tables, and Calum stepped away from the mic and stood for a moment as the current of music drained from his body. Then he picked up the pint glass beside his mic stand and downed it in three deep draughts.

Johnny had already settled his guitar into its case and begun to unplug mics and wind up cables. He looked at Calum with quiet eyes, assessing his frame of mind by the set of his jaw and the little tic beside his left eyebrow.

'All right?'

'Aye.' Calum squatted beside him, wincing as his knee cracked, and put his fiddle away. It would be painful to stand up again, so he lingered there on his heels, dusting rosin from the instrument's dark, cracked shellac finish, his mood deflating like a punctured tyre.

Just keep moving, Son, his dad would've said, draping a heavy arm over his shoulders, encouraging him as they toiled up a hill. Don't look back and, whatever you do, don't look at what's coming for you.

181

'Dad.' A hand landed on his shoulder. 'Oh gross, you're all sweaty.'

He looked up at Catriona; it might have been the first time since she'd arrived that she hadn't called him by name. Her hair had collapsed with the humid air and there were black make-up smudges on the pale skin below her eyes.

'It's hard work. You surely didn't dance much.'

'Nobody to dance with.'

'That guy was interested. What's his name? I've seen him around a few times.'

'Dunno. Didn't like him.' She shuddered. 'Creepy. I'm gonna take Gran up the road, okay? She's wanting her bed.'

'Okay. I'll help tidy up here.'

'Don't wake us up when you come in.' Obviously she didn't expect him to come straight back.

'Don't worry, Sleeping Beauty.'

She nodded. 'You sounded good tonight.'

He stood up with a grunt. 'Thank you.'

'I just thought, you know ... you needed to hear it. You haven't seemed seventy-six per cent okay today.'

Unexpected insight: he'd considered himself a better actor and her a less astute observer. He would hug her for it, if he had a dry shirt. 'Down to about fifty per cent today, kiddo. Tomorrow will be better.'

Or not, he thought, watching her take Mary's arm as they stepped out the door. Then he squeezed his eyes shut and opened them again, trying to refocus on things outside his head. Cat was good with her gran. She was tolerant and gentle and she hid her frustration at having to answer the same questions over and over. She wasn't opening up though. At least not about anything that mattered, and certainly not about whatever had gone on at university. When he looked at her, he could see himself before his breakdown, trembling and fearful, clinging to a tenuous

182

hold on sanity but knowing it was only a matter of time before he had to let go.

She wanted him to help her, otherwise she wouldn't have come. Finn had wanted his help too, when he'd called and asked to go climbing. Finn had wanted to patch things up but Calum didn't know how. He still didn't know how. The only thing he could do now was speak to Jenny.

SKIMMING STONES

Even here, Kyle insinuated his way into her sleep, appearing in dreams that should have had nothing to do with him, laying a hand on her shoulder and turning her around, laughing in her face, calling her Sleepy Cat and Kitten. Sometimes she woke with a surge of fear and knew he'd been there, stealing through like a thief even though she couldn't remember the content of the dream.

A noise downstairs. A door opening, closing. Footsteps. She lay rigid, frozen in that place between dreaming and waking. Bumps in the kitchen, the rush of water in the pipes. She breathed in, emerged fully from sleep, looked for reassurance in the now-familiar bookshelves on the far wall. Then she closed her eyes again to better tune in to the sounds downstairs. These were familiar morning sounds: Calum grinding his coffee beans, pouring cereal, clanking his spoon off his bowl, making a show of having breakfast as normal although she was almost certain he had only just come home. He'd been next door with Julie all night – her smell would be all over him – and this knowledge brought a flicker book of unwelcome images. Catriona had wanted to believe he was clean, above having sordid animal instincts even in spite of what she knew about her own conception, and now she would have to find a way not to be disgusted with him all over again.

She lay on her side and stared at the shelf of file boxes. These were neatly labelled according to date and content: mostly bills and invoices, tax forms and all kinds of other equally mind-numbing institutional documents by which adult life was apparently defined. However, at the far end of the top shelf was a box labelled *Finn*, and this often drew her eyes. When Calum spoke of his childhood he would say *we* instead of *I*, acknowledging the existence of a sibling, but otherwise he rarely mentioned his brother. Finn was a name, an evocation of loss, a mystery. Mary made reference to him more often, imbuing him with a saintly quality but never fleshing out the details. Maybe she couldn't remember them, or maybe she was ashamed. Catriona could grasp only an echo from long ago, something she'd heard but which hadn't been meant for her, Calum telling someone, *Finn was looking for a good way to die.*

She slipped out of the sofa bed and stepped as lightly as she could, touching the floorboards only with the balls of her feet, drew the box down and brought it back to the bed. It was like opening a forbidden book; she might almost have expected a dusty ghost or voices to rise out. The box of memories was disappointingly sparse, and the photographs she found were silent and mundane. She lifted the top one: Calum, long-haired and very much younger, standing with feet apart, holding a rope, staring up at the climber on the rock face above him. A more solid memory materialised. That was how he'd wrecked his knee, in some kind of climbing accident before she was born. He'd told her that once, or maybe her mother had. He was still recovering when they'd met. This was making sense, though she couldn't remember ever having a conversation about any of it.

The climber's face wasn't clearly visible behind damp, blowing hair, but he looked almost feline on the rock, his hand reaching upward, the toe of one foot stretching down.

Around them, the light of a golden evening, a shimmer of sea beyond the grey walls of rock.

A second photo of the two of them standing at the back of an old red Vauxhall, kitted up in parkas and gaiters, a snowy landscape spread around them. Finn was taller and slimmer than Calum, his cheeks hollow below prominent bones, his eyes very dark under his brows. His wide mouth turned up slightly at one side: more of a sneer than a smile. There was an old, faded picture of both brothers, kilted, playing the pipes at what looked like a Highland Games. Calum was already stretching towards his full height and Finn was pre-adolescent and very slight, maybe ten or eleven years old.

Below the photos she found an old cassette tape in an unlabelled box and five flat grey-brown pebbles. At the very bottom, a funeral programme for Finlay James Macdonald, 26 January 1972 –3 July 1993. Inside was a photograph of the same rock-star skinny, not-quite-smiling face, and then a poem or a song in Gaelic, an unfathomable assemblage of consonants. On the back, another photograph: Finlay as a black-haired boy on the beach just in front of the house. It was a perfect moment in time: the perpetual motion of a small boy frozen, imprinted on paper. His left hand was extended in front of him, balancing, while the right hand drew back, forefinger cocked around a flat, round pebble. The hair was blown back from his forehead, the face a scowl of effort and concentration. There was an impression of barely contained energy. Catriona stared at the picture and willed the hand to release the stone so that it could skim out over the water: six, seven, even ten bounces before disappearing.

Calum's feet creaked up the stairs. She hid the box under the duvet and lay down, muffling thick breath in the pillow. Water ran in the bathroom. While he was in the shower, she replaced the box on the shelf and got back into bed, not much wiser about Finlay James Macdonald, the unsmiling young man who would have been her uncle, except that he was a climber and that he died at only twenty-one. She was more curious now, not less, and she wondered why she shouldn't just ask straight out. Maybe she could, if Mary wasn't here. The old woman's presence made everything delicate, as though the wrong words could shatter her.

'Calum, you're going to make me late for Mass.' Mary was banging on the bathroom door.

'It doesn't start till ten, Mum,' came the reply.

Catriona glanced at the clock. It was half-past seven.

'Where have you been? I heard you come in the door.'

'I went for a paddle.'

Liar. Cat bit her lip.

'I want to buy flowers for the graves.'

There was a pause before he said, 'I'll be out in a minute, all right? You'll wake up Cat.'

'Who?'

'Catriona. Your granddaughter. Could you wait till I come out, please?'

Mary waited a moment, then knocked again and said something in Gaelic. Calum didn't reply this time, and Mary tried again. She was like a child who couldn't wait. The shower switched off and eventually he emerged, presumably to find Mary waiting outside the bathroom door.

'We're going to be late,' she said again. 'I have to go to Morrison's for flowers.'

'Pick some outside. I'm not driving to town this morning.'

'They die as soon as you pick them.'

'Oh for Christ's sake.'

'Calum! You're so unhelpful. I don't know why you're so unhelpful.'

'Would you please just let me get dressed?'

'I'll make porridge.'

'I've had my breakfast.'

187

'You don't want porridge?'

'No. Thank you. S'cuse me.'

Cat heard him creak along the short landing and shut his bedroom door, and Mary's lighter but slower footsteps making their way down the stairs. She clattered around in the kitchen, opening cupboard doors and closing them noisily because she forgot where things were from one day to the next. Cat lay a bit longer, guilty at her eavesdropping, guilty for being an added complication in Calum's life. He'd been noticeably downbeat yesterday and she wondered if it was her fault, even if he would never say so. How far down might he go?

As if her questions had seeped through the wall, he knocked on the door and called softly, 'Cat? You awake?'

She sat up and ran her fingers through her hair. 'Yeah. Come in.'

He pushed the door open. 'Sorry about that before.'

'It's fine. Granny doesn't give you much of a break, does she?'

'Not much, no.' He shut the door behind him and sat on the edge of the bed, seeming to relish a moment of refuge. 'This is only the beginning. I never thought much about getting old until she came to stay, and now it scares the crap out of me. Anyway ... how are you? Did you sleep all right?'

'I guess.' She saw shadows under his eyes. 'I take it *you* didn't do much sleeping next door.'

He closed his eyes, laughed softly. 'Oh, we slept ... a bit.'

'Oh my God. Too much information.'

'Uh huh. Sorry.'

'When were you going to tell me about her?'

'I don't know. I just hadn't got around to it yet. Julie and I are ...'

188

'Fuck buddies. Yeah, she told me.'

'Jesus, Catriona.' His eyebrows shot up and his cheeks flushed visibly. 'You don't have to be so rude, and I think you're old enough to respect my privacy.'

'Fine.'

'Fine,' he repeated.

She hesitated and stared at her fingers. The cuticles were torn and red. 'So ... are you better?'

'Better than yesterday, you mean?'

'Yeah.'

'Probably.' He shrugged. 'I'm all right.'

'Is it me? Is it because I'm here?'

'No, of course it isn't.'

'You'd tell me, right? If you didn't want me here?'

'I do want you here.' He patted her knee through the duvet and stood up. 'I'll be taking Mary to church in Arisaig this morning. You can come or you can stay, it's up to you.'

'I don't do church.'

'Neither do I. But you can see where five or six generations of our family are buried, if that interests you. There are Macdonalds stacked upon Macdonalds in that churchyard. My dad's there. And my brother.'

'What happened to your brother?'

'I thought you knew about that. Your mum never told you?'

'Not properly, no.'

'He had a climbing accident.' He paused and corrected himself. '*We* had a climbing accident.'

'So you were with him when he died?'

He sighed. 'Yup.'

'Oh.' What were you supposed to say? 'So is that why you're afraid of heights?'

'I was afraid of heights before that, but it didn't help. Can we talk about this later, Catriona, please?'

She cringed. 'I'm sorry.'

'It's fine. I will tell you about it. Just . . . later.'

'Look at the state,' Mary muttered, lowering herself onto her knees beside her husband's grave. John 'Jack' David Macdonald was overgrown with dandelions. She arranged her small cluster of wildflowers – the subject of much protest and disgruntlement – against the headstone and began pulling out tufts of grass and weeds. 'When was the last time you paid your Da any attention?'

It wasn't the brightest of days, but Calum had on the mirrored sunglasses that he wore when he wanted to keep out more than the sun. He turned them on Mary.

'We were here not that long ago. A month maybe. Just before the fire.'

'What fire?'

'Your kitchen fire, Mum.'

She stared at him, puzzling over this. 'There was no fire. I'm having a new kitchen in.'

He pressed his fist over his mouth and turned abruptly, stalked away from both of them, and stood against the wall that separated the churchyard from the copse of woods beyond, arms over his chest.

This was more than just her memory problem. Whatever it was between them, Catriona thought she recognised it as the same thing – the same fundamental fear – that existed between herself and her own mother. It was the reason she couldn't tell Jenny about Kyle. It was the fear of being exposed as weak or careless, or maybe just stupid. Families were the ultimate lie, she decided. The pretence of love was really just judgement. It hurt badly, whether it was spoken or only implied in a look or a shake of the head. Maybe she should go, she thought. Away somewhere, anywhere that nobody knew her. She could find some total stranger, in a bar

190

or on a train, and she could tell them about what Kyle had done to her, and they would only be kind, not disappointed.

The church bell began to ring and she looked back towards the road. Parishioners were arriving, a slow procession of the grey and the dowdy, wee women with fat ankles and bad perms. Mary hoisted herself from her knees with a grunt, dusted her stockings and stowed her little spade in her handbag. 'He is lost to God,' she said to Catriona, nodding in Calum's direction, 'but you would be very welcome, dear.'

'Oh. It's not my thing.'

'Your mother raised you Protestant, I suppose.'

'We didn't go to church at all.'

'Oh aye.' She had no need to speak her disapproval. 'You make sure he doesn't forget to come back for me at the end.'

'He won't.'

'He's done it before.'

'I'll make sure he doesn't, Gran.'

Mary only jutted her chin. From the other side of the churchyard, Calum watched her make her way over the damp grass and take the arm of another elderly lady who had just arrived. When they had disappeared behind the grey granite edifice, Catriona stepped towards the two graves, Jack's now tidied and Finn's still harbouring weeds. She knelt and began pulling the long grass with her fingers.

CIRCLES

'You don't have to do this,' Calum said when Mary went into the church. He watched Catriona rip tufts of grass and dandelions from around Finn's grave. Her jaw was clenched; she seemed to need a physical task to fill her mind.

'I don't mind weeding.'

'If that's true, I'm happy to put you to work at home.'

'Aye, sure.'

'I'm just going to sit in the car and make a phone call. Back in a few minutes.' He placed his hand on her shoulder, just for a moment. 'Thanks Cat.'

She looked up at him, eyes full of ambivalence, then went back to work.

He shut the graveyard gate and sat in the passenger seat of the Land Rover facing out so he could see Catriona coming, and brought up Jenny's number. It seemed impossible to speak to her in the house without running the risk of being overheard. His breath quickened as she answered.

'I wondered when I'd hear from you,' she said. Cool but not hostile.

'How are you, Jen?'

'I'm surviving, Calum. As I always do. You?'

'Well ... ' He wondered how much to tell her. 'Okay. Surprised by the sudden appearance.'

'Surprised? You didn't know she was coming? She told me she spoke to you.'

He rubbed at his forehead. 'She didn't tell me.'

'The lying wee minx! I'm sorry. Send her back if you want to. I know you've got your mum with you as well.'

'I don't mind having her. I do mind the fact that she's not well.'

'Depressed, you mean?'

'Aye. Depressed. Distressed. Anxious. I take it you've seen it too.'

'Of course I have. She's been like that since she came home from uni. Before that, even. She was all right all year. I don't know what's kicked this off, but I hope it's not ... you know ... a family thing.'

He laughed softly. 'Thanks Jenny.'

'I don't mean it that way.'

'I'm sure you don't.' He couldn't quite manage to keep the spite out of his voice. 'She's never been like this before?'

'Not really.'

'So something's happened.'

'Probably, but she hasn't told me what.'

'She hasn't told you anything at all? Because I'm a bit desperate here, Jen.'

'This is new. I find it interesting you're so concerned all of a sudden. What's it about, Calum?'

'Oh don't start, for Christ's sake. I'm calling you for help, not an argument.'

There was a pause. He could hear her sighing into the phone. 'I shouldn't have said that. There's a boy from university called Kyle. He called the house a few nights ago, looking for her. When I told her, she got all agitated and told me not to tell him where she is.'

'Why?'

'She just said that he was creepy. He'd stalked her a bit or

193

something. She swore to me that he has nothing to do with it, but I'm not sure I believe her. Trust me, if I knew anything else, I'd tell you.'

'Okay. You said his name was Kyle?'

'Aye.'

'I'll ask her.'

'If you get anything out of her, please call me.'

He softened. She sounded alone and fearful. 'I will. Thanks Jen. Look, I'd better go. You . . . keep well, okay?'

'You too. Calum?'

'What?'

'I'm sorry I snapped at you.'

An apology from Jenny. That was new. 'It's okay. Listen, I'll talk to you soon, all right?'

Ending the call, he sat sideways in the car for a few minutes more, watching Catriona work her way around the grave. She was steady and meticulous, and certainly not handless. He'd worked with plenty less careful roustabouts over the years.

Jenny's question resonated around the vehicle's greasy interior. *What's it about, Calum?*

What was it about the day Finn died, he wondered. He could still hear himself saying, 'Not on my watch,' as if to say, 'Go ahead and kill yourself but don't make me watch you do it.'

What was it about now? What if the situation was reversed? If Jenny had phoned him and asked for help, would he give it? Had he ever done it before, when she'd asked?

The answer to that last question was so obvious that he didn't even want to think the word.

Life went around in such tight little circles you barely had time to untangle one disastrous mistake before you made it all over again. Jenny was right to ask what it was about. It couldn't be about himself anymore. He had to make it about

194

Catriona. If he wanted her to give up her secrets, he would have to give up his.

He went back to the graveside and squatted beside her, lifted his fingers to the headstone and let them move over the engraved letters of Finn's name. 'I never thought he'd make twenty-one.'

THE WORST THING

Mary watched stained-glass light playing on the church wall, pink and blue patches slowly following each other across grey stone like dying butterflies. She remembered so clearly the way the last beautiful pink tinge subsided from Jack's cheeks. Father Daniel prayed. Mary's mind drifted from one question to another.

Did your soul rise immediately from your body when you died or did it emerge slowly like a snake shedding its old skin? She'd often wondered this. Would you be aware of your journey to heaven or simply wake up in the house of the Almighty? Or some other place she hated to imagine.

Jack had never been a believer. He'd turned from the church at a young age, and had succeeded in turning Calum. But still, she prayed that God had seen his goodness and claimed him anyway. He was a good man. He was the best of men in every way but one: he had not died in the grace and friendship of God. Surely a merciful God wouldn't have condemned him to eternal damnation for that.

Then there was Finn, who was always faithful but never the good man Jack was. He had made so many bad choices. He had sinned against God, possibly in the worst way of all, by going too willingly to his death. And yet, at every Mass she was reminded: *He gave himself up to death, and, rising from the dead, he destroyed death and restored life.* Just like Jesus.

How could you square it? She knew she shouldn't question, but lately she did. What would God have done with Finn?

Mary tried to pray but all she could do was remember the things she wished she could forget.

The worst thing about the day of the accident was facing Calum. She had seen Finn first, on the slab in the hospital, still in his climbing gear. What she remembered most was his absolute stillness. The twitching mouth, the exploratory eyebrows, the busy eyes. His bonny, uneasy face, which had never stopped moving, now inert and white as her mother's china. It would have been very quick, they told her, and perhaps there was consolation in this. He'd been in pain, her child. He'd been carrying the weight of his own being like a cross on his back for so many years now. You could see it in the hollows under his cheekbones and in the grey hairs that had already started to appear amongst the crow-black.

In this private, frozen moment, she might have experienced the faintest sense of relief. She might have whispered a prayer of thanks, that He had lifted Finn's burden. Perhaps she had, but now, sitting in the chapel in Arisaig, she couldn't remember. All she remembered now was how she had begged Calum not to let Finn climb.

She also remembered that when she saw her remaining son, she wanted to hurt him. She wanted to beat him with her fists, drag him from the bed and throw him down the stairs, and with the strength of her anger she might have managed it. He was deep in a drugged sleep, his leg splinted, his face swollen and badly scraped. The nurse said his knee would take some fixing but he wasn't in danger.

She had pulled the curtain and stepped towards the bed, stood beside him, her hands hanging by her sides.

'Wake up,' she said sharply. She couldn't say his name or bring herself to touch him. His eyelids fluttered but didn't open. She waited a moment and tried again. 'Damn you, wake up.' Receiving no response, she had turned and left the ward.

The light coming through the stained glass dulled, turned from pink to silver. She moved her eyes to the left and saw gulls flying through the clear glass, rising on a draft above the churchyard where Jack and Finn lay. Where did she go that night? Where did she sleep? Was she alone? Did she cry? Did she pray? What did she pray for? She couldn't remember. She couldn't remember any of that.

Why did she lose the details? She was so cloudy. They were giving her something to make her cloudy.

Father Daniel prayed.

Mary asked: *Are you with your Da, Finn? Have you told him the truth about what happened that day? Maybe you'll tell me when I see you.*

HEADSTONE

Catriona looked at him, chewing her lip and waiting for the story. Anticipation jangled around inside her and brought out moisture on her hands. 'You don't have to tell me now.'

'I should have told you a long time ago.' He took a deep breath. 'My brother was a drug addict. He was also manic-depressive. Bipolar, they call it now. Do you know what that is?'

'Sort of, yeah.' She'd heard the term, but it was a bit of an exaggeration to say she fully understood what it meant. She could look it up later. It was embarrassing to make him explain any more than he had to.

'He was up and down his whole life, but he got really bad after Dad died. He was fourteen then, and by the time he was eighteen he'd become a total speed freak and tried to kill himself twice. He stole stuff from Granny, he stole stuff from me, he was a total disaster.'

'Why was he like that?'

'Nobody knows why. Losing Dad so young was a massive part of it, obviously, but I'm not sure it was all down to that. He was always a bit vulnerable. He might have gone that way regardless. But then, this one time, I took him climbing and he could just ... do it ... like he'd been doing it all his life.'

'Probably because he was too crazy to be scared.'

Calum glanced at her, then nodded. 'Maybe. When he was really hyper, he thought he was invincible. The thing about climbing is it takes such concentration and focus, you can't think about anything else while you're doing it. So I took him climbing because it brought him out of his own head. When he was climbing, when he was up there on the rock and for a few hours afterwards, he seemed happy. He was calm, like his mind had finally cleared. And he was just so bloody good at it. Complete strangers used to stand and watch him. By the time he was your age, he was properly making a name for himself.'

'You must have been good too.'

'I was okay. He was a lot lighter than me, longer limbed, perfectly made for it. I was like a gorilla clambering up after him. The stupid thing was, the route that killed him wasn't even that hard. Well within both our ranges. It was summertime in the Cairngorms, a warm quiet Thursday morning. He was agitated, the way he often was just before one of his downswings, and we were pissed off at each other. We'd completely fallen out a few weeks earlier.

'The whole walk in, he was muttering to himself and I should have known he wasn't in the right state of mind for climbing. I should have bailed on that climb before we started, except it would have caused a stushie. So, as usual, I let him lead ... I thought ... I believed I could keep him safe from himself. But he took off like some kind of weird phantom, sprinting up this chimney of rock on his fingers and toes. He never liked being belayed ... he'd have preferred to free climb without any protection. He had this delusion about a guardian angel who lived inside the rock. Anyway, I'm shouting at him to chill and slow down, but he's like fifteen feet up before he places his first cam.'

'Cam?'

'It's a safety device you wedge into cracks in the rock and

clip onto. They work fine if you place them correctly so they can't slip, and if you have a whole line of them. He didn't. We were both too complacent; he never fell. It happened that fast, he ... reached up for a hold and missed, but his body was already committed to the move and he peeled off. The cam pops loose and he decks hard, right on top of me. I broke his fall to a certain extent. If he'd been wearing a helmet he might have survived, but his head cracked off a stone. I'm battered all over, concussed and my leg's bent the wrong way at the knee and he's just ... lying there, not moving. And that was him ... in the blink of an eye. When I look back I realise that day changed everything. Sometimes something happens and it sets your life onto a new track forever.'

'Aye.' She wanted to tell him she understood. Instead, she forced herself to imagine how the scene must have played out. How did they get down from where they were? Were there other people around? How long did he have to wait there with his dead brother before someone came to help? Questions that were too graphic to ask.

'It must have been just ... horrible.'

He nodded and placed his hands flat in the damp grass at the base of the stone, as if feeling for vibrations. 'I've always told my mother it was an accident, but actually I'm pretty sure he knew exactly what he was doing. He wanted to die. And my mother wonders why I won't go to Mass with her.'

She couldn't look at him. His voice was deliberate and steady, but something was screaming just out of her earshot and she was frightened of it. 'I don't blame you.'

He acknowledged this with a grim smile. 'It properly messed me up but I pretended it didn't, until I couldn't pretend anymore.'

'That was when you came back here.'

'Yep. After I'd lost my marriage and my career.'

'But that was years after the fact.'

'Aye. The human brain is remarkably capable of saving up bad shit for a long time.'

'So would you have stayed in California if you hadn't got ill?'

'Maybe.' He shrugged. 'Probably. Can I ask you something, Cat? Just ... answer me honestly. Do you think there's a chance you might be pregnant?'

'No,' she said as forcefully as she could. Her face flushed. It was bad enough being asked by her mum. Staring at the ground she said, 'I'm not.'

'Were you worried that you were?'

If she said yes, she'd be admitting to having let someone between her legs.

'No.'

He looked like he was trying not to appear relieved. He dusted his hands and stood up. 'Let's get out of here.'

Catriona followed him, away from the gravestones and onto the road, down the hill towards the village. A west wind drove whitecaps onto the shore, and beyond the harbour the water undulated like a blanket shaken by a giant. A band of rain obscured the islands. A few tourists wandered up and down the small promenade. She wondered whether Anna had made it to John O'Groats yet. They had exchanged email addresses. Anna had invited her to visit her in Denmark, and perhaps it was a genuine invitation and perhaps it could be a sanctuary, a bolthole with a safe expanse of sea separating her from Scotland. She could make an excuse. She could ask Calum for enough money to get there. Maybe she could find work.

He led her to the single open cafe. They took a small table upstairs beside the window, ordered bacon rolls and a pot of tea, and sat quietly as the sky darkened and rain began to fleck onto the glass. Cat looked down and watched people scurrying for cover. Opposite her, Calum was impossible to read: he might have been thinking about Finn or about his mother, or thinking about making love to Julie or about something less tangible than that. Or he might not be thinking about anything at all.

His meaty silences had been unsettling at first. Two nights ago, after a long stretch without speaking, she had asked if he was angry with her.

He had seemed surprised. 'No. Should I be?'

'You haven't said anything to me for an hour.'

'Do you leave the tap running when you don't need water?' he had asked in return.

So words, like water, were not to be wasted. This was a new thing to consider. Uni was all about words, the incessant blether of students and the intellectual pomposities of the academics. Now she found these interjections of silence liberating. He had told her what she needed to know about Finn, and the rest would come later.

There was music playing, just audible over the other customers, a fiddle sweeping and wheeling like a swallow over the water.

'That sounds like you,' she said.

'Good call.'

'Honestly? You're like ... some kind of West Highland pop star or something.'

He laughed. 'Aye, you know you've reached the heady heights when you're going out to the tourists in Arisaig. Haven't you noticed the paparazzi at my back?'

'How can you be so good at something and be so dismissive of it?'

'It's only music. I've made a mess of everything that matters.'

This surprised her. As far as she had seen, he was good at everything he did and he knew it. 'Like what?'

He paused before answering, a dark half-smile on his

203

face. 'Like being a dad. I've made kind of a cock up of that, haven't I?'

If she had been in the mood for a fight, she might have agreed, but all she felt at this moment was the need for him to accept her. To wrap his arms around her and be her shield, to be an old-fashioned father who would threaten any encroaching man with a shotgun. She'd never felt this way with Mum; Mum had always just been there at her back, telling her how to be and reminding her of what she wasn't. Poor Mum didn't deserve her resentment, but she could only admit this from a distance.

'You never hit me or molested me, so you can't have been that bad.'

'Surely you could set the bar a bit higher than that.'

She shrugged. 'My experience of men hasn't been exactly wonderful up till now, if you want to know the truth.'

One of his eyebrows arched. 'Catriona, has somebody hurt you?'

Catriona sat very still, her fingers tucked under her thighs, and she felt like a droplet of rain quivering on a metal railing. One touch, one breath even, and she would burst, ooze down into the collective pool on the ground and be lost.

'A little bit. A guy I went out with at the end of term didn't turn out to be very nice. I'll get over it.'

'What did he do?'

'It doesn't matter.'

'Cat, it won't hurt as much to say it as you think it will, I promise.'

'Fuck's sake, you want me to respect *your* privacy. Let's just say he's somebody I never want to see again.'

'What happens when you go back to uni?'

'I don't know if I want to go back.'

'You can't drop out of university because of some guy.'

'Would you go mad if I did?'

'No, but I think your mother would. She's worked bloody hard to help you get there.'

'I know, but ... ' She took a deep breath and blurted, 'It just seems completely pointless. It's just a game someone says you have to play, and I don't want to anymore. Maybe you'd let me stay here ... until I figure some stuff out.'

'Do unto others, eh, Cat?'

'What?'

He smiled and looked at his hands on the table. 'We've been here before, only the tables are turned.'

'I know, Dad ... I'm sorry.'

Calum sighed and she could see the dilemma playing itself out in his mind. Their tea and rolls arrived and she nibbled hers, feeling sick, realising she'd put him into an impossible situation. He wanted her to leave but couldn't say it. He wouldn't lower himself to that.

'I'm not asking you to apologise for anything,' he said.

'I feel like you want me to. I know what you think but ... I like it here.'

'But you're not exactly going to learn anything here, are you?'

'I could work for you. I could be like your apprentice or something. You could teach me how to build stuff.'

He looked dubious. 'Is that what you really want to do?'

'Aye, why not? Or ... if you don't want me to stay, maybe I'll go travelling for a while. I met this woman from Denmark and she said I could come stay with her anytime I wanted.'

He sipped his tea and offered no response to this, most likely trying to hide his disappointment in her. At least he tried. Mum would just come out and say it for the whole cafe to hear. The photo of Finn throwing the stone into the water came into her mind. There were times in her teens when she went down to the beach alone, brimming with things that nobody would want to hear about even if she knew the right words for them. Sometimes she would stay there for two or three hours, skimming stones or just throwing them as hard as she could into the waves. She would imagine each stone was something bad that had happened to her: nasty words from Rachel Merrick who bullied her at school, an argument with her mum, another one of Calum's broken promises. She would throw and throw until she could barely lift her arm. Then she would go home and for a little while would feel better. Now she understood why the relief never lasted: because you could never throw away the bad stuff. You became it.

CRUX

'It's looking good, what do you think?'

Mary followed him through the dried out, freshly plastered and painted rooms of her flat, head quaking as though she'd just come upon the scene of a crime. Having eventually found her insurance documents in an envelope under her mattress (along with her passport, National Insurance card and will), Calum had been able to bring men in to fix the place. The damaged wiring had been repaired, the carpets replaced and the kitchen entirely reconstructed. Everything was bare, clean and ready for reoccupation, but her face was a projection of dismay.

'There's a bad smell.'

'Aye, it'll take a while for that to go.'

'I don't like this flat. It's cold and there's a bad smell. I couldn't imagine wanting to live here.'

'But you *do*. It's your flat.'

'No it isn't. My flat is ... ' she stopped, looked around, ' ... I have things. I have Mum's old desk, and ... where *is* everything? Jack's armchair? What have you done with my things?'

Calum breathed in. She was right about the smell. An ominous hangover: melted plastic, overheated chemicals, burnt hair. You never realised how sinister the aftertaste of a house fire was until you experienced it.

He tried to keep his voice even. 'Your furniture's in storage. The kitchen table and chairs were burnt, and I suspect you'll probably need a new suite for the living room because it'll hang onto that smell forever. Mattresses and pillows too. This is why we've been washing all your clothes and towels, and the rest. Remember?'

Stupid question.

The headshaking started again, a gesture of confusion that was threatening to become a palsy. 'I still don't understand how the fire started. Did they properly investigate it? Was it something to do with those voices on the telephone? They were putting things inside my walls. I don't know who they were.'

'How many times do I have to explain this?' It was out through gritted teeth before he could stop it. 'You started the fire. You did it. Nobody was ever in your flat, don't you understand that?'

'I was frightened.' She took a step back from him and her eyes filled with tears, her head still quivering side to side. In Gaelic, she said, 'I don't understand why you're so angry, Calum.'

'I'm angry because you can't remember,' he said in English. It was like having to haul her back into the present. It felt like it hurt her, but he didn't have the words in Gaelic.

Her brows drew together. 'I don't know what's wrong with me these days. I'm out of sorts. I feel cloudy. I'm sorry I make you angry. I'm sorry you're lumbered with me; I know you'd rather you weren't.'

'I'm trying as hard as I can, Mum. You're angry with me all the time. I think you can't stand me. I am trying to help you and all you can ever do is insult me.'

'No, I don't. You don't like helping me, Calum, you never have. You left home at the first possible chance. I told you people were coming into my flat. I told you I was frightened

208

that something bad was going to happen, and I was right. There's such a terrible smell here.'

She was turning into a goldfish and he was only making it worse.

He always panicked at the crux: terror, sweats, the Elvis shakes.

All you could do was breathe.

He closed his eyes, pressed his fingertips into his eyelids, spoke into his hand. 'Mum, I'm sorry. It's not your fault. You have Alzheimer's. Do you remember that much? Do you remember what it is?'

She snapped. 'I know what Alzheimer's is, Calum, I'm not ignorant. I don't have it. I don't know where you're getting that from.'

'You do. I wish you didn't. I can't lie to you and pretend it's not happening. You've been covering it up, probably without even realising it, for a long time. That's why your memory is cloudy. I shouldn't have sworn at you. I'm ... finding this very hard. I want to help you, but I can't give up all my work and be with you full-time.'

She turned away from him and walked to the window, looking down over the street, processing this devastating news with her back towards him. Maybe within the day, or within the hour, she'd have forgotten it again and would just go back to being cloudy without knowing why.

'What will happen when I get worse?' Right now, at least, she understood.

'I don't know. I suppose we'll have to talk about that.'

'Jack made me promise that I wouldn't let him die in hospital.'

'I know.'

'I kept that promise, but it was terrible. I was exhausted. He was exhausted. All I could do for him was tell him it was okay to let go.'

'I know, I remember.'

'You weren't there.'

'I *was*. Of course I was there. Can't you remember that I was there? Finn and I both.'

She only shook her head. 'I don't want you to nurse me.'

Was she trying to save him from that burden, or was it because she didn't trust him? Probably the latter, but at least it offered him a window through which to escape, dragging the guilt of obligation behind him like a shackle.

He stepped up beside her but didn't touch her. Lately, she seemed to find even the gentlest touch a threat. 'Look, it might be a long time before you need someone to nurse you. You'll probably be all right here for a while longer. Once everything is back in, it'll feel more like home. We can get a carer in to help you with bits and pieces.'

'Calum, I don't want to stay here.'

'You don't have to,' he said, trying to keep his voice steady while everything inside him was threatening to crumple inwards. He had no idea what alternatives were available in the area. 'So what do we do? You want to stay in Glendarach?'

'Maybe ... for a little while longer. We could find someone else to help. A nice young lady who doesn't have rings in her lip.'

Who did she think Catriona was, a live-in care assistant?

'And when the time comes ... ' she shrugged, 'I don't suppose I'll know the difference.'

Planning for her future was as unsettling as sinking a drilling rig into the Pacific seabed, where at any time, an earthquake could change the shape of the earth beneath you. 'Mum, can I tell you what scares me?'

'What is it?'

'We can talk about it now, and maybe we can make a plan that you're happy with, and then ... when it comes to it, you'll have forgotten that we ever had the conversation and

210

you'll think that I've coerced you into something you don't want. I'm afraid you'll blame me.'

'Why would I blame you?'

'Because you have before.'

She looked at him, her brows beetling towards each other, and began shaking her head again. 'Calum, I don't know what you're talking about.'

ABERDEEN, NOVEMBER 1993

'Oh, please don't tell me you've just got out of your bed. It's past noon.'

'I've just got out of my bed.' Calum shuffled to one side to let Mary in. She left two bags of shopping on his kitchen table and sniffed around his flat like a terrier, nostrils flared, lip curled into a grimace. He followed slowly, bleary and hot in his dressing gown. After five months and three operations, his leg could finally take his weight and he could hobble stiffly around the flat. He was still using the crutches when he went out, but the three flights of stairs were a monumental prospect and he wasn't yet fit to return to work, so it didn't happen often.

'This place is worse than a piggery.'

'I'd have cleaned up if I'd known you were coming.'

'You shouldn't be living like this. If you can't manage, get someone to help you.'

He chose not to respond to this. 'D'you want tea?'

'Is there a cup that won't give me a disease?' She lifted a dirty mug from the table and peered inside.

'Feel free to wash one.' Calum lowered himself onto a chair, holding his left leg in front of him and letting the right take the burden. In his physio sessions, he could now bend his knee to ninety degrees, more or less the angle required to sit comfortably on one of his kitchen chairs, but not without a torrent of expletives.

'I'll not bother just now,' she decided, and began rolling up her sleeves. 'I'll get this kitchen cleaned up before I make us some lunch. Maybe you'd put those messages away, Calum, if it's not beyond your capabilities.'

He didn't get up. 'I will in a minute.'

She ignored him, filling the basin with soapy water and dumping dirty dishes into it. Several minutes passed and he hadn't moved from the chair, so she turned on him. 'What is the matter with you?'

'I'm just tired.' And he was. The pain was tiring. The energy his body required for healing was tiring. The extra effort he had to put into basic living was tiring. The repetition of Finn's fall, running in a continuous loop around his mind, was crushing.

She pointed the sponge at him, foam splatting onto the floor as she punched the air. 'When you've spent more than a decade caring for your dying spouse and your sick child and you've them both buried, then you can speak to me about being *tired*.'

Mary the Widowed Bereaved Mother. She had made these things into a cloak, wrapped it around herself and refused to take it off. He was tired of this too. 'You say that like I haven't been through all of this with you.'

Mary gave a breath of joyless laughter, the colour draining from her lips as she drew them into a hard frown. She seemed too disgusted with him to speak.

Calum continued. 'You know how much time I spent with Finn. He practically lived here most of last year. He trashed the place. He chain-smoked, he drank himself stupid and puked in his bed. He brought his nut-job associates back here to get hammered the whole time I was offshore. I bought a new guitar last spring and guess what?

212

It walked. He gave it to his dealer. Just like he did with all your jewellery.'

'I can't believe you would accuse him, Calum. Your *brother*. He wouldn't have done that.'

'He did. I know he was ill, Mum, but he did that stuff. I didn't tell you about the guitar because I knew you needed a break. I tried to help him. I went through his pockets when he was sleeping and tried to keep him off the hard stuff. I fed him, I bought him everything he needed. I took him climbing just about every week I was off work.'

'And I wish to God he'd never gone with you.' Her eyes fluttered as tears rose. 'Just once in your life I wish you could have listened to me. It was madness, teaching him to climb mountains. You were as bad as he was, in your way. Just as self-obsessed, just as unable to heed anyone except yourself. One might have thought you actually *wanted* him to come to grief. Or were you so arrogant you couldn't see what was bound to happen?'

If he could have stood up easily and stormed away, he would have. As a theatrical alternative, he let his head thump against the wall behind him. Her eyes shot blame at him and it cut him in half.

'You can't answer that, can you?'

He didn't try. Silently he wondered what kind of a mess a case of spontaneous human combustion would make right here in this kitchen.

'God didn't make the mountains for us to climb. He made them to remind us of our frailty.'

'Well then, consider me fucking reminded!'

'Calum!'

'That is bullshit, Mum. You never saw him climb. He had a gift, all right? If you want to believe God had anything to do with it, believe that. Climbing gave him a reason to keep living.'

'Until it killed him.'

'Aye. But better that than an overdose or stabbed in some junkie's flat.'

She closed her eyes, bit her lip, gripped the edge of the work surface so hard her knuckles paled. 'He might have got better. He might have found a better treatment eventually.'

'Or he might not.'

'Is that why you didn't take better care with the ropes, then?'

Now he did get up, straight off the chair and into lounge. Rosy late-autumn sunlight was pouring in through the bay window and people were laughing on the street below. It was the first time the sun had come out in weeks. Or maybe he just hadn't been looking. Maybe rage brought the clarity he'd been missing for a while. It was time to get out.

He showered, shaved for the first time in days, dressed, put on shoes and a jacket. Mary was still in the kitchen, the messages still in their bags, the dishes still unwashed. She was sitting at the table, hands wrapped around a mug of tea, her eyes and nose red.

He pointed at her and punctuated each word. 'It. Was. Not. My. Fault.'

Mary looked up at him. He didn't want to know if she was going to accept this or renew her accusation. He didn't want to hear her equivocate or try to justify. He didn't want to hear her voice at all.

'If you ever try to blame me again, you will lose your other son as well. Do you understand?'

She only looked at him, neither confirming nor denying.

'I'm going out.'

Mary took a deep, shaky breath. 'Would you like me to leave?'

214

'Do what you like. I'm going out.' He ignored the crutches, mostly hopped down the stairs and tried as hard as he could not to limp as he walked up the street. The bright, clear air brought the smells of ice and the North Sea, coal smoke and petroleum (or maybe the smell of petroleum was so permanently up his nose already that it would flavour everything for the rest of his life). Two blocks away was a pub he liked, unselfconscious and functional, wooden floor-boards cured with beer, a lively hum of conversation, music sessions which he joined when he was onshore. It was quiet this afternoon: a couple of old guys at the bar, a group of younger women in the snug, bags of shopping around their feet.

He ordered a pint and a nip of Grouse.

'Fit like, Calum, ma man,' Louise said as she pulled his pint. 'Havena seen ye for donkey's.' She tilted the glass under the tap and it looked tiny in her hand. She was oversized in every feature, from her breasts to her put-on North-East patter, but also had a barmaid's expansive kindness. 'Are ye back among the living?'

He reckoned it was obvious to anyone looking that he wasn't, so he didn't bother to lie. 'I can see the living from where I am, but I'm not sure I'm quite there yet.'

Louise squeezed his hand as he handed over a fiver. 'We've been missin' yer tunes, doll. Get yourself doon this week.'

'Aye, maybe. Ta, Lou.' He let the whisky slip down his throat, then picked up his pint and turned around. The girls in the snug were very young, probably barely old enough to be in here. Oversized jumper and legging types, teasing each other, laughing, vigorously living the life of new students. One of them looked up and met his eyes. Her hair was short, bleached almost white, her eyes heavily framed with black make-up. They were pretty though. Big and shiny, and her face was shaped like a heart, with wide cheekbones and a small, delicate chin. Plump red-painted lips, which smiled at him.

He smiled back.

He took the kayak out, fixed his sights on the Sgùrr of Eigg and paddled hard. He wanted to exhaust himself enough to sleep tonight. He wanted to clear his mind but the conversations continued, tipping into arguments, going round and round just like the debates about Scotland's future. Mary was firm on that one: there was no such thing as independence. Human beings relied on each other, communities were woven together over centuries. In a muddled, not-quite-clear-on-the-concept sort of way, she was right. He couldn't cut her loose, either to live alone or to be looked after by strangers. You couldn't simply walk away this time. You couldn't tick a box on a paper and turn your back on your family.

Except for Finn. Finn, the mad, laughing poltergeist.

She blamed him for Finn. He'd be within his rights to dump her in a nursing home and wash his hands of her.

Did Mary remember that? What did Mary remember? Did she remember how blame and threat had formed a kind of magnetic force between them, locking them into a tense, quivering stasis? They hadn't discussed it for years. He thought about it, though. He thought about it every time he looked at her.

Had she forgiven him? Had he forgiven himself? You shouldn't have to forgive yourself for something that wasn't your fault.

But.

But what if it was? Because maybe it *was* his fault, strategically if not technically. Because maybe his plan had been wrong from the beginning. Because he'd thought climbing could make Finn better and he should have known that was never going to happen. Because maybe climbing was only a display of testosterone-driven arrogance and you deserved to be smacked down for it. Like she said, maybe God didn't think kindly of men who tried to conquer his handiwork. Maybe.

Maybe if he believed that, some part of this would make sense.

He stopped paddling and let himself drift, and slowly the current carried him away from shore. Out here, accompanied only by the sloshes and slaps of the water against the kayak, he could answer one question with confidence. With the absoluteness of English, not the relational bend of Gaelic. No.

No, he hadn't forgiven himself. He had simply drifted away from the event, lame and dazed even if he no longer looked it to anyone else. Maybe this was where the vertigo came from. Maybe some part of him would be falling forever, until he found a way to absolve himself.

Where would an atheist seek absolution? It was a problem.

He and Mary couldn't talk about it, and that was always going to be the other problem. That was the way it was between them: hierarchy and silence. They'd never had anything that might have been called a friendship. Finn would sit there between them, and he would laugh at them and squeeze them against the walls until they couldn't breathe, but they wouldn't talk about him. And maybe as the disease progressed Mary would properly forget and Finn wouldn't exist anywhere except in Calum's own head. Eventually, Calum would die or become senile, and it would all finally disappear. Individual losses eventually merged into something far bigger, and their own family's grief would become part of that great collective absence. Death truly was the only socialist republic there was ever going to be.

BURGLARY

Calum said she had Alzheimer's. He was lying. Once again, he was lying. He said she started the fire. He said nobody else had been into the flat.

He had forgotten that she had been the victim of a crime before. He had obviously forgotten about the burglary. He didn't know she remembered that more clearly than he did.

At the time, he told her to call the police. He would have put his own brother in prison. Now he tried to tell her she was losing her memory. How could she be losing her memory when she remembered that perfectly well?

FORT WILLIAM, 1992

What Mary noticed first was the smell. There was always a smell in the flat when Finn had been there: cigarette smoke, unwashed hair and something sweetish, almost like the stink of a dead animal. It was repulsive and embarrassing. When he stayed with her she gently reminded him to shower every few days, but he ignored him more often than not. His hair was long and matted, nearly forming itself into dreadlocks. His beard sprouted in thin, dark tufts on his pale cheeks. Such a beautiful boy he'd been; it was heartbreaking to look at him now.

'Finn?' she called into the flat, putting down her bags and hanging her coat on the hook. 'Are you here?'

There was no answer. That in itself wasn't unusual; he could be sleeping or locked in his room with headphones on. She hadn't been expecting him. Normally he stayed in Aberdeen when Calum was offshore. He seemed to get by well enough on his own there, although Calum complained about the mess he left behind.

'Finlay?' She went into the kitchen, the living room, Finn's bedroom. The bathroom door was open. There was no sign of him or any of his usual clutter, but the door to the hall cupboard was ajar. She wouldn't have left it like that. Open cupboard doors were one of her pet hates, along with toilet seats left up and clothes sticking out of drawers. She'd nagged the boys about these things on a daily basis all their lives, to no avail. She opened the door fully and looked in. Her stacks of tidily folded towels and linens had been knocked over, some of them crumpled on the floor as if someone had shoved an arm past them to pull something out from the back.

The wooden box containing her silver cutlery set had been removed from its safe place behind her old towels.

It had to be somewhere. She moved the remaining towels and sheets aside, knocking most of them onto the floor in her growing distress. Maybe she'd moved the box last time she'd tidied. She searched the other shelves.

Her legs felt as weak as they did when the doctor broke the news of Jack's cancer. She began to shake all over and sweat broke out on her forehead. She went into her bedroom and knew immediately that he'd been here too. The quilt was rumpled and two of the photographs on top of her chest of drawers had been knocked over. She opened her jewellery drawer.

She'd never had much; she'd never been one for jewels and gold, apart from her plain wedding band and the little crucifix she kept close to her heart. What she had was mostly sentimental and she rarely wore it: her engagement ring, her mother's pearls, the elegant silver necklace Jack had bought her for their twentieth anniversary. He was already ill by then and knew they wouldn't make it to their twenty-fifth. It was gone, all of it.

It had to be Finn. If he'd been a little bit more careful, she might never have noticed anything for weeks. But he always left a mess behind him. And a bad smell.

Mary sat down on her bed and wept, wailing into her hands, overflowing with tears that she'd held in for so many years. She cried until the sun went down and she began to shiver with the cold, and then she got into bed and lay there until morning, drifting in and out of a troubled sleep.

The next day she folded all her linens and towels and organised what was left of her jewellery: glass beads and broken earrings. She opened the windows and cleaned the flat as thoroughly as she could, removing Finn's smell and fingerprints. As she cleaned, she debated whether to confront him. He wasn't a criminal, he must have been desperate to do it. He needed help and forgiveness and he could only steal things, not memories.

He wouldn't do it again; there wasn't much left of any value. Only Jack's pipes: the Highland pipes which had belonged to his father during the war, and the small pipes that had made her fall in love with him. Surely Finn would never take those.

Just in case, she hid both sets of pipes inside an old suitcase and wedged it into the eaves behind the panel in the loft.

'I've remembered where the pipes are,' she said when Calum came in the back door, trailing his dripping gear after him.

220

'Behind the panel in the eaves, inside a suitcase. I put them there after the burglary.'

'So Finn wouldn't take them,' he said softly.

'Finn would never have done that.'

He gave her a strange look and asked 'You're sure they're there?'

'Yes, I'm sure.'

'Okay. We'll go get them.' He placed his hand very lightly on her arm. 'Well done. That's a relief.'

'I'd hate to have lost them. I'm losing everything else.'

'Oh Mum.' His voice wobbled. 'They'll be all right. They'll be safe up there.'

Tears rose in her eyes, and for the first time in years she stepped in close to him and allowed him to put his arms around her. He was sweaty and smelled of salt and mouldy waterproofs, but she didn't mind.

LIFE CLASS

Calum worked Catriona hard, but it was a relief to be able to think about the ache in her arms and back, rather than the dark labyrinth inside her head. They were fixing up a shed for some rich guy's yacht, and he had her carrying wood and tools, ripping out old rotted timbers, hammering and painting and varnishing, even climbing around on the roof. He didn't chat very much when they worked, except to issue instructions and ask for things. Sometimes he sang under his breath, just like Granny Mary did, probably not even realising he was doing it. His voice brought her back to those nights in his flat in Aberdeen, when she was scared of the dark and he sang her to sleep. They were good times, maybe even the best of her life. She didn't know anything then. She was too little to look into the future and understand what she was about to lose. The unfulfilled promises of California seemed insubstantial compared to that.

Sometimes she wanted to ask Calum why he never brought her over there like he promised, but she knew it would lead to an argument and she didn't have the stomach for it. They had come to an unspoken agreement: he didn't ask about *that boy* and she didn't whinge about his paternal absenteeism. In this unquestioning silence, days slipped by more easily. The labour opened a valve in her skull and released some of the pressure. She began to sleep again.

Mary usually went to bed early. The efforts of social interaction seemed to weigh heavily on her by eight o'clock. A carer was now coming to help her while Calum and Catriona were at work. They went shopping or to the church, or sometimes just to the pub for tea or a bowl of soup. On Thursdays she was picked up in a minibus and taken to lunch with other pensioners in Mallaig, complaining as she departed and complaining as she returned, about the saltiness of the food, the senility of the company, the bingo, the mediocrity of the accordion player, the fact that Calum would rather pack her off with a load of elderly fools than have her in the house.

After tea Mary would watch the news, still trying to keep up with events the way she always had, and she would doze on the sofa until Calum turned the telly off.

Catriona was grateful for the evenings without her. She began to explore the woods and the beach, following the rocky headland as it curved out of the bay, opening up the view of the islands, and then in again to another smaller cove. She watched the waves, watched terns and gannets dive into the water, sometimes saw one of the sea eagles unfurl like a roll of dark cloth and rise over the far hillside. She almost never saw another person. Her fear subsided a little, although creaks and rustles in the woods still made her startle, pause and listen for footsteps.

Making her way home one evening, she saw Julie digging in her garden, man's shirt knotted at the waist, hair tied up in a forties-style headscarf. She waved and Catriona went over hesitantly, smoothing her sweaty T-shirt and raking her fingers through putty-spiked hair.

Julie hugged her as if they'd known each other for years. 'How you doing, my love? Sorry, I'm covered in muck.'

'I'm permanently covered in muck now,' Catriona said, showing Julie her broken and stained fingernails. 'You still look glam, though. Most people don't look that good hoeing a garden.'

'Oh,' Julie looked down at herself, 'I'm just a scrawny waif and a slave to my red lippy. I'd give anything for a pair of decent tits.'

Catriona allowed herself to laugh. 'You can have some of mine.'

Julie looked at them, let her speech broaden comfortably. 'You're a sculptor's dream, hen.' Then she ran her hand up Catriona's arm. 'You're a braw lassie. Calum says you look just like your mam.'

'Aye, I guess I do. More than him, anyway.'

'There's something about the eyes. Maybe the shape of the forehead.' She scrutinised Catriona's face for a few seconds, then smiled. 'I was just about to crack open a bottle of red Spanish plonk. You want some?'

'I was just on my way home.'

'Oh, go on. Just the one.'

Catriona glanced over her shoulder. 'Yeah, okay.' She followed Julie in through the kitchen door and copied her in removing her shoes. The kitchen was small, plain and square, and when Julie opened the cupboards to bring out the wine and glasses, Catriona noticed that they were nearly empty: a couple of boxes of muesli, a few jars of spices, a packet of chocolate biscuits. She must barely eat. There were, however, at least twenty wine glasses.

The living room was mismatched and chaotic. It led your eyes on a manic ramble from one thing to another: art that didn't adhere to any kind of theme, surreal contemporary paintings next to folksy driftwood crafts, ethnic rugs, old wooden chairs that had been painted and covered with beads and bottle caps, conflicting colours and textures. Nude women, lots of them: little statuettes on the shelves, paintings and drawings on the walls. The smell of incense covered up something more pungent, probably cannabis.

Julie motioned to a worn lime green velvet sofa. 'Have a seat. Is it warm enough in here? Should I make a fire?'

'I'm fine,' Catriona said, trying not to stare at the painting of a naked pregnant woman on the wall directly opposite her. She sipped her wine and her gaze darted from place to place.

'I know it's a bit of a riot, but I can't live without colour.'

'I like it.'

Julie laughed. 'It's not everybody's taste. I'm not exactly an accent wall and matching cushion kind of woman. My landlord won't let me paint the walls. If I did, I'd have every one different. The only thing he's ever let me do to the house was put the shells around the front door.'

'They're beautiful.'

'He thinks they look traditional, whereas purple and yellow walls are just ... you know ... ' she shrugged, 'vandalism.'

'So how did you end up here? You seem more of a city person.'

'I am, but I need my bolthole.' Julie drank deeply, put her glass down and picked up a pencil and a small sketchpad from the table beside her chair. She opened to a blank page and began to draw. 'May I?' She glanced up at Catriona.

'You're drawing me? Why?'

'Because you're bonny.'

'Hardly.'

'Aye, you are. You're right, I am a city person. My heart belongs to Glasgow, as they say. I do a lot of teaching and workshops down there, but ... I can't live there all the time. I don't have a place there, I stay in my pals' spare room. I'm a migratory bird, I guess. Glendarach is my sanctuary when my head starts to overload.'

'Doesn't it feel weird to move back and forth so much?'

There was something intriguing about Julie, something deep and magnetic like a blossom full of nectar. Catriona wasn't sure how much curiosity was acceptable.

'I'm used to it.' She tilted her head, closed one eye, looking at Catriona as her hand moved across the paper.

'You've never been married?'

'No. I don't have a good track record with men. I lived with a guy for a few years in my twenties. Stuart was a fair bit older than me. He was ... a very well-established artist and teacher, he was passionate and brilliant and gorgeous. I was totally enthralled by him. The first year was like the most perfect honeymoon and then when he thought I was his forever, he let his out inner bastard. He was controlling and abusive. He was known for it, apparently, but none of our so-called friends could be bothered to tell me until I found out for myself.'

'Oh God, I'm sorry, I'm asking too many questions.'

'No you're not.' Her hand stopped moving, the sharp point of the pencil poised above the page, and her eyes were open wide and round. Catriona's breath quickened. Julie knew something. Calum had told her something. He suspected ... what? What did he suspect? It wouldn't be so hard to guess. He'd sent Julie to fish it out of her.

'He shoved me around and slapped me. Someone pissed him off at work, he had a glass too many on his way home, he overheard me arranging a meeting and thought I was two-timing – any old time he felt like it, really. It took him breaking my arm before I got off my arse and left.'

'Honestly?'

It was hard to imagine. It seemed like something so bad would show – like you could look at a person and read the history like words tattooed on their skin – but it didn't. Not on Julie.

'Where did you go?'

226

'The women's shelter first. Then London. Then Paris. Then Sydney. I was afraid to stay in any one place too long. Maybe I still am.'

'So where is he? Glasgow?'

'Yip. Married, with a son. I bumped into him and his wife at an opening a couple of years ago. He made out that we were old friends, and she made out she was the adoring wife. Fuck, I wanted to get her alone and ask her if he was still at it.'

'You could have just told her, right there in public.'

A slow nod, and for the first time a shadow of regret crossed Julie's face. 'I could have. I was too weak to confront him. I didn't want to make a scene. I doubt he has any idea how badly he hurt me. We're not fully human to men like that. I couldn't be with a man for years after that. I had a lot of girlfriends before I hooked up with your dad.'

She started drawing again, a long spiral of hair hanging over her forehead. Catriona leaned forward a little to try to see the paper, but it was tilted away from her. 'So why my dad?'

Julie lifted one shoulder. 'He doesn't ask for more than I can give him. He's gentle. He knows what it's like to have this monstrous black thing inside you. He has his weird moods and so do I and we get each other. I might even go as far as to say I love him, but don't tell him I said that.'

'How come?'

Julie picked up her wine glass and smiled at it. She took a moment to think about how to answer this, but before she could, there was a soft knock and Calum came in the front door.

'Speak of the devil,' Julie said. 'His ears must have been burning.' She laughed at him. 'Did you lose someone?'

'I wondered where you'd got to,' he said to Cat. 'You all right?'

Catriona raised her wine glass towards him. 'Just fine.'

Julie put down her pencil and gently tore the sheet out of the pad. 'Here. Your daughter.'

Calum looked at the drawing and smiled. He stared at it for ages. Catriona could see his body sway with each breath.

'Let me see, Dad.'

He handed it to her. She saw a girl with full lips and deep eyes. She was intelligent, rebellious, strong. It looked like her but didn't feel like her. It felt like who she wanted to be.

'I wish I could draw like this,' she said, offering the drawing back to Julie.

'It's for you.'

'Oh ... okay. Thank you.' She stood up. They'd want to be alone. They'd want time to talk about her. 'I'll just go. I think I'll have a bath. Thanks for the wine, Julie.'

Sitting on the edge of the tub as the bath filled, she thought about Julie's story. Julie would be around Calum's age, maybe slightly younger, and it had taken her since her twenties to want to be with a man again? That was as long as Catriona had been alive, or maybe more. A life sentence.

Maybe women were the answer. Who really needed men anyway? She didn't think she wanted children, so why bother with men at all?

It had never crossed her mind to be with another girl.

She swirled her fingers in the water and wondered what it would be like.

She didn't suppose it mattered. A girl would still touch her. A girl would still say *trust me*, and that was the problem. That was never going to happen.

NIRVANA

'I want you to have it,' Julie said. She set the sculpture of Finn and the angel on the coffee table in front of him. 'I don't care what you do with it. You can bury it, you can put it on his gravestone, you can leave it out in the woods somewhere, it doesn't bother me. It's up to you.'

'Are you sure?'

'Of course. It's yours.'

Calum wanted to tell her to put it back into the studio, chip the images away and use the remaining stone for something else. Or otherwise just take a sledgehammer to it. He could wait until she went down to Glasgow and do it himself. Except it was Julie's art and he was no iconoclast. She had her own reasons for making it, and for giving it to him. She wanted him to do something meaningful with it.

'I don't know where it should go.'

'It'll come to you.' Julie turned him by the shoulders and began to massage his back, making circular motions down his spine with her callused sculptor's fingers. 'I told Cat about Stuart.'

He glanced back at her. 'What did she say?'

'Not much.'

'She's good at saying not much.'

'I think she wants to. She asked me a lot of questions. She's not antisocial, she's just afraid.'

'Afraid of what?'

'I don't know. Of being judged? Maybe of being let down.'

'Or dropped.' He touched Finn's stone face.

'You didn't drop him.'

'Mmm. I know I didn't. I just about killed myself trying to catch the bastard and he didn't even want me to.'

He turned and slipped his arm around her shoulder. She nestled into his side and they sat together for a while as the light outside dimmed and the water turned from turquoise to gold to silicon. They sipped wine and didn't talk. They didn't do this very often – maybe it was too domestic for comfort – but it was nice for as long as it might last.

Julie dozed. She reminded him of the cats they'd had as children: affectionate but only on their own terms. They might sit in your lap and purr for twenty minutes and then slash your hand open without warning.

He closed his eyes. Julie's drawing of Catriona materialised behind his eyelids. It was Catriona without the personal storm cloud hanging over her. It was also the spitting image of Jenny as she'd been at eighteen, that first hungover morning in his flat in Aberdeen.

ABERDEEN, NOVEMBER 1993

The girl was there again when he went back to the pub with his fiddle the following week. The girl with the white hair and kissable lips. Tonight they were painted dark burgundy. She'd done herself up a bit: motorcycle jacket, black and white striped skirt, purple tights, ankle boots with kitten heels. She and her pal had settled themselves at the table nearest the snug where the musicians sat. They were already merry with drink by the time he arrived. He threw back a whisky at the bar, carried his Guinness over to the table, went through the obligatory meet-and-greet and got his fiddle out. He fielded a hundred questions about the accident and his convalescence as he rubbed rosin on the bow and tuned up, replying that he didn't want to talk about it but would accept drams of condolence. These were supplied with such generosity that he knew it would rapidly become a messy night. He was not going to be capable of moderation. All the while, the girls watched him. When they played, the girl with the white hair tapped her heel and rattled her thumb on the table. She looked like she wanted to get up and dance. Sometimes she and her friend would lean in and say something, and they'd both giggle. Her face turned a brighter shade of pink as the night went on.

After a while he went outside for a smoke, hoping a blast of icy air would settle the tide of whisky already running high in his blood. He inserted the fag into his mouth, flicked the lighter, drew deeply, exhaled an opaque lungful into the night. The smoke hung there in a shocked cloud, like it was having second thoughts.

'Hey,' she said, materialising behind him. There was no mistaking it; she'd come looking for him. She tapped her own packet of cigarettes and slid one out. 'I've lost my lighter. Have you got one?'

He pulled his Zippo from his pocket and she bent towards the small flame.

'Ta.'

'No worries.'

They stood there as smokers do, united in vice. 'Where did you learn to play fiddle like that?'

'Home.' He drew on the cigarette again and wondered what had happened to his chat. Even on a relatively good day, the structure of language seemed to melt into a formless puddle as soon as he tried to articulate it.

'Where's home?'

'West coast. Glendarach. Near Arisaig.'

'Never heard of it.'

He shrugged. 'Most people haven't.'

Her lips flickered into an uncertain smile. His bluntness had unsettled her. I'm not really like this, he wanted to say, but what would be the point? She'd be scared off before he would manage to explain himself.

'So what brings you to Aberdeen, then? Don't tell me oil.'

'Oil.'

'No! How come the only guys I ever meet are roughnecks?'

'You must be hanging around the wrong bars,' he said. 'Anyway, I'm an engineer, not a roughneck.'

'It's all the same to me. I'm Jenny, by the way.'

'Calum.'

'Nice to meet you.' She offered him a hand. 'Sorry, my fingers are frozen. Why'd you come out here to smoke?'

'For the fresh air.' He laughed. 'Why did you?'

'To talk to you, obviously.'

'Oh good. These things can be misinterpreted.'

He woke up beside her, the bed listing on an unstable earth. After that first conversation amidst the frosty night vapours, he remembered thinking or perhaps saying *bugger it* and launching into a headlong drinking session, embracing the whisky like a cliff diver reaching for the deep water beyond the rocks. It had been a long time since he'd allowed himself to get so drunk.

Somehow they'd made it back to his flat. He couldn't remember inviting her, couldn't remember coming up the stairs, couldn't quite remember what had happened next. There were lingering sensations: mouth on mouth, skin on skin, her smell: clove cigarettes and Poison perfume. The fact that they were both now naked suggested that they had not stopped at polite first-night exploration, and a throbbing ache in his knee hinted at the kind of exertion it had become unaccustomed to.

A faint sense of unease added to the hangover. In the cold light of morning, with eyeliner smudged below her eyes, she looked vulnerable and very young. Far too young, in fact. The queasiness in his gullet threatened to become full-blown nausea. He sat up slowly, let his feet rest on the floorboards for a few seconds before testing his ability to stand without falling over. The effort brought a sweat to his forehead; it was going to be a grim day. The best thing would be to go back to bed, but he suspected he didn't smell very good and didn't want to lie beside her anymore. He scooped up last night's jeans and shirt, washed his face, dressed, forced down a couple of paracetamols with a pint of water, filled the kettle and smoked out the window while he waited for it to boil.

Tea brought some of the details into sharper focus. They'd walked her friend (name now lost) home and then Jenny had said, 'I'd invite you back but I'm in halls. The bed's barely big enough for half a person.'

'They do that on purpose. It's called contraceptive furniture.'

She'd laughed at this: a joyful sound. They'd walked slowly, holding on to each other, ending up back here without any real discussion. He remembered trying not to limp obviously; he didn't want questions or a sympathy shag, and he didn't want Finn spoiling the party like he'd been doing for years. You could never have a girl back here when Finn was around.

Jenny appeared, wearing his dressing gown, her hair standing up on one side of her head and flattened on the other, her cheek creased from the pillow. He lifted his head from the wall. 'There's tea in the pot.'

She poured herself a cup and wrapped her hands around it. 'How are you?'

'Penitent.' He closed his eyes and crossed himself for emphasis. 'And a bit sick. I hope we didn't . . . '

'We did.'

'Do anything you didn't want to do.'

'No . . . don't worry.' She sat down across from him and almost managed to make the morning after look sexy. 'And I *am* eighteen, because I know you're wondering.'

'That's . . . good to know.'

She sipped her tea and looked around his kitchen, surveying gig posters and clutter, a peroxide-dipped detective gathering titbits, waiting for him to offer further conversation. 'You don't talk very much, do you?' It wasn't a challenge, just an observation.

'You're not seeing me at my loquacious best this morning.'

'Loquacious? That's a good word.' She raised a thin black eyebrow. 'Are you ever?'

'Not often.'

'I like your flat.'

'My mother was here a few days ago and cleaned it for me. You wouldn't have liked it much before.'

'Do you always get your mum to clean your flat?'

'No. She's just trying to be helpful since I broke my leg.' *Helpful.* Maybe Mary thought so, with her bags of shopping and her venomous advice. He was still nursing the wounds from their last conversation. She'd phoned him twice since then, but he'd taken to screening his calls and wasn't in the mood for making up.

'I was going to ask you about that. What did you do?'

'I had a bad day climbing in the Cairngorms, back in July.'

'Oh.' She shrugged this off with the carelessness of her age. 'D'you mind if I look around?'

'Go ahead.'

She wandered off and he stayed in the kitchen, gingerly swallowing tea and exhaling anxiety. The flurry of visitors

234

he'd had immediately after the accident had died down quickly, and the flat had become quiet and still as a monastic cell. He could spend days on end alone. He could spend a day without uttering a word and another talking to himself in Pig Latin if he wanted. He couldn't see his life any more, he could only feel it from the dark place in the middle. He didn't know what she might see.

The strum of a guitar came from the lounge. He was protective of it after the disappearance of his predecessor, and he hurried to its rescue. Then he stopped abruptly in the doorway. She was playing Nirvana, gently but competently. 'Lithium'. Jesus, of all the hundreds of songs she might have chosen.

'Can you sing that?' he asked, stepping into the lounge.

She lowered the guitar. 'Sorry, I should have asked.'

'It's all right.' He sat down across from her.

'You like Nirvana?'

'Not really, but go ahead.'

Pink splotches appeared on her cheeks. 'You're making me nervous. I don't sing in front of people.'

'Close your eyes and pretend I'm not here.'

She picked up the guitar again, shifted on the sofa so that her shoulder faced him, and sang in a husky voice that might fly if she allowed it to. Her hair fell over her eyes as she played and there was a raggedness in her expression that spoke of more than a hangover. She understood the song, and for the first time in six months, he was curious about someone.

When she finished, he said, 'You're not a bad singer.'

'Thank you.'

'My brother used to think that song was about him.'

'That's worrying.' She held the guitar close against her chest, her fingers still on the strings.

'Aye, it was.'

'I hope he's better now.'

'He killed himself.'

Jenny lifted her eyes and met his. 'Oh fuck. Honestly?'

Suddenly he knew it was true, as if he'd seen the event again in slow motion: Finn's deliberate neglect of his protection, the breakneck speed, the wild reach for a hold that was so far above him he never stood a chance, his body launching itself upward, then out, then down. It was always going to happen. Finn knew it was going to happen, if not that day then another. Maybe that had been the whole point of his climbing from the very beginning. He had been practising the art of a beautiful suicide.

He carried the stone angel home, wrapped it in an old towel and stowed it at the back of his wardrobe. It couldn't stay there forever; it would sing at him every time he opened the door and he'd be compelled to unwrap it and look at it. It would have some weird hold over him, like a magical object in an old story. Julie had no idea what power she had.

He listened at Mary and Catriona's doors. Both rooms were silent, so he felt safe to bring out the little bag of cannabis and roll himself a thin joint. He smoked it in his bedroom with the window open, watched the moonlight shimmering on the black water and tried to figure out what to do with the damned statue.

THE PIPER OF
GLENDARACH

The birches had developed their first golden fringes. Mary
looked up from the sink and thought of Jack. Every year, the
first signs of autumn brought memories of his final weeks.
After he died, she pinned up her hair and carried on. Just
keep going: that was what he did, and what he would have
wanted her to do. She was praised for her strength. That was
something to be proud of. But still, she would never know
how she survived that first winter without him.

She washed four carrots, topped and tailed them, and
chopped them into small cubes. They went into the pot with
the onions and turnip. She poured in hot water and crumbled
a stock cube with her fingers, watching the yellow powder
dissolve into the liquid. The smell of soup filled the kitchen.
She put the lid on the pot, poured herself a thumb-width of
whisky and added water and an ice cube. She'd never cared
for the taste of whisky but it stopped her mind tumbling
around so much. It helped her to relax. It was only a tiny
dram and surely Calum wouldn't miss it. He drank too much
of it himself anyway. He was his father's son that way, and
in many others.

Both of the boys were far more like Jack than they were
like her. They had inherited his extremes: his wild joys and

237

red rages. His busy legs and his busy mind. As children, they could never sit still. The worst behaviour always happened at Mass: poking, kicking, bumping around like monkeys, sliding down onto the floor, making rude bodily noises. Arched eyebrows and disapproving looks came from every direction. Jack, God rest his soul, was no help. He refused to come. He said if she was going to insist on subjecting his sons to that weekly torment, she would do it on her own. Finn was only young but Calum should have been able to control himself. Around his brother, he seemed to regress.

She tried banishing them to their rooms after Mass, but within a couple of weeks they found a way to rig up a rope and climb out the window. Off they'd go with their dad, the three of them, away into the hills for the rest of the day. Jack must have given them the rope. He was a wicked man. 'Incorrigible' was the word her mother used. He had the devil and too much whisky in him. She'd been well warned from the first time Jack came courting. He's not for you, *a ghràidh*. All the little sayings. The finer the musician, the poorer the husband. You will never be done saying goodbye to him.

The warnings had come true after all, but not in the way her mother had predicted.

The sound of the pipes entered her ears. Mary closed her eyes and listened. Sometimes her imaginings were so real it seemed like she could reach out and grasp them, except when she tried she found out they weren't there.

Sometimes imaginings did actually become things. She imagined Finn's death, many times over, before it happened.

She followed the sound, through the garden and around to the front of the house, over the road onto the beach. Calum was standing on the stones at the end of the beach where Jack always used to play, the drones over his shoulder, the Black Watch tartan bag under his arm. Jack's pipes had been lost or stolen years ago, but from a distance these looked just like them.

And Calum, standing there with his feet slightly apart like that. If she let her eyes fall out of focus he became Jack. They had been the best times, those long light hours of early summer, mild evenings with just enough breeze to keep the midges from flying. She would sit with a book and Jack piped, out there on the rocks so the sound went out to sea. The boys dove around the water like seals or disappeared into the woods. They could be out of sight and out of mind for a little while. That respite had always been her precious time. Perhaps she had been selfish that way. A mother wasn't supposed to be grateful when her children were out of sight, but she was.

Jack had wanted to move to Glasgow, where the work was more plentiful and the children would have opportunities they'd never have here. But they wouldn't have this, she said. A grey terrace somewhere, broken tarmac to play on, the noise of city traffic day and night. She would look out across the bay and tell him, not for my boys. Not for any money. So they would grow wild and they would be fine.

Except they weren't.

She returned to the present and focused on Calum again. The tones were punctuated by squawks and wrong notes. Jack never made a noise as awful as that. Catriona was sitting on the rocks behind him with her fingers in her ears. She looked over as Mary began to pick her way over the rounded stones.

'Stay there, Gran,' she called, skipping over on her toes. 'It's too slippy. You'll fall.'

'Where did he get those pipes?'

'They're my granddad's.'

'Your granddad's pipes were stolen.'

'No they weren't, Gran. He found them.'

'I don't think so,' Mary said.

Catriona shrugged but didn't argue. They stood together on the sand and Calum started to play a march. Mary watched his fingers flicker over the holes. The sound was wrong. They couldn't be Jack's pipes. She scowled and remembered her soup.

'The soup will be boiling over.' She turned away from Catriona and went back to the house. The pot lid was rattling and spewing steam. She turned down the heat, lifted the lid, stirred the contents. She could smell that it had burned at the bottom. Tears came to her eyes. She couldn't keep track of anything, couldn't even focus her mind long enough to make a pot of vegetable soup.

Calum and Catriona followed her in.

'You've made me burn the soup with all that racket.'

'It'll be fine.' He didn't even look at it.

'It won't taste good.'

'It will. Don't worry, Mum. See, I found the pipes.'

'Where were they?'

'Just where you said. In the suitcase, in the eaves.'

'Whose eaves?'

'Yours, Mum. In your flat.'

'Who put them there?'

'*You* did. Look ... come here.' He showed her the instrument.

She touched the frayed black tassel at the end of the chord. 'Jack's pipes were stolen.'

'No they weren't. They're right here. I've had the reeds replaced.'

It was impossible to know whether he was telling the truth. 'They don't sound the way they did when your father played them.'

Calum laughed. 'That's because I can't play them. I haven't lifted a set of pipes since before he died.'

240

'Finn was always the better piper.'

'I know he was. I never liked them, to be honest.'

'Didn't you?'

'No. You look upset, Mum.'

Her eyes were watering again, but she couldn't explain it to him. It felt so new, all this loss. She shook her head, trying to dislodge it. 'I've burnt the soup. It won't taste good.'

Catriona dipped a spoon into the pot and sipped a little. 'It tastes fine to me.'

She was a sweet girl, Mary thought. There was a kindness in her, underneath all that silly get up. 'Will you have a bowl?'

'Yes please, Gran, I'm starving.'

'Calum?'

'Aye.' He put the pipes into their case.

'It's burnt a wee bit. I heard the pipes and I thought ... well ... I got distracted.'

Calum sighed. 'It's fine, Mum.'

AXE

Life moved at a different speed in Glendarach. Nobody rushed for anything, nobody cared about being late, nobody checked their watches or their phones. It was the light and the land that reminded you of the hours and the weeks passing. Catriona counted the yellow leaves and knew that the time for a decision was coming: stay or go. Aberdeen or Edinburgh. Back to university and to hell with Kyle, or quit and let him win.

They worked most of the day in the woods, removing low branches, clearing excess undergrowth, creating space and allowing light to reach the young trees. Calum turned his axe on a dense thicket of rhododendrons, merciless in a way that made her almost pity the bushes. Why he had to bust a gut with the axe when there was a perfectly good chainsaw in his shed, she had no idea. If she asked, he'd probably lecture her about the virtues of doing things the hard way. Catriona decided that sometimes it was better not to ask.

She'd been cutting smaller branches with a bow saw and loading them into the trailer to drag back to the woodshed. She was weary but satisfied by her expanding stack of firewood. It had taken her a while to find a stance that gave her enough purchase with the saw, but now it was feeling more comfortable and her cuts were long and smooth. Her arms didn't ache as much as they had when she'd first arrived and she'd lost some of the weight she'd gained at uni. It happened so effortlessly when you did physical work. Your mind cleared and your body took over. Hours could pass and you could think about anything you wanted, or nothing at all. Edinburgh was dreary student rooms and interminable lectures, waking up sticky after half-forgotten nights out and everything coloured with the dark red shadow of threat. But from here, those things were irrelevant. Waking up was easy here.

Maybe this was the point of not using the chainsaw.

She paused, picked a couple of blackberries and ate them, watched Calum swing the axe with brutal efficiency. 'Remind me not to fall out with you when you've got that thing in your hand.'

He backed out of the devastation and straightened up, rubbing his right shoulder as he came over to the trailer and looked in. He didn't look displeased, and she'd learned to take that as a compliment. Then he held out the axe. 'I call this the Mood Adjustor. You want a shot?'

'Does it work?'

'Absolutely.'

She slipped her fingers around the handle. 'Okay.'

'Swing it hard.'

'Uh huh.' At least he didn't patronise her by reminding her to keep her body parts out of the way. She walked around the far side of the thicket and found a stretch of clean, smooth trunk. The rhododendron had grown into a bonny tree, but Calum was determined to keep the invaders off his land. She supposed that centuries ago, the Macdonalds of old would have been swinging their axes at less inert enemies: Vikings, Campbells, Redcoats, others she had no idea about. She knew nothing of their history, but she thought the name was one you could be proud of. Catriona Macdonald sounded good. Better than Smith, which had always felt so workaday.

Macdonald evoked something – this place, the language he and Granny Mary spoke, a kinship with all of those people in that graveyard. It would be an almighty slap in her mum's face if she decided to take Calum's name now. Jenny didn't deserve that.

She faced the wood and fingered the blade, remembering. Remembering Calum the way he'd been five years ago. Remembering the way she'd treated him that day. Remembering Edinburgh, and that house in the woods. The laughter of those girls at that party. Their horrid, high-pitched laughter. Remembering the shock of the cold water hitting her.

Then she clutched the handle with both hands, touched it to the trunk, drew it back and swung as hard as she could. The blade embedded itself deep in the wood and sent jarring reverberations up her arms. With a grunt, she pulled it out and swung again.

At first the axe bounced and refused to hit the same spot twice, and it seemed like the wood had some impervious inner core. Her arms hurt and felt too weak to keep swinging. She had stopped fighting Kyle because she'd been too tired, too wasted by the stuff they'd both been smoking. Maybe she'd stopped fighting because she'd thought it would be easier just to let him have her at last and then forget about it. Like a child pestering for a toy, he'd play with her once and realise how boring she was. It was only sex.

Eventually the axe began to land cleanly in the same cut and small chips began to fly out. She chopped until her muscles turned to liquid. A wedge opened up and the giant shrub began to creak as it leaned toward her. She stepped to the side, then pushed on the trunk and watched the rhododendron subside, its shiny green foliage rustling and crushing under its own weight. Wiping sweat from her forehead, she lifted the cut end and dragged the full trunk out of the thicket.

Calum was sitting on the back of the trailer, whittling at a stick with a pocketknife, singing under his breath.

'Glad one of us is working, anyway,' she said, and dropped the axe at his feet. 'You knackered, auld man?'

'Just on my break, boss.' He poured tea into the cap of his flask and handed it to her. 'Tell me you don't feel better.'

'Aye, I was pretending the tree was somebody's neck.'

'Pity the poor bastard who gets you as an executioner. It'd be a long, painful death.'

'Excuse me, I cut that thing down in ten swings.'

'Fifty swings, more like.' He held up a rough-hewn implement that might eventually resemble a spoon. 'What do you think?'

'Aye, great, if you want a muckle big skelf o'wood in your tongue with every bite.'

He laughed and swung it toward her face. 'Good for beating insolent teenagers with, though.'

'Don't even think about it. I've still got the axe.' She picked up the handle and danced away from him, notes of laughter escaping when she opened her mouth. They subsided and the forest gathered around them again. She thought back on that scene at home five years ago. The way he couldn't look at anyone and seemed so humiliated by himself. He'd been ill and she'd been cruel. 'I wish I'd come here before now.'

He looked at her curiously. 'Why didn't you?'

'I don't know. I guess I felt ashamed about the things I said to you last time.'

'You were fourteen.' He shrugged. 'You were right. I wouldn't have been fit company for you or anyone else.'

There was little relief in this, only more shame. 'I never understood what happened to you. How did you get like that?'

Calum sighed, folded his knife and slipped it back into his pocket. 'I don't know. There isn't always a reason. Since

Finn died, or maybe before that, I felt like I was just ... play acting at being normal. Like I was wearing the costume of a sane person, and actually beneath it I was this big messy ball of ... barely contained stuff, like a reactor core, and I went through my life shit scared of being exposed.'

It was as if he'd peeled back her own skin and described what he'd seen. The air cooled against her damp shirt and made her shiver. She wanted him to know without having to tell him. Why couldn't somebody invent a way to transfer information from brain to brain, like you could between computers? It was the saying of it that hurt. She glanced towards the treetops.

'I feel like that all the time.'

'I thought you might.' His look was sharp, full of intention. 'It's not nice when you melt down, Cat, trust me. I should have got help after Finn died, but I didn't. I was pretty near the edge then and someone managed to pull me back.'

'Who?'

'Your mum. I don't think she fully realises.'

So why didn't you stay, she wondered. And why didn't you tell her? And why didn't you tell me? Questions opened like wrappers onto more questions, a never-ending game of pass the parcel. How would you know when to stop? What if you kept asking and unwrapping until you ran out of questions and found out there was no answer?

'What about now?'

'It's an easier act now.'

She sat beside him. The woods whispered and creaked, and the breeze brought the smell of low tide into their clearing. There was a cooler edge to the air today, a moist autumnal smell on the breeze. She propped her elbows on her knees and pressed her sticky hands over her eyes. 'I'm scared about going back.'

'What are you scared of? Is it this boy?'

246

'Yeah. And I'm afraid . . . of myself . . . that I won't be able to cope with things. I'm scared I might . . . do what you did. Lose my disguise.'

Calum's hand fell onto her back and rested there, a broad, reassuring warmth. 'Catriona, what did he do to you?'

'He . . . ' she took a deep breath. If she was ever going to name the thing, it had to be now. 'He raped me. I was drunk, at a party, and he carried me into the shower and made me suck him off. And then he held me against the wall and . . . you know. Fucked me.'

EDINBURGH, MAY 2014

Kyle wasn't just drunk. He'd taken something, some kind of tablet that she didn't know the name of, and it made him crazy. Wild, horny crazy that was hilarious and terrifying at the same time. He held forth in the kitchen, proclaiming Scotland's forthcoming liberation while two girls painted his bare chest blue with their fingers. Enjoying the job enough to call it foreplay. Catriona didn't know where the paint had come from, or the tablets, or the girls. Somebody was laughing, freaky shrieky laughter, a girl or a high-pitched boy. It might have been that they were laughing at her, but she couldn't tell where it was coming from. It might have been coming through the air vents like gas.

She didn't know whose big modern house this was, in the woods at the end of a long, dark drive. Somebody's parents were loaded, and clearly absent. She wanted to leave and walk home, but they'd come in a taxi and she didn't know where they were. Kyle claimed these were 'his people' but she had never met them before. He hadn't bothered to introduce her to anyone.

The combination of vodka and hash had tipped the whole

world to one side. She had to concentrate to stay on the sofa and re-order her surroundings. While the world keeled, the party continued, a dark and sweaty scrum of bodies and music. She tried to focus on what Kyle was doing with those girls. She leaned into the sofa cushions and tried to think herself back straight, but strands of her mind kept spinning off out of control. There was something wrong with gravity. It felt better when she closed her eyes, but she was so sleepy and you couldn't go to sleep at a party. Nobody was bothering her, though. It was like they couldn't see her. Maybe a wee doze would make her feel better. Just for a minute.

A girl said, 'Aw, bless! Look, it's Sleeping Beauty.'

Another said, 'Sleeping, anyway. Don't know about Beauty.'

More squawking laughter, looming music, a jolt as a body dropped onto the sofa beside her. Catriona opened her eyes and realised it was herself they were talking about. Kyle, now with half his face painted, shoved his hand between her back and the cushions and hauled her onto his lap.

'Come here, sleepy Cat.' He bumped his lips roughly onto hers.

'Kyle . . .' she pushed him away. 'How long was I sleeping?'

'Hours and hours! Is it past wee Kitty Cat's bedtime?'

She squeezed her eyes shut and opened them again. He looked like a demented clown. His lips were red with someone else's lipstick. She was bursting for a pee. She tried to squirm off his lap, but he held on, his fingers digging into her waist.

'Come on, Kyle, let go.' The words came out in a breathy gust.

'No. I'm not letting you go. Anything could happen to you in this den of iniquity.'

She thought she might be sick. 'Kyle, I need the toilet . . . please.'

'I'll take you to the toilet.' He gripped her more tightly and stood up, cradled her in his arms like a toddler, bashing her knees off the doorframe as he staggered out of the room. She wrapped her arms around his neck. At least he was hers again. Just hers. Whatever those other girls thought they were going to get, he had come back to her.

They went down a long corridor, bumping against walls. Bedrooms on the right and left, writhing bodies in various stages and combinations of intercourse: two, three, more people in a bed, girls and boys, legs and breasts and arses all tangled and layered. None of them seemed to care about being seen, but she didn't want to see. She didn't want to connect any of these bodies with the face of someone she'd have to sit beside in a lecture. She stopped struggling and turned her head into Kyle's chest. In a large, entirely white-tiled bathroom, he fumbled for the shower door and dumped her inside. Her legs collapsed under her and before she could stand, he turned on the water. She screamed as the cold stream hit her.

'Kyle!' She struggled to her feet but her legs were so wobbly. 'What the fuck? You bastard!'

He was leaning on the door so she couldn't push it open, laughing madly and stripping off his remaining clothes. 'Let's have a shower, Cat. We're dirty. We're so fucking dirty. We need a shower.'

Catriona managed to turn off the water, but Kyle kicked his boxers aside and stepped in, pressed himself against her, pinning her to the wall. He hit the tap again and the water cascaded over both of them, now warming.

'Cat, my love, relax.' He kissed her and petted her hair. Blue paint ran in streaks down his body and pooled around his feet. 'This is good, baby. Trust me, you want this. Come on, let's get your clothes off. What are you playing at, having a shower in your clothes, daft girl.'

'I don't want to do this,' she moaned.

'Of course you do.' He caught the bottom of her dress and pulled it over her head, then unhooked her bra. 'Jesus, girl, look at those peaches. So sweet. Cat, you're beautiful, what are you afraid of? I won't hurt you.' He pressed his face into her breasts and his dick against her belly. Then he put his hands on her shoulders and pushed her down to her knees.

'Have a taste, Kitten.'

She closed her eyes and gave in.

She'd held it in and held it in and held it in for so many weeks, and now it came out like a fully armed torpedo. The most overused word in the English language, or at least in the Scots one. It rolled off the tongue so easily most of the time that it became meaningless. But that's what Kyle did: a deed, not a word. He fucked me. He. Fucked. Me. He did that. To me.

She couldn't look at Calum to tell whether he had winced or closed his eyes or paled with paternal fury. He was so still beside her, he might have been holding his breath or he might have become petrified and cracked and turned to ash. He didn't speak. There was half a minute of poisoned, droning silence. She stared at the ground, and out of the corners of her eyes she could see movements in the woods: birds and insects moving, brave because of their stillness, gathering back into the space. If they stayed still long enough, the insects would crawl over their skin and lay eggs and hatch out, and their clothes would rot away and fungi would grow from their damp skin. They would be subsumed into the moist bed of leaves and moss like those people who had lived here long ago and left only rectangles of stone behind as evidence.

He took a deep breath. 'Oh Cat.'

She swallowed hard and wanted so badly not to cry.

'Did you report it?' he asked.

'No. I mean, how could I? We'd gone out before. How could I make anyone believe he forced me? I couldn't face that.'

'Your mum doesn't know?'

'No. Don't lecture me, okay, I know I should have told her. I should have told you. I couldn't. I'm sorry.'

'Why are you apologising?' He stared at her, his face almost childlike in its disbelief. 'Dear God, Catriona, why are you apologising to me?'

'Because I've ruined the way you'll think of me forever.'

'Don't say that.' His hands were in his hair, tufts emerging from between his fingers. Did he put his hands to his head to keep something out or hold something else in?

'That's why I came here,' she said. 'He kept trying to call me and I was afraid if I stayed at home this summer he'd find me.'

'Tell me his name.'

'Kyle. Kyle Hunter. Why?'

'Because if he ever shows up here I will do something to him with that axe, I promise you.'

She knew that he meant it, if only for the moment. 'It doesn't make me feel better to hear you talk like that.'

'Well it makes me feel better.'

'He won't come here. He doesn't know where I am.'

'You can't hide here forever.'

'Why not? I like it here, and I'm not hiding any more than you are.'

'This is where I live. What makes you say that?'

'Because I can see that thing in you too. I can see you the way you were five years ago. It's like...a shadow sitting beside you. You know he's still there, and you're scared of him.'

'I can live with him. He reminds me not to take anything for granted. This isn't about me. You shouldn't have to live

251

with what this bastard did to you. You shouldn't have to live with letting him get away with it.'

'I have no choice. Things happen. They happen to girls all the time, you know that. And they always will.'

'There's no justice in that. He should face the law.'

'I can't go through that. It's too late now. Can you just accept that, please?'

'I don't know. I've failed miserably at keeping you safe, and now you're asking me just to accept it, and I don't know if I can.'

She lurched to her feet and put three long strides between them, before turning around and shouting, 'You were never there! You were away my whole life! You know nothing about me. Don't you dare say anything about keeping me safe, like you ever once cared about that. So you have no right to tell me what to do, Calum. That's what you have to accept, because that's the choice you made, and at least you had a choice!'

There were so many more things she could say. Things she could scream into the woods about lies and broken promises and how things that looked so shiny from far away always turned out disappointing. She could hurt him with these things, perhaps irreparably, and maybe she wanted to, but she didn't want to have to leave.

'Okay,' he said, very quietly, and his voice was on the verge of breaking. He threw his tools into the trailer and the gloves on top of them. 'Let's get this put away.'

He pulled the trailer out of the woods, and she walked several feet behind him with the axe over her shoulder. They stacked the cut logs in the woodshed and he began cutting up the smaller branches for kindling. He worked without looking up, a horse turning a wheel, keeping his thoughts to himself. What would he do with the thing she'd just told him? She didn't want to be responsible for him getting ill again.

'Dad . . .'

He paused, mid-cut. 'What?'

'I'm fine, all right? I don't want you to worry about me.'

'That's bullshit.' Calum left the saw twanging deep in a log and glared at her.

'What?'

'Fine is the disguise.'

'Honestly, I am.'

'No you're not. Fine is what you say you are because if you say *I'm in pain*, everyone runs a mile. We live in a world where people take Prozac in secret because it's too embarrassing to say to anyone, no, actually, I'm not fine. Don't tell me you're fine, Cat. Don't lie to me.'

'What do you want me to say, then?'

'Tell me something real. Tell me how you really are.'

'Okay!' she almost shouted. 'I'll tell you then. I feel disgusting. I feel like something died inside me. I feel like if I ever slept with anyone again, they'd smell it, and all this . . . rotten stuff would come out of me.' She stopped short of saying *out of my cunt*.

He waited. Did he really want to hear more of this?

'I feel like I'll never be able to have a normal relationship with anyone now. I feel like I hate everybody in the world except you and Granny Mary. I feel like I'd rather die than go back to university and have to pretend I'm *fine*.'

He paused for a moment, chest rising and falling as if he couldn't quite get his breath, cleared his throat and said, 'That's better.'

EAGLE

Calum left a note on the kitchen table, I HAVE GONE FOR A PADDLE in black capitals, and went out the back door, a bottle of water, a flask of tea and a cheese roll in his rucksack for later. His stomach wasn't ready for food and his eyes stung at the brightness of the morning. Nausea hung around, the taste of whisky lingering at the back of his throat. A shadowy memory of hurling into a gorse bush halfway home from the pub, rinsing his mouth, falling into bed. He'd slept badly, drifting between nightmares before waking in sweaty clothes, the bed listing port and starboard.

Eejit.

This shit's hard enough without a hangover.

He tried to swallow but didn't have enough saliva. The hangover hadn't even started yet; he was still hammered.

He needed to forget. He needed to bail. Everyone had to, some time or other. Julie's bed would have been a better escape, but she was away back to Glasgow and would be there until she finished the Simpson commission. It might be weeks.

He'd been sick. Then he had crumpled onto his knees at the side of the road and told Abby and Johnny everything about Cat, and about Finn and his mother. 'I can't do this, Abby. I can't deal with this shit. I'm gonna lose the plot, I know I am. I can't go there again.'

Abby had her arms around him. She rocked him and stroked his hair. He'd been blubbering like a baby. Honestly? Had he really done that? Jesus.

He dragged the kayak down the drive, almost blind with alcohol and embarrassment, faster than was comfortable for either his head or his body. His knee cracked and crunched with each step. The other one grumbled too, having carried more than its share of the load for twenty-one years. It hurt. They both hurt, more than usual. Bits of himself were grinding together, the structure was weakening, just starting to creak. Nearer fifty than forty, you have to start to expect these things. Nearer fifty than forty and you're on your knees spilling your guts and a skinful of whisky at the side of the road, what do you expect?

He needed not to think. He paddled fast away from the shore, pulling against the flood of the early tide, and alcoholic sweat oozed down his forehead, nipped his eyes, dripped from the end of his nose. Leaving the bay, he rounded Bert and Georgie's headland, eyes seeking the top of the eagles' tree. One of the juveniles was visible from this distance, hulking on the edge of the platform, an early riser waiting for his breakfast. The other one was out of view. It must have fledged already.

He forced himself to maintain the pace, and finally ran out of steam far to the south of his normal turnaround point. He collapsed forward, lungs heaving. Whisky-flavoured bile burned his throat and rose into his mouth. He spat it into the water and listened to his own breath. It rasped a bit, but less than his head.

The water was very still, the breeze yet to wake with the warmth of the day. A salty haze hung low, blurring the skyline of the islands to the west and the long, jutting silhouette of Ardnamurchan to the south. To his left, a stretch of uninhabited coastline, broken by burns that spilled over shell

255

sand beaches, a long way from any road-end. He grounded the boat on a tiny arc of beach, took the rucksack and walked uphill from the southern end of the beach, through a ring of beech trees, towards the rounded hump of the hill. On top, he found a tumble of stones, the remains of an ancient dwelling or fortification that commanded the view of the surrounding lower ground and sea. The scattered slabs of slate poked his feet through the thin rubber soles of his water shoes as he climbed over them, and the combination of alcohol and the sweeping vista made him feel dizzy.

A small curve of wall remained standing towards the back of the structure. He approached it gingerly and looked for a comfortable place to sit among the stones, stirring up a gathering of crows. As they flapped into the air, he saw something where they'd been, just down the hill, on the grass at the base of the structure. A soft brown heap. Feathers lifted by the breeze from an otherwise motionless corpse.

He whispered, 'Oh crap,' and closed his eyes. His eyelids formed a screen, and on it he could see Finn lying just like that, on his back.

His heart skittered. He half climbed, half slid down to it, legs almost buckling beneath him as he knelt. It was the second young eagle; there could be no mistaking a bird that might have stood almost half his height. Its massive hooked beak was open, revealing its tongue as though it had been panting. He didn't dare touch it, but the only injury he could see was the eye, which had been taken by the crows. Black-flies gathered in the socket.

Finn had bounced and slid about ten metres further down the hill. Calum launched himself off the ground and collapsed again, his own scream repeating around the walls of the corrie. Pain drew black curtains at the edges of his vision and filled his ears with a droning zoom. He managed to haul himself down to where Finn lay before he passed out, face pressed into his brother's shirt.

The crows chattered behind him, little ghosts hopping around the peripheries.

'Go on, fuck off.' He flapped his arms. They lifted themselves a few feet further down the hill again, but not away.

He sat down heavily beside the eagle and tried to work out what he was supposed to do, kicking his feet towards the crows that sidled closer whenever he stopped moving.

'It's poisoned, you idiots!' he shouted at them. 'You want to die?' And then worse possibilities materialised. If one of the parents had brought poisoned meat back to the nest, the whole family could die.

'Oh my God, are they dead?' A female voice. Geordie accent. Footsteps, scrambling through the scree field, the chuffing breath of the person running towards him and Finn. He opened his eyes and saw Finn's outstretched hand, fingers open like they'd been reaching for something. He lifted his head and tried to move. A sledgehammer came down on his knee.

A man appeared at his side, brown beard, red cheeks. A moment later, a woman.

'Help my brother,' he managed to say. He was fading out again.

The woman felt Finn's neck. Her mouth opened but she didn't say anything. She shook her head at her companion.

'I'll go for help,' the man said. He stood up and dropped his backpack beside her. 'Try to keep him awake. Give him some tea.'

'Hurry, Dougie,' she said. Then turned back to Calum, her breath shaking. 'It's okay. Dougie's fast. It won't take him long to get down. Let me give you some tea.' With trembling hands, she unzipped Dougie's pack and pulled out a flask. 'My name's Alison. Can you tell me yours?'

'Calum. My brother's Finn. Can you please help him? I'm all right, I've just done something to my leg.'

'Your leg's broken, Calum. Try to stay still. Here.' She was trying to force the cup into his hand. 'Drink some of this.'

'Would you just please try to wake Finn up?'

She began to cry, tears streaking down her scarlet cheeks. 'I can't. I'm so sorry, but I can't.'

He learned later that Alison and Dougie followed the ambulance to the hospital. The next week they drove all the way to Arisaig from Newcastle for Finn's funeral. It had been years now since he'd spoken to them, but their number was still in his address book. If it was still their number.

There was nothing to do but leave the eagle where it lay and paddle back. At home he pulled out an Ordnance Survey map and found the place where the eagle was. He marked it with a red pen and phoned the police.

WHEESHT

You'd think a person had been murdered. Police came and went over the following days, notices appeared around the village, accusations trickled. The eagle and the referendum jumbled themselves together in conversations, so that the fate of the bird began to represent the fate of the nation. Everyone they met had a different spin.

If we can't look after our wildlife, we can't look after ourselves.

It's hard enough for crofters already. A bird like that would take a lamb, and do we really want to live in a country that cares more about animals than people?

This is the work of the absentee landlords who own all of us.

If we vote Yes, we can kick them out forever.

If we vote Yes, we'll be even more reliant on them than ever.

Catriona grew tired of the arguments and stopped listening. She and Calum worked on a loft conversion and the repair of an old byre. He was quiet, even quieter than usual, scarcely issuing a word beyond necessary instructions or requests, and everything became still except for the sounds of their tools and footsteps. Even when the stillness threatened to freeze her, she found she had nothing to say.

She lifted potatoes and weeded the garden and cut kindling

while he taught fiddle lessons. Bert and Georgie kept a vigil watch on the nest and reported that the parents were still dutifully bringing food to the remaining youngster, showing no sign of illness. It was determined that the fledgling had scavenged poisoned meat, and the investigation into the source continued.

Around midnight, Catriona knocked on his door. A full week had gone by since she'd told him about the rape. She hadn't slept properly since, and they hadn't spoken of it again. She felt like a balloon that was running out of helium. She drifted just above the ground, neither rising nor sinking, pushed by the changing breeze, bumping between obstacles, unable to control her own direction.

'Dad?' The door was closed but she could see light beneath. He was playing the guitar, very quietly.

The guitar stopped. 'What?'

She pushed open the door and was hit immediately by the tang of dope. He was sitting in a chair beside the open window, wrapped in a quilt, holding the guitar, smoking. On a little table in front of him, a pad of paper with musical notation.

'Oh my God, is that a joint?'

He glanced at it and put down the guitar. 'Aye.' It didn't seem to bother him that she'd just caught him getting high. 'What's up, Cat?'

'I can't sleep.' Outside, a heavy wind was sweeping around the woods. It whistled down the chimney. Lines plinked against metal masts. Branches creaked. Cold breath blew into the room.

'Join the club.' He held out the joint. 'You want some of this?'

'No! Where did you get that?'

'I have my sources. For medicinal purposes, obviously.'

His voice was croaky and the corner of his mouth turned up. 'You sure you don't want some? It's good.'

'I don't like it.' She sat on the bed, watched him take a hard toke and felt uncomfortable. Everything was the wrong way around. She was the one who was supposed to get caught doing things she shouldn't. He was supposed to lecture her about right and wrong, about the dangers of turning to substances for consolation, about slippery slopes, all of that. Had he forgotten that he was the parent? She turned away and surveyed his bedroom. A stack of dusty books, jumpers and jeans draped over the bedstead, a couple of empty mugs, guitar picks, CDs, coins. Blue badges that said Yes and Aye. A framed picture of herself as a wee girl: a scrappy tot in red wellies, dragging a stick in the sand. Another of himself on a stage, hair falling over his face as he bent forward, pulling the bow across the fiddle strings, a moment of joy captured like a butterfly in a jar.

She picked it up. His hair was fully dark then, his face unlined. He looked happier than she'd ever known him.

'It's been a fucked-up week,' she said finally.

'Yup.'

'Are you all right?'

He laughed in his throat, stubbed out the roach on the outside sill, shut the window. 'Better than I was half an hour ago.'

'Give me a percentage?'

A detached shrug. 'Twenty-one point four.'

'That's crap.'

'I know that, boss.'

'What are you going to do about it? Apart from getting completely off your face.'

'Can I come back to you on that? Further exploration is required.'

'I need you to do something for me.' She drew a long

261

breath. 'I need you to take me to see Mum. I have to tell her.'

Calum stared at her for a moment, suddenly reconnected with reality. Then he took off his glasses and pressed his fingertips into his eyes, squinting like he couldn't quite focus. 'Are you asking me for a lift, or are you asking me to be there with you?'

'I want you to be there. And I want you to be ... ' She trawled for a word that wouldn't embarrass him. 'You know. All there.'

'Sober, you mean.'

'Aye. No offence.'

'What are you trying to say?' He had a dopy wee chuckle to himself and his hand made a scraping noise as it moved across his cheek. 'It's fine, Cat. I'll just need to sort out someone to look after Granny.'

'Will you do that? I want to get it over with. And there's something else. Would you ... take me down to Edinburgh? I want to talk to Kyle.'

'Ah. Are you sure that's a good idea?'

'Dad ... I can't get him out of my head. Every time I see someone walking towards me, I think it's him and I can't breathe. This is just going to go on and on. I have to tell him what he did. He probably doesn't even realise.'

Calum chewed his lower lip and said nothing.

'I've thought about this. I'll meet him somewhere public. I'll be fine.'

'I'm not sure I will.'

'It's not about you.'

He closed his eyes and swallowed hard. 'Okay. Aye ... if that's what you want to do. I'll take you.'

'Thank you.' She shivered. 'It's freezing in here.'

'Get under the cover.'

Catriona pulled back the duvet and lay down in his bed, and he lifted the guitar and began to play again, a tune as delicate and soft as a lullaby. She let her head sink into the pillow and remembered staying with him when she was wee. His flat had strange sounds and shadows that made her scared, and he'd sit on the floor beside the bed and play the guitar to keep her safe until she fell asleep. Sometimes he sang in Gaelic, and the meaningless syllables would wash around her like warm water, his voice soft and smooth as sanded oak.

'Dad, can I ask you something? Have you ever been climbing again?'

'No. Hillwalking, but not climbing.'

'How come?'

'I don't think my knee would take it.'

'Isn't that just . . . you know . . . a handy excuse?'

'Probably, but I'm sticking to it.'

'I don't want to go back to university.' She hadn't planned to say it like that, but it was the foremost thing in her mind, a relentless alarm going off, making sleep impossible.

'Then don't.'

She shifted her head on the pillow so she could see him. 'D'you mean that?'

'Aye. You've a home here as long as you want it.'

Alert again, she scurried to find a purpose for herself. 'I was thinking I could do like . . . the Open University, or . . . maybe there's a college, or . . . '

'When you're ready. You need to be okay first, that's the most important thing.'

'Are you sure I'm not in your way?'

'Catriona, wheesht. Just . . . ' he sighed and sounded unbearably sad. 'Wheesht now. Lie down. We'll talk tomorrow.'

He started playing again, a sweet melody that sounded more American than Scottish and made her think of a long straight road across the desert. Tears pooled in her eyes, ran down her nose, and wicked into the pillow. She let them, felt her breathing become thick and congested. She turned over, pulled the other pillow against her face and cried until eventually the convulsions in her body subsided and let her slip into sleep.

CATCH

He sat there with his fingers in his hair. For two or three seconds, gravity pulled him forward and he felt like he was sitting on the edge of a precipice. Like the time he dangled his feet over the rim of the Grand Canyon. Michelle had dared him, and you couldn't refuse one of Michelle's dares unless you wanted to be taunted for weeks. Maybe she thought it would cure him. It didn't, it only caused him to break into a cold sweat and become ashamed of himself in front of hundreds of tourists.

The dizziness passed. Jenny poured more wine and took a greedy drink, shuddered slightly. She had stopped crying but looked stunned, like a wounded rabbit waiting to be attacked by gulls. 'I feel sick.'

Calum nodded silently and left his glass on the table. Any more wine and he would lose control over the things that came out of his mouth. There was enough venom swilling around the room already.

Catriona had disappeared upstairs and taken shelter in her bedroom, leaving her parents to negotiate the fallout. They argued about it because it was their habit to argue about everything to do with her. After a volley lasting more than an hour, they'd fallen into an exhausted ceasefire.

'I don't want to fight with you, Jen.'

She turned away from him, as if his words came with a bad smell. 'Are you and Cat actually getting on?'

'Aye, we are.'

'That's nice for you.' Her lip curled with cynicism.

He bristled. 'It *is* nice, actually. It's long overdue.'

'You can't blame me for that.'

'I don't.'

She stared at him hard, looking for the lie, possibly preparing to open a whole new line of attack. 'So, you two are all cosy again, and you've let this go all summer without telling me.'

He kept his voice as low as he could. 'Jenny, she only told me last week.'

'But you knew something was wrong when she came to you. You knew she was hiding something.'

'Aye, and I spoke to you about it, as you'll recall.'

'I wish you'd just brought her home, Calum.'

'As far as I was concerned, she *was* home.'

'Well you were wrong. She lives with me.'

'Catriona made a choice to come to me. She's an adult, I can't control her any more than you can.'

'Oh my God, you're so bloody irresponsible. Have you taken her to the doctor? What if she's pregnant? This is so typical of you.'

Typically irresponsible: always her favourite line. She'd hauled him over these particular coals so many times, they didn't even hurt anymore. 'She isn't pregnant.'

'You know that for sure?'

'I have one bathroom in my house. I know she's had her period.'

She got off the sofa and he followed her into the kitchen, where she began loading the dishwasher so furiously he thought the plates would break.

Jenny started in again. 'So that's it for you. She gets raped.

266

She gets fucking *raped* and she drops out of university, but hey, she's not pregnant. She isn't going to repeat *my* mistake and ruin her life by having a kid at nineteen, and so everything's just peachy. You've won. You've got your daughter working with you and she wants nothing to do with me, and God only knows what you've said about me to make her feel that way. You've won, Calum. Good for you.'

'Jesus Christ, Jen, there is no possible way for anybody to win out of this situation.'

She whirled around, a paring knife in her fist. 'Don't do that. Don't you dare step up on the moral high ground and try to lecture me. Don't talk to me. If you speak to me right now, I might stick this knife into your stomach. I mean it.'

Jenny's temper always had an edge of drama in it. In the past, he'd been able to call her bluff, but right now he wasn't quite brave enough. He slid away from the kitchen doorway and returned to the living room, sat down again, closed his eyes, and tried to listen to the tempo of his own breathing. Tried to focus on slowing it, opening his lungs slowly, closing them slowly. It felt like if he breathed in too deeply, he might either scream or vomit. There was a pain in his chest.

How did you distinguish heartbreak from a heart attack? He supposed if he keeled over, he'd know.

She was sobbing in the other room. Clattering the dishes and sobbing, not bothering to keep it quiet. Then the sound of breakage and a curse.

He went back to the kitchen. She was hiccoughing into a tea towel with a broken wine glass at her feet. Pushing the glass aside with the instep of his boot, he wrapped his arms around her shoulders and pulled her against his chest. She kept her arms folded up between them like armour but let him hold her, her body jolting with each intake of breath.

He stroked her hair. 'I'm not trying to win anything. I

should have been here for you. For both of you. If I had the time back, I'd stay.'

'Well you don't get the time back! So say it all you like, it doesn't mean anything.' Her voice was muffled against his jumper. 'You didn't want to stay with me, and that was the end of it.'

He spread his fingers in her hair and didn't try to deny it. 'I'm sorry.'

'Sorry doesn't change anything, Calum.'

'You're right, okay? I'm admitting that. We have to stop fighting. She needs us. It's not going to get easier for her. She hasn't dealt with it yet, in her head. She'll need us both, Jen. Believe me.'

She looked up at him, face a scarlet, swollen mess. 'What do we do?'

He brushed her cheeks very gently with his fingers, wiping away the tears and pushing the moist hair out of her eyes. 'Just be here to catch her, that's all.'

AFTER

Catriona took off her headphones and listened. Her parents had gone so completely silent there could only be one possible explanation: he was gone. Either Jenny had thrown him out or he had taken off, to the pub or even home. In spite of his promise to take her to Edinburgh, to stay with her, to keep her safe, he was gone again. He couldn't stop himself. Disappointment burned like a fever across her face. She should have known better than to trust him. Well, that would be the last time. Trust was overrated anyway, she'd known that all along.

She lay on her back, trying not to cry, trying to convince herself it didn't matter. It wasn't so bad, being back here. Surely Mum would go easier on her now that she knew the truth. She could find a job and make the best of things, and at least Kate and Eilidh were here. Maybe eventually they could all share a flat together. She listened to the familiar creaks of old Mr Stoddart climbing his stairs next door. Beyond that, she heard the hiss of car tyres on the wet street. Geese flying overhead, a noise that announced the coming of the darkness and always made her sad. From somewhere outside, a peal of feminine laughter, a boy's voice, the scrape of high heels on pavement.

It was the time for gathering in and sheltering down. She should be getting ready to go back to uni. Her friends would be packing and celebrating their final days at home, drinking, clubbing, shagging, laughing. She felt like an invalid who could only look on from afar, gradually losing any desire to join them.

Now there was only one last person to confront. Calum was supposed to drive her down in the morning. Damn him, now she'd have to ask her mum for money for the train and explain why she needed it. *And* she'd have to face Kyle alone. As much as the thought terrified her, maybe it was for the best. This way, at least she'd know that she'd stood up for herself. It wasn't how she'd imagined it, but she'd called him to ask for the meeting and she wasn't going to back out now.

He'd been his typical smooth self on the phone. 'Jesus Bloody Christ, it's the Stray Cat. Where you been, girlfriend?'

'Visiting family,' she said. The word *girlfriend* made her shudder, but she kept her voice steady. She had to give him enough truth to stop him asking any more questions. 'Uni was pretty full on at the end of term. I needed a break.'

'I phoned you a hundred times. Everyone's saying you like ... went a bit mental and were in the psych ward or something.'

'I haven't been in the psych ward, Kyle. Don't believe every bit of gossip you hear. My mum told me you phoned the house.'

'I was worried about you.'

'Really? Okay, look. I'm coming down to Edinburgh tomorrow. Meet me at Peter's Yard at three. We'll talk then. Can you do that?'

'Yeah, all right. I'm going to a Yes rally at Holyrood after that. You should come. Unless you've changed your colours.'

'I haven't, but I'm busy tomorrow night. I'll see you at three.'

'I'll look forward to it.'

You do that, she thought as she hung up.

270

She might have crumbled at the sound of his voice on the phone, but she didn't. She'd given away nothing, and she was proud of that. If she could make that call, she could face him.

This time tomorrow night, it would be done.

There was a noise downstairs: the rustle of a body moving around on the leather sofa. Catriona got up, slipped on her old pink dressing gown and poked her head into the corridor. Jenny's bedroom door was shut and there was silence from within. She moved as quietly as she could along the landing and down the stairs, and looked into the living room.

Calum was asleep on the sofa. Relief flooded her. 'Thank God,' she whispered. She sat on the arm of the sofa, feeling weak and guilty. Very softly, because she didn't really want him to wake up, she said, 'I'm sorry, Dad.'

His face was resting on one arm, his other arm hanging down to the floor, knees at a sharp angle, feet draped over the arm of the sofa. His blanket had fallen off. It looked uncomfortable and she considered waking him, offering him her bed. She was almost a whole foot shorter than him; she could stretch out on the sofa without a problem. His knees would hurt him in the morning if he slept there all night.

But he was sound, breathing heavily, clearly long past any discomfort. She smiled in the darkness, picked up the blanket and draped it over him, tucked it in at the side. Then she went back up the stairs and got into her bed.

YIELD POINT

They were driving south on the A90, passing Laurencekirk. The particular combination of land and sky – fields of ripe wheat, rising west to the hills under a stormy purple canopy – reminded him of the road trips he'd taken across America before he got married. They were the best times of his life, riding across deserts and plains and farmlands, camping out, stumbling across jam sessions in unlikely bars, meeting his fellow travellers: men and women who loved being on the road more than anything else in the world. Out there he could understand why oil was so fundamental to the American idea of freedom. Without it, there was no onward movement. No movement, no escape. No escape, no freedom. That open road was everything.

In Scotland, you could move but you could never escape. Everything here was more controlled, more claustrophobic, always hemmed in by the sea. Space was an illusion. You could never be out of anyone's reach, not even out on his remote little fringe. He'd loved all that American distance for the first few years. He'd loved the freedom of wheels and money, but eventually it left him hollow and lonely for something he couldn't name. He had never properly connected with anyone in America, not even Michelle. He spent those hazy months after his breakdown lying in the Southern California sun, reading old books of Scottish poetry that he'd had since school and they made him so homesick that he was willing to give up everything and come back.

He glanced at Catriona, who had barely spoken since they left Aberdeen. She stared out the window, scraping her cuticles with her teeth, brooding on the confrontation she had set up for herself. She was also fighting with those big decisions that would determine the course of her future. We all are, he thought. Especially now, with the referendum less than a week away. You could get caught up in the debate and forget that any identity mattered except that of your nation.

But things that seemed so important one day could be overshadowed the next. Wherever you drew your lines on a map, you owed your allegiances to the people closest to you.

White veins of lightning ripped across the sky and a shadow of rain fell. Heavy droplets began to splat onto the windscreen. Calum rolled up his window and turned off the radio.

'Cat, I want to try to explain myself.'

She pulled her eyes away from the window. 'How?'

'I made a decision after Finn died. I was never going to get married and I was never going to have any kids. I didn't want to have to be responsible for anyone, and I didn't want to have to watch anyone else I loved die.'

'So what happened?'

'Sex, I guess.'

'Gross.'

'I was a young man. I wasn't going to take an oath of abstinence. Jenny and I were careless, that's all.'

'I know I was a mistake. I don't need to be reminded on a daily basis.'

'Look, the point is we loved you. I loved you so much that it terrified me. When you were little I sometimes thought I'd go into your room and find that you'd died in your sleep. Sometimes I'd just have to go in and check on you, and sometimes I'd just sit there and watch you sleep and think that if I could only watch you forever, nothing bad would ever happen to you. I can look back now and see how irrational it was, but at the time ... I didn't know how to deal with that feeling. So I did what I thought I had to do at the time, which was turn my back and walk away.'

'Which makes no sense at all.'

'I know.'

'You don't think Mum ever felt like that?'

'At the time, it didn't occur to me that she would.'

'Then you're stupid.'

'I was very stupid, Catriona. There's nothing I can do now except tell you that I wish I'd done things differently. I know it's not enough.'

She folded her arms across her chest: armour up, tender parts pulled deep into her core. Everything about her was geared for defence. 'So why bother saying any of this?'

'Because I want you to know!' His voice edged upward. His nerves were frayed after last night's arguments and an uncomfortable sleep on the sofa.

'But you can't just come out and say that you loved Michelle more than me. She didn't want me around and that's why I never got to come to California.'

'Michelle would have had you over there in a heartbeat. It was me, Cat.'

She took this in without any response except a clenched jaw. She stared out the window, her breath making a steamy patch on the glass as the rain ran down the outside. She might understand better if he told her the rest: the full details of his breakdown and how close he'd come to the edge in the months afterwards. He was more like Finn than he ever wanted to admit.

GLENDARACH, JUNE 2011

A mild and unusually dry night, barely touching darkness, scented with gorse blossom and wood smoke. They were a foursome for the first time: Johnny, Abby, Calum and Julie, who had arrived months earlier in a rented van and filled Donald's old cottage with mismatched art and unformed lumps of stone. Calum had watched her with detached curiosity, attracted and frightened at the same time. They'd taken their time getting to know each other: chatting across the fence for weeks before moving on to cups of coffee and, only last week, a pint in the pub.

'I am not getting involved with her,' he'd promised Abby.

'Oh my God, Calum, a single woman your own age moves in next door, she's hot as shit, and you're not interested.'

'I said I'm not getting involved. I didn't say I wasn't interested.'

Now they were on the beach, watching each other from opposite sides of the bonfire, waiting. Heady with music, smoke and whisky, he could almost touch a feeling he'd forgotten himself capable of. Happiness. The word itself seemed pointless except to describe fleeting moments attached to specific things: a fiddle reel, a good film, a fine meal. But as for intrinsic happiness – the ability to be a happy person all day or all year – he figured that he would just have to muddle through life without it.

This is also just a moment, he thought. Tomorrow it will rain and the fire will be a charred ring on the sand. He wanted to keep this and hold it. But how did you? He could feel his hold slipping already.

He was drunk. The bottle of Ardbeg passed into his hands again and he took two big swallows. He wanted to be drunker. While he still had the ability, he put the fiddle into its case and zipped it, then got up and wobbled away from the fire.

From what felt like too far a distance, he could hear the others laughing. Johnny commentating: 'Oh ... a little wobble there ... He's gonna fall ... oh ... no, he's saved it ... doing the pisshead's shuffle ... Mind the rocks there, boy!'

He waved back at Johnny and tried his best to control his muscles. 'Going for a walk. Back in a minute.'

He climbed barefoot over the kelp-slick rocks until he was out of view of the fire. Then he sat down and let his feet hang into the water. They were so white they seemed to phosphoresce like strange creatures from the deep. The water was mild, barely cooler than the air, and everything was still. A becalmed respite, like when you dropped down into a sheltered hollow after a day on the mountain and the howling suddenly stopped.

He didn't know how long he'd been sitting there when Julie announced herself with a soft breath.

She eased herself down onto the rocks beside him. 'I hope you're not pondering the meaning of life or anything deep and pretentious like that.'

'Why would I do something as silly as that?'

'Because you're like me. Your default colours are dark. We can't help it.'

He smiled. 'You've figured me out.'

'Mmm.' She sat for a moment, looking across at the dark profile of the Cuillins. She was a hot ember beside him, restless and combustible. 'Can I ask you a question? It's a biggie.'

'Do I have to answer it?'

'No.'

He shrugged. 'Okay then.'

'Do you ever just sit here and think about diving in and floating off into oblivion?'

'You mean suicide?'

'Yeah. The S word. The ultimate sin against thy father, thy mother and thy God.'

'Do *you*?'

'Yes.' Her eyes were hard on him, sparking coals.

He shrugged. 'I guess I do too. Not . . . like I want to do it. Two years ago I really wanted to. I sat beside the sea, just like this, and played Hamlet. To be or not . . . and all that shit. I actually wrote down the reasons for and against. I still have the list.'

Julie giggled. 'You wrote them down.'

'It's my engineer's head. I need to put a plan on paper. I planned myself out of doing it.'

'What swung it?'

'Probably the idea that I wouldn't be any bigger loss to the world than a bug splatted on the windscreen.'

'Okay. That's not arrogant or anything. Jesus.'

'That's not quite what I meant.' He laughed, mostly at himself, ran fingers through moist, salt-stiffened hair, swished his ankles in the water. 'I have a daughter. I thought . . . if I jumped off that cliff, I'd only be confirming all the bad thoughts she had about me. Nothing would change for her. If I didn't jump . . . if I came home . . . maybe I could fix things with her.'

'But you don't see her. Abby told me.'

He sighed. 'I think we're both . . . waiting for the right time.'

'When will that be?'

'I don't know.'

Julie went quiet for a minute. Then she said, 'I have a daughter too.'

He looked at her.

She took a deep breath. 'She was a glitch in the experiment. I never got regular periods. I thought I couldn't get pregnant, but then I did. She was mine for nine months, and when she was born I handed her over to a stranger. I remember they let me hold her. She was a scrawny wee thing with black hair that stood straight up from the top of her head, and she was ugly as a troll. Then they took her away and I'm sure she made some other family very happy.'

'And you've never heard of her again?'

'No.'

'Would you want to?'

'No. Am I awful?'

'No. So . . . what swings it for you, then, Julie?'

'It's pretty simple. In between all the shit that happens, I actually quite like being alive.'

'And do you like it *here*? Has it been a good move for you?'

She turned towards him, placed her hand on his cheek and moved her thumb along the ridge of his cheekbone. 'The neighbours are okay.'

Catriona stirred, shifted in her seat, rubbed her eyes and looked out the window at the patchwork of fields. A blue sign in a green field said Yes, and on the other side of the road a red sign in a field of yellow wheat shouted No Thanks! Scotland felt like a rig straining into a North Sea howler, fighting with itself while far bigger forces assailed it from all sides. Support for independence was slipping as last-minute fears took over. Calum knew how it would go. The 18th of September would bring a result of almost-but-not-quite, and everyone would shrug their shoulders and say, Ah Scotland. We play our democracy the way we play our sports, he thought: in pursuit of second best. Still, a process was happening that could not be undone. People were asking questions they had never asked before. Something would change, eventually. What would Scotland's yield point be? Mechanical engineering lesson number one: all things have their yield point.

'Will you come to the café with me to meet Kyle?' she asked abruptly. 'I want you to come.'

His eyes darted off the road and he had a briefly thrilling vision of himself landing a right hook on Kyle's nose. 'I don't want to end up getting done for assault.'

'You won't. You don't even have to sit with us. Sit nearby and pretend you don't know us. I just . . . I'd feel safer if you were there.'

'Okay, if that's what you want.'

She nodded. 'That's what I want.'

AS IF NOTHING BAD
COULD EVER HAPPEN

She had picked the café deliberately. It was light, expensive, scented with cardamom and cinnamon, populated by academics and creatives who held forth in a dozen languages. You could sit all day on a sofa or at a communal trestle, reading and drinking strong coffee, and be forgiven for thinking nothing bad could ever happen in the world. They got there before three and she chose their seats strategically: a table for two tucked in a corner for herself and Kyle, a stool for Calum at the bar just behind her. He could sit with his back to them and watch their reflections in the window without appearing to.

Calum settled himself with his laptop and his coffee. He'd gone quiet and she could see by the pulse of his jaw muscles that he was grinding his teeth. She watched for Kyle out the window, her stomach churning, and rehearsed what she was going to say. It was the only way to do this: to script her words and rehearse them like lines of a play. Except of course there was no way to know what Kyle might say. He wouldn't touch her here in a café that he and his friends frequented. Probably he would try to sweet talk her, and certainly he would deny it. He might laugh. He might even cry. What would she do if he cried?

She couldn't allow it to matter. She had to control the conversation, say what she needed to say and leave. Nothing Kyle said could be allowed to make a difference.

Bang on three he appeared from the direction of the Meadows, walking with that same floaty, untouchable stride, tanned and gorgeous, the sun casting a golden sheen over his hair. He saw her by the window, waved, grinned broadly. He had no clue. Not a bloody Scooby.

'Here he is,' she muttered to Calum.

He didn't say anything, but his eyes followed Kyle with lupine attention. Catriona opened her lungs and drew in as much air as she could. Kyle drifted over and paused to see if she was going to stand up and hug him. She didn't, so he slouched onto the chair across from her and leaned forward.

'You look fit. You been working out?'

'I've been working,' she said vaguely.

'Do you ... uh ... want a coffee or anything?' Her icy tone had unsettled him.

'I've got one.' She tilted her mostly empty cup.

'Oh. So ... ' he raised an eyebrow, bounced his knee, 'I take it we're ... not cool.'

Catriona pressed her hands flat onto the table top. 'I wanted to talk to you about what happened at the party.'

'What party?'

What party. Jesus. 'That party at your mate's house out of town. In the woods, wherever the fuck it was.'

'Mikey's?'

'Yeah, that's it. That party. The last time I saw you.'

'Oh what? I can't even remember that night, I was so far gone. That was out of control. His mum and dad were completely ballistic the next day. He's gonna be paying that one back for ... '

Shut up, she thought. *Shut up shut up SHUT UP!* 'Kyle, I think you probably remember carrying me to the shower.'

'Did I?' He grinned with half his mouth. 'And what did I do to you in the shower?'

'You had sex with me. I said I didn't want to and you didn't listen to me.'

His smile vanished. She watched his Adam's apple bob up and down. Calum was watching their reflections intently. Catriona hoped he was watching Kyle's life change forever.

'Cat . . .'

'I said no and you held me against the wall, Kyle.'

'What are you trying to say?'

'I'm not trying to say anything. I *am* saying you raped me.'

He laughed, but it was a terrified sound. He looked around to see who was listening but the conversations around them were boisterous and unheeding. His voice dropped to a whisper. 'You can't just . . . Catriona, you can't just say that. I was drunk.'

'So was I, but I remember perfectly and so do you.'

'No, I . . . didn't do that.'

He looked pitiful but she couldn't let that in. She hoped his guilt would follow him forever, silently, like one of Doctor Who's Weeping Angels. She hoped that it would petrify him slowly from the outside in, cock first. It was a vengeful thought, and a comforting one.

'You did.' She leaned forward. 'That's all I wanted to say to you. I want you to know what you did. I want you to know that because of you, I'm not coming back to university and I may never want another man to touch me ever again. Maybe you'll find a way to live with yourself or maybe you won't. I really don't care. Don't say anything. I don't want to hear your voice.'

'Are you going to . . .' His voice was barely audible. 'Are you going to the police?'

Catriona paused before answering. Facing him changed things. It brought that night into sharper focus. They had

282

not been alone in that house. Of course they hadn't. Other people had seen him carry her into the shower. There were witnesses. She had screamed and shouted at him to stop. Somebody had heard. Surely, somebody had heard.

'I don't know, Kyle. I'm still thinking about it.'

'You could destroy my life.'

All she could do was stare at him. Three or four stunned seconds passed before she stood up and took her hoodie from the back of the chair. *Yes*, she thought. *I could*. Kyle started to rise but she poked a finger towards him. 'Stay there and stay away from me.'

As she turned to leave, Calum slid off his stool, placed his big hand heavily onto Kyle's shoulder and whispered something in his ear. Kyle's face lost the last of its colour and he looked genuinely horrified. Catriona began to shake. She shot out the door and walked away as fast as she could without breaking into a run, back towards George Square where they'd parked. She subsided against the bonnet of the Land Rover, legs burning, holding herself up with her hands. A wave of nausea came over her. She closed her eyes and tried to breathe it away.

Calum came up slowly behind her. 'That was some performance. I couldn't have done what you just did.'

'What did you say to him?'

'I told him if he ever came near my daughter again I'd rip his prick off and shove it so far up his arse it would come out his mouth.'

'You didn't actually say that.'

'I had to. I'm sorry.'

Catriona dropped her elbows onto the bonnet, covered her eyes and shuddered with spasms of something she couldn't describe if she tried: laughter, devastation and profound relief.

Calum stood beside her and waited until it subsided.

When she could breathe again, she straightened up and looked around, scrubbing below her eyes with her palms, smearing black mascara onto her hands. The new term hadn't started, but there were still groups of students buzzing back and forth, laughing, English and American voices cutting sharply over the din. The square seemed distorted, the sun too bright, the people too cheerful or busy or oblivious. She could never be one of them again. She was a ghost here. She remembered what Calum said that day in the graveyard. *Some things happen and they set your life onto a new track forever.* She understood now. You didn't just make different decisions than you would have done otherwise. You actually became somebody new and stepped into a different life. Nothing could ever be as it was.

But that didn't mean it had to be awful. She felt lighter, as if she'd handed at least some of the burden back to Kyle. She wondered what else he might have said if she'd allowed him to respond. He might even have apologised. She was glad she hadn't given him the chance.

'How do you feel?' Calum asked.

'Better.'

He stared straight ahead, smiling at something he saw through the trees of the square.

'Dad, maybe we should get out of here now.'

He came back from wherever he was and took his keys out of his pocket. 'I think that would be a good idea.'

They got back on the road north. Around Stirling, as they turned off the motorway and headed toward Callander, she started to cry. Huge shuddering sobs that came up from somewhere deep inside. She pressed her cheek against the window, her tears forming a film of moisture on the glass. Snot ran from her nose and she wiped it with the back of her hand.

Calum pulled an old red bandana out of the glove box and handed it to her. 'Sorry, it's not the cleanest.'

'It's okay.' She pressed it over her nose. It smelled of oil and pine resin.

FLOWN

The question came back to her just before bed one evening, like a lost thing that turned up when you'd stopped looking for it. With the question itself, Mary remembered how afraid she had always been to ask it. She wasn't afraid anymore; she just needed to know.

'Did Finlay mean to take his own life?'

Calum's eyes opened wide, his face reflecting the horror of the question. 'What did you say, Mum?'

Finally, she had his attention. He'd been ignoring her all evening, nose down in a book. As if those pages were more important than his living family. He'd always been that way, single-minded, silent except when it suited him to speak. At last he looked up. When did he start wearing glasses? Mary had never noticed him wearing them before. He was middle-aged. He looked tired, like he wasn't taking care of himself. Mary didn't look that old when she was his age. He'd let himself go so grey, he was starting to look like an old Labrador. He hadn't shaved for several days.

He looked just like Jack, but Jack shaved every day. He was proud of his strong features. Women turned their heads to look at him.

Calum was older now than Jack was when he died. Was he ill? He probably wouldn't tell her if he was. He never told her anything. He was too preoccupied with that lassie of his.

She looked ill as well. All that make-up around her eyes made her look like a corpse. Or a whore. She should be back at school by now, but showed no sign of it. All she wanted to do was sleep, and he let her. She'd come to no good; Mary could see that a mile off. She'd take drugs, or she'd end up pregnant. It would serve him right. It would be of his own making.

'Did Finlay commit suicide? Did he let go of that rock on purpose?'

'Why are you asking that, Mum?'

'Because I think maybe he did.'

'You know it was an accident.'

He was pretending to be shocked, and so was Catriona. Mary didn't know why they should be. She wondered why people could never see what was right in front of them.

'It's a terrible sin, to take your own life.'

'Could you really have blamed him if he had?'

'It's a cowardly act.'

'He didn't do that, I promise you.'

'Then you let him fall.'

'No, I didn't. He didn't use the safety equipment properly, Mum. I've told you this until I've run out of breath. Climbing is dangerous. People make mistakes. Finn made a *mistake*.'

'Then you should have made sure he didn't. You were the responsible one. You were meant to look after him.'

'Mum, I tried my best. You have to believe that.'

Mary couldn't stop herself. The words were alive now. They couldn't be swallowed.

'You didn't, Calum. You didn't keep him safe. You didn't do what your father asked you to do. Remember? He told you to look after your brother. *One* thing he asked you to do, and you couldn't even do that. You betrayed both of them.'

'Oh come on, Gran,' Catriona said. 'You're being cruel.'

Mary shot a look at the poor stunned girl. Who was she in

286

all of this? She didn't even look like part of the family. 'You should keep your nose out of other people's business, young lady.'

'And you should give my dad more respect. You treat him like a piece of dirt.'

'Cat,' he said sharply. They looked at each other like they were hiding something. 'She doesn't know what she's saying. Let it go.'

'Don't tell her to let it go, Calum. I know perfectly well what I'm saying! Yes, I do treat him like dirt. Because that's what he is to me. That's what he's been to me, ever since Finlay died. I hate him.'

Mary glared at Calum. She wanted him to hate her back. She wanted him to leave her house. She couldn't make him go. He just stayed and stayed. She hated him so much she could hurt him. She picked up the cup with an inch of luke-warm tea in it and threw it at him. He blocked it with his hands and the tea splattered across his face and shirt.

Catriona shrieked. 'You horrible old bitch!'

Calum swiped at the tea. 'Oh for fuck's sake!'

Mary clamped her hands over her ears and rocked forward. 'Don't use that language!'

Calum stood up. 'Catriona, could you go upstairs, please? Just for a few minutes, please?'

Catriona stumped out of the room. Mary felt panicky. She tried to get off the sofa but her feet slid out from under her. Why was he sending Catriona away? What didn't he want her to see? What was he going to do? He got onto his knees in front of her, trying to pull her hands away from her ears. She rocked away from him. He pulled harder and said, 'Mum, calm down.'

'Get off me!' She slapped his face as hard as she could.

He let go and sat down on his bottom. He didn't say anything. He just sat there on the floor. She could see her finger marks across his cheek, reddening. Did she do that? Did she just hit her son? She'd never hit either of them when they were children. Never. She didn't believe in hitting children. The other teachers thought she was soft, but that wasn't her way. She'd lost her way.

She was so angry she'd just slapped her own son on the face. He must have done something to make her so angry. She should apologise. She didn't want to apologise. She didn't feel sorry.

A silence stretched out between them. They might never have anything worth saying to each other again.

'Finn flew away, Mum,' he said. He was rubbing his jaw and his face was wet. He was crying. Or maybe it was the tea. He couldn't be crying, surely she couldn't have hit him that hard. She was old; her hands had lost their strength. A man his age should have more control of himself.

'Don't you remember how he told you about his guardian angel? She caught him. She took him. She . . . reached out her hand just as he slipped off, and she caught his fingers. And they flew away. I saw them.'

'I saw his body, Calum.' He was lying again.

'That was only his body, you know that. She caught him. He's with her now. He's fine. All that . . . stuff he had in his head. It's gone. He's with her. Just, remember that. If you forget everything else, try to remember that.'

What did he mean, if you forget everything else? She didn't understand why he said that. Why would she forget?

'You saw Finn's angel? You really saw her?'

'Aye, I did.' He sounded so weary, as if this truth had cost him a great deal. 'I want to show you something. Stay there.' He went upstairs, came back down with a heavy object cradled in his arms like a baby. He stood it upright on the coffee table. 'This is them. Finn and his angel.'

Mary leaned close and stared at the frozen image: two

beautiful faces, one set of fingers reaching down, another reaching up. She touched the stone Finn's face.

'Where did this come from?'

'Julie made it.'

'Who's Julie?'

He sighed. 'Julie, who lives next door. The sculptor. She's a good friend. I told her what happened to Finn and she made this for me. And you.'

'It's a beautiful thing,' she said. The anger that had come from nowhere had now pulled back like a spring tide and she was exhausted. Her hands were shaky. She clutched them together, knitted her fingers, seeking the reassurance of her own warm skin. 'Mìorbhaileach,' she whispered. *Miraculous.*

'Will we bring it to his grave, Mum?'

She thought about this. It might be a comfort to see it each week, but it wouldn't mean anything in that place. It would be a folly sitting there in the weeds. At last she said, 'It should go to the place where he died. Tell me the name of the place again.'

'Coire an t-Sneachda.'

'The Corrie of the Snow. Was there snow, Calum?'

'No, it was summer. It was a warm day.'

'Take it there. Leave it, for others to remember that a miracle happened there.'

He was silent for a long time.

'You don't want to do that?'

'I've never wanted to go back there.'

'Well, it's up to you.'

'Okay. I will. I'll take it. But I don't think you'd manage the walk in.'

'I don't have to go.'

'You wouldn't get to see it.'

'You can take a photo, can't you?'

'I can, but . . .'

'That's where it should go.' With this decree, a heavy weight fell away from her. Something she'd been carrying for such a long time. She began to cry with relief.

'Are you all right, Mum?'

She wiped tears with the back of her index finger. 'I'm just being silly.'

'No, you're not.'

'We've had our hard times, haven't we, Son?'

'Aye, we have.'

He placed his hand over hers and squeezed gently. It felt nice. Warm and strong, just like Jack's. She let him hold her hand for a little while.

Then he stood up. 'I'm going to bed. Will I put this away?'

'Leave it here,' she said. 'I want to look at it a bit longer.'

COIRE AN T-SNEACHDA

Mary went to bed early the night of the 18th, refusing to say which box she'd ticked on the ballot paper. She scolded when he asked: a person's vote was a person's business and if he was going to live with her, he would have to learn to keep his opinions to himself.

Calum stayed up most of the night, watching the results with Julie, Abby, Johnny and Catriona. Johnny got more despondent as the night went on, slouching lower and lower on the sofa, curses subsiding eventually into snores. Abby analysed and predicted Tory vengeance on Scotland. Julie sat Catriona on a stool and cut her hair, sculpting the renewed spikes with relish. Sometimes she said something softly and they both giggled. Later they drank shots of tequila and wandered off somewhere, laughing and forgetting. Calum turned his back on the television and played Guy Clark songs on the guitar, hauled himself upstairs to bed around four and crashed hard. He slept through Cameron's smug announcements and Salmond's resignation, and woke up thinking, almost but not quite.

He thought about Mary's question again. Independent from what? It was a good question. He'd declared his own independence all those years ago, but it had always been a charade. It was time to grow up. Step up and assume his place within the family. Mary was staying in Glendarach. This was her home, as much or more than it was his. He would look after her and his friends would help; he was lucky to have them. There was a good community here, and he was lucky to have that too. It would be okay. He breathed in as much air as his lungs could hold and let it out slowly. If he could learn to be more tolerant, it would be okay.

And Catriona? Right now she was adamant that she was not going back to university. Maybe that would change eventually, but she needed time. There was no telling how much time.

Before any of that, he had his own trip to make: a drive to the Cairngorms, a reunion with English friends and a walk up to the corrie.

'Are you sure you don't want to come?' he asked Julie.

She spooned against him, pulled his arm around her and held onto his hand. Her hair tickled his nose. They were in his bed, next door to Mary and down the hall from Catriona. This was a big enough step for her just now. It was as much of a declaration as either of them could make.

'I'm sure.'

He kissed the top of her head. 'Okay.'

'What do they look like?' Catriona asked. Anxious in her crisp new jacket. It was a good one, scarlet red, the same colour as her hair. He'd bought it for her at Nevisport in Fort William, and not from the sale rack. A random un-birthday present like all the cuddly toys he used to send, except a lot more expensive. This would serve her better. You had to learn to sort the things you needed from those you didn't. A good jacket to keep out the wind and rain was a thing you needed.

'I haven't seen them in a very long time, I can't quite remember.'

They were in the car park beside the ski centre at Cairn Gorm, waiting for Dougie and Alison. It was a fine afternoon, bright and clear, a breeze sweeping down from the plateau bringing the smell of snow. He laced up his boots and loaded his rucksack with essentials: gloves, hat, sandwiches and chocolate, water. A hip flask of whisky. Julie's granite angel.

Catriona scuffed her boot over the small stones at the edge of the tarmac. 'They should be here.'

'It's a long drive. Maybe there was traffic. They'll be here.' His stomach did a turn. The road across from the west had been quiet for a Saturday morning, as if all of Scotland was nursing a hangover. He stared down the hill, watching cars come and go – mostly tourists heading for the funicular – remembering the last time he'd been here. Finn muttering all the way up the road in the old red Astra, conversing with his reflection or the voice in his head. Dread filling him like water leaking into a diving mask.

You off your meds again?

Aye, Finlay's off his meds and Big Brother thinks Finlay's mad. Big Brother's embarrassed. Big Brother wants Finn to take his tablets and stare at a fucking wall. Big Brother is watching . . . but Big Brother doesn't understand. Finlay sees the truth. Finlay's the only one who sees the truth. That means he's the only one who isn't mad.

Maybe reading Orwell isn't a very good idea just now, mate.

Maybe Orwell was as mad as me, eh, Big Brother? Maybe he got it.

All right . . . fine. Let's not climb today. Let's go to the pub and talk about whether *Nineteen Eighty-Four* has or hasn't come true.

Oh it has. And we're climbing today. I'm climbing today. You don't have to.

Catriona stepped up in front of him, lifted his gaze from the ground, pulled him back into the present. 'You okay?'

'Aye.'

'You sure? We don't have to do this. Gran won't know the difference.'

He couldn't lie to Mary again. Not about this, although he didn't regret lying to her when she'd slapped him. It had calmed her immediately, like magic. Like the superstitious bullshit it was. The truth or falsehood of it was irrelevant. Her disease would break down any distinction between the two, and one day she would forget all of it. Whatever reminders he might give her, she would eventually forget everything. But right now, she was capable of believing in miracles.

He squinted up toward the corrie, following the line of the new path. 'I'll be fine. It's a walk in the hills, that's all it is. I have to do this for her.'

'What about you?'

'After you faced up to that bastard last week? I've got you with me, right? You're like Wonder Woman.'

'You can borrow my force field anytime you like.' She turned as a green Skoda sped up the hill. 'Is this them?'

'I think it is.'

The couple in the car were waving and grinning as they swept up beside them, apologising simultaneously as they got out, about temporary lights at Dunkeld and a slow tractor at Blair Athol. Then the apologies stopped and silence fell as they allowed themselves to observe the effects of almost twenty years. Dougie had lost most of his hair and Alison was stouter, but these things were like thin overlays against a backdrop that stayed fundamentally the same. Calum saw old mountaineers, solid and fathomable, people who changed in geological time.

'Calum,' Alison said. She pressed her palm into the corner of her eye and hugged him tightly. 'Oh bloody hell, I've started already. Thank you so much for asking us.'

'Aye, mate,' Dougie affirmed, gripping his hand.

'Better late than never, eh?'

'These things take a while,' Alison said.

'Twenty years might be too long a while, but ... you know.' Calum was grateful for his sunglasses. Poor Cat would die if he started bubbling before they'd even left the car park. 'This is Catriona. She's changed a bit since the last time you saw her.'

'Hi,' Cat said, holding up one hand. That single embarrassed syllable, like a shield stuck up in front of her.

'All grown up,' Alison said, and wrapped her arms around her. 'You were just a little baby the last time I saw you. Oh God, where's the time gone?' She let go and laughed tearfully. 'Your hair is just fabulous, by the way. Isn't it, Dougs? I love that red.'

'Don't you be having ideas,' said Dougie, beginning the usual pre-walk routine, pulling off trainers and putting on a second pair of socks. He glanced at the Yes sticker on the back window of Calum's Land Rover. 'Condolences on the vote, by the way. We were all ready to swim across the Tweed and claim political asylum.'

A chipper comment offered as a distraction. Until now, Calum hadn't really thought about how painful this journey might be for Dougie and Alison. They hadn't heard from him in two decades but had agreed to come as if they'd been waiting for his call all these years.

'I reckon anyone who's walked across as much of Scotland as you have must qualify.' He swung the pack onto his back and shifted the heavy weight into a comfortable position.

Angels were supposed to be made of light. 'We weren't quite ready to go yet.' He felt suddenly certain of that, just as he was that the old order of things was irrelevant. Catriona's generation understood that, even if his own didn't. 'But Thursday won't be the end of it.'

'A single day is never the end of anything,' Dougie said. He shouldered his own pack and locked up the car. 'Are *you* ready to go?'

'As I'll ever be.'

The walk in was a steady climb for over an hour, the path breaking and eventually giving way to heather, scree and boulders. Alison kept his mind occupied with conversation, just as she had on the way down Ben Alder, but she fell silent as they stepped over the brow of the corrie and looked across the little dark lochan. Calum glanced back down at the route they'd come up. Dougie had run all that way back down for help. It was a longer way than he'd remembered.

He couldn't remember the spot where Finn had landed with any clarity, but Dougie and Alison did. A small hummock of grass and heather surrounded avalanche-strewn boulders, high up the shoulder of the corrie. Falls of sharp scree spilled all around. The buttresses towered above them, empty except for a couple of ravens.

He eased the rucksack from his shoulders and hoisted out the sculpture. Dougie, Alison and Catriona lingered behind, waiting for him to find the right place for it. A flattish slab of granite seven or eight steps up the slope. He set it upright there and piled some smaller stones around it, making a cairn to anchor it in place. He'd considered bringing a tub of pre-mixed cement to hold it down, but something about the permanence of that felt wrong. Finn would never have wanted to be stuck down anywhere. It was secure enough in its little cairn, but it might fall eventually if other rocks tumbled from above or if heavy snows avalanched over the top of it. Or it might sit there until the elements eroded the details and reduced it back to the rough, shapeless lump it had once been.

He took a photo and walked back down to where Cat stood with Alison and Dougie. Silently, he sat down, slipped the hip flask from his pack and swallowed a mouthful of whisky. They climbed up to look at the sculpture, the three of them standing side by side. After a few minutes, they came back and sat beside him, sharing the flask and a bar of chocolate, speaking quietly. Catriona leaned into his side and allowed him to place his arm around her shoulder. The angel and Finn stretched out their fingers and almost touched, and wind skimmed like a flat stone over the surface of the water.

ACKNOWLEDGEMENTS

My thanks go first to my family, who inspire and encourage me, even though it means sharing me with an evolving cast of fictional characters. Thanks once again to the editorial team at Sandstone Press, Keira Farrell and Moira Forsyth, for their patience, insight and attention to detail. Finally to my writing buddies, Moira Cormack and Stella Hervey Birrell: writing can be a lonely road and I am very grateful to have good friends to travel it with.